PRAISE FOR SORAYA M. LANE

'With stunning imagery, historical detail, and a clever plot, *The London Girls* is a book not to be missed. I couldn't put it down!'

—Andie Newton

'Soraya M. Lane brings history to life in ways that take readers into the heart of some of the most frightening, challenging, and inspiring WWII experiences. Unputdownable!'

—Patricia Sands

'*Under a Sky of Memories* is a thrilling novel full of suspense, intrigue, and romance . . . Highly recommended for fans of World War II fiction.'

—Historical Novel Society

'I became so easily immersed in Soraya's poignant, vibrant, visual story, *The Secrets We Left Behind* . . . I loved this novel!'

—Carol Mason

'*The London Girls* is one of those stories that grabs you by the heart and doesn't let go until long after you've turned the last page.'

—Barbara Davis

T0026878

The
SECRET
MIDWIFE

OTHER TITLES BY SORAYA M. LANE:

The
SECRET
MIDWIFE

SORAYA M. LANE

LAKE UNION
PUBLISHING

Text copyright © 2023 by Soraya M. Lane
All rights reserved.

Published by Lake Union Publishing, Seattle

www.apub.com

Amazon, the Amazon logo, and Lake Union Publishing are trademarks of Amazon.com, Inc., or its affiliates.

ISBN-13: 9781662504068
eISBN: 9781662504075

Cover design by The Brewster Project
Cover image: © Abigail Miles / Arcangel;
© DavidSamperio © Kozlik © Athena Plichta © jax10289 / Shutterstock

Printed in the United States of America

*Heroes do extraordinary things. What I did was
not an extraordinary thing. It was normal . . .
You see a man drowning, you must try to save him,
even if you cannot swim.*

*—Irena Sendler, a Polish social worker
who saved more than 2,500
Jewish children from the
Warsaw Ghetto during WWII.*

This novel is a work of fiction that was inspired by real-life events. It contains descriptions and references to the Holocaust, Auschwitz and the treatment of women during this period.

The Holocaust represents one of the most atrocious acts of persecution in history, and my hope is that in writing this story, it helps to keep the past alive, and specifically pays tribute to the prisoners who risked so much to help others, particularly women. I have such huge respect and compassion for all the survivors of Auschwitz (and all other camps during WWII), their families, and of course those who lost their lives to this atrocity. More than 6,000,000 Jewish people were killed during the Holocaust, and millions of non-Jews perished in concentration camps, too. This is a part of history we must never, ever forget.

PROLOGUE

Auschwitz-Birkenau,

January 27th 1945

Emilia heard the shouts of men as she leaned heavily against the rough wall. Coaxing the baby into the world, she strained to stay upright. She squinted in the dim light, instinctively knowing something wasn't right when the infant didn't cry as she cut the cord then turned him over, feebly patting him on the bottom.

She fought tears, looking down at him, her fingers so frigid from the cold she could barely move them. Smoke clung to the air, the barracks around them still smouldering.

'What's wrong?' the exhausted mother whispered, still lying flat after the exertion of labour.

There was a noise outside, more shouts, but Emilia ignored them even as her legs trembled. The Nazis were gone, but who knew if these men who'd arrived were any better than the guards who'd fled in the night and set so much of the camp alight before they'd left? She refused to be frightened, she'd faced death too many times now to fall to her knees; all she cared about was saving the little life in her hands, because he had a chance to live when so many others had not. He was already a survivor, and she would not let him die, not now. But he was so tiny, his body fraught from lack of nutrients, and his mother likely incapable of feeding him, if she survived at all.

She glanced to her left, as if expecting Lena to be there, waiting to take the baby so she could attend to the mother. *Lena is gone.* She had to tell herself sometimes, remind herself that Lena existed only in her memories now, memories that swirled at times and tricked her, like dust in the air creating illusions that she had to fight against believing were true.

She patted the infant's back more firmly then and carefully scooped her finger into his mouth, gasping in relief when he finally cried, but as she went to lift him to the mother, lying on top of the crude stove, her legs still parted, Emilia realised she was now slumped over and silent.

'No!' Emilia croaked.

Blood coursed from between the woman's legs, a sign in these primitive conditions that she was only minutes from death unless Emilia could act quickly.

The calls outside continued, and Emilia listened as a man spoke loudly in a language she couldn't understand. But then he called in Polish. And as hope lifted inside her, he said the same words in English. He was repeating the same words in different languages.

'We are the Allies. We are not here to hurt you.'

The accent was strong, but the words were clear. Emilia shuffled to the door, her bare feet aching on the snow-covered ground as she stepped out, wishing she could go faster, seeing soldiers wearing thick olive coats, mounted on ponies as they rode through the camp. Some of the remaining prisoners had come to the doors of their huts, those who'd been too sick to leave with the others who'd been marched from the camp, their skeletal bodies hunched as they stared out. If these soldiers killed her, so be it; at least she'd tried.

'Help!' Emilia cried, her throat dry, lips cracked and painful. She still carried the baby, tucked in her arms and barely making a sound. 'Please, help me!'

The alarm on the soldier's face closest to her was obvious, and he yelled something to his men. He was Russian, she recognised the dialect from others she'd met in the camp. When he turned to her, she saw the sadness in his expression, and when she followed his eyes, she could see that he was taking in the naked newborn in her arms and her blood-soaked apron and ragged skirt. Or perhaps it was her stick-like arms and sunken face that alarmed him most.

'I need water, and towels,' she croaked.

'We will get your supplies,' he said, dismounting and passing the reins of his horse to another soldier as he followed her into the barracks. 'Let me help.'

She thrust the baby into his arms and scurried back to the mother, taking her pulse and then reaching for her knife. For so long, it had been the only tool at her disposal, the one thing that no one had taken from her. The bleeding hadn't slowed, and Emilia knew she barely had time to save her; even if the conditions were better it would be difficult. But for the first time since she'd started delivering babies at the camp, this infant had the chance to truly *live*, which meant she wasn't going to let this mother die on the stove, not when mother and son had a chance to survive together, not without doing everything in her power.

'What is your name?' the soldier asked.

From the corner of the room, hidden by shadows, came a raspy reply.

'Her name is Emilia,' Aleksy gasped, as he shuffled forwards on spindly legs barely able to hold him, his cough telling Emilia just how sick he'd become. 'She is the midwife of Auschwitz, and without her, hundreds of babies would have died.'

Tears started to fall down Emilia's cheeks as the hot water arrived, as she sterilised her knife and lifted it. *Because of me, hundreds of babies never had the chance to live.* But bless him, Aleksy only reminded her of the lives she'd saved, not the ones who'd perished because of what she'd been forced to do.

Her legs shook, barely strong enough to hold her as she prepared to save a life. Aleksy wasn't able to help her, so sick he could barely make it across the room, but the soldier beside her cleared his throat.

'Tell me what to do,' he said.

Emilia nodded and gave him instructions, using a towel to stop the bleeding, wishing she had more at her disposal. By the time she was finished, as she completed her final stitch using cotton they'd painstakingly unthreaded from a blanket months earlier in case of emergencies, Emilia was starting to wobble. Strong arms caught her and cushioned her fall as the ground rose to meet her, the first kindness ever shown to her by a soldier at the camp since she'd arrived.

'Rest,' he said, when her eyelids fluttered open. 'I will bring you food.'

He placed a warm jacket over Emilia, *the soldier's own jacket*, and she folded herself into it as a familiar form crawled closer to her. He had a threadbare blanket clutched to his shoulders, his cough rattling as he collapsed beside her.

'We're going to make it,' Emilia whispered, as Aleksy's breath wheezed in and out of his chest. 'Don't give up, you need to stay alive. You can't die on me now, Aleksy, I won't let you.'

She found a strength she didn't know she had and moved the jacket to give him some extra warmth, holding his hand while they shivered beneath it. They were both so small now, so skeletal, that it was easily big enough for them both.

Aleksy didn't say a word, but his fingers tightened around hers. It was all she needed – to know he was still alive. That there was still hope.

CHAPTER ONE

EMILIA

LONDON, 27TH JANUARY 1995

Emilia would have changed the channel if she could have reached the television remote. As much as she appreciated the efforts of most major networks to pay tribute to the fiftieth anniversary of the liberation of Auschwitz, it was a memory she'd spent most of her adult life trying to suppress. What had happened there, all the lives lost, wasn't something she needed to be reminded of by a documentary.

She was about to call out to her daughter when something flashed across the screen, overlaid across the often-used images of the gates from the notorious concentration camp and the skeletal prisoners who'd survived until the bitter end. Images she usually did her best to avoid.

'Mum, are you ready for—'

'Lucy, turn the volume up please,' she said, leaning forwards in her chair as her daughter walked into the room, the blanket that had been folded over her knees falling to the floor.

'It is rumoured that from late 1943 until the liberation by Russian soldiers in January 1945, a Polish midwife worked with a male prisoner doctor, who himself was also Polish, to save hundreds of babies within the camp. While the fate of Jewish infants was predetermined, many non-Jewish babies were taken and given to Nazi families, after a change in policy in 1943. It has been said that this midwife secretly tattooed the babies immediately after birth, in the hope that they might one day be reunited with their mothers.'

Emilia stared at the screen, her skin clammy as she listened to the reporter, fingernails digging into the arm of the chair. She leaned closer. Sometimes her mind failed her, sometimes lately it had been like trying to think through mud, but the memories that she'd fought so hard to forget never left her. Those had remained crystal clear, despite all the years that had passed.

'Despite our best efforts to find out the identity of this courageous midwife, we have been unable to discover any information about her whereabouts, or whether she even survived. If you have any first-hand knowledge of the prisoner midwives or doctors who worked at any of the Auschwitz concentration camps, we urge you to contact the number on the screen. Any survivors are encouraged to make contact to help us piece together what happened to these children, to share their stories of survival with the world.'

'Lucy,' Emilia said, hastily writing down the phone number on the newspaper beside her, forgetting all about the crossword she'd been doing previously. Her hand was shaking so much, the numbers were barely legible. 'Would you please get me the telephone.'

Her daughter had been watching the television too, standing in the middle of the room, but she glanced back at Emilia now.

'Dinner's ready, Mum. Could you wait until after?'

'Please, I need to make a phone call,' she said. 'It won't take a moment.'

Her daughter gave her an impatient look, but eventually she sighed and nodded, as if she'd been asked to run to the shops instead of step into another room. But Emilia knew she couldn't wait any longer; if she didn't call now, she might never muster the courage.

It's time we told them what we did, Aleksy, before it's too late. We can't keep it a secret forever. What if my memory disappears completely and what happened there, what we survived, is lost forever?

Emilia held out her hand for the phone, not surprised at how much she was trembling. It had been a very long time since she'd said the words she was about to say, and she knew they were going to come as a shock to her daughter. To her, she was just an old woman, a mother in her seventies who needed looking after, an elderly lady who forgot to lock the front door and sometimes got lost on her way back from getting groceries. It was why Lucy had insisted that she come and stay for a while, not liking her mother living on her own after she'd become widowed, convincing her that it would be nice for them to spend more time together. What she really meant was that she didn't trust Emilia to live independently any more. But when it came to what had happened at Auschwitz, to the things she'd done in order to help her fellow prisoners under her care survive, she didn't need help remembering. It wasn't something one could ever forget.

She took a deep breath and gripped the telephone when Lucy returned with it, carefully dialling the numbers she'd written down.

'Mum, who are you calling? Are you sure there's nothing I . . .'

Emilia pressed the receiver to her ear, her heart racing as she waited. It rang six times before a woman answered. Her daughter gave her a tired smile that only reminded Emilia how trying it must be to have her mother living with her, even though it was Lucy who'd insisted she move in.

'Hello?' the woman said. 'Is anyone there?'

She gripped the phone tightly, trying to stop it from shaking.

'My name is Emilia Bauchau. I am the midwife you're looking for.' She paused, glancing up at her daughter. 'I believe it's time for me to tell my story.'

7

CHAPTER TWO

MONDAY

Emilia sat at the table, listening to her daughter greet someone. She clasped a small gold cross in her palm, a present from her husband that she'd always found comfort in holding, that she'd barely put down since his passing. Lucy often asked if she'd like her to clasp it for her, so she could wear it around her neck, but she preferred to hold it, liking the feel of it in her hand.

'My mother is through here,' she heard Lucy say, still audible even when she lowered her voice. 'But I have to tell you, her memory isn't what it once was, and whatever she wants to tell you, it's not something she's ever talked to me about before. To be honest, I don't know anything about that part of her life.'

'Please don't worry. I'm grateful for whatever she wants to share,' the woman said. 'And to be honest, many of the people I interview, even as they age, the past is often more clear to them than the present, and it's not uncommon for them to have kept their memories to themselves, either. Your mother might just surprise you.'

'Perhaps,' Lucy said. 'I'll make tea and join you in a moment.'

When the woman walked into the room, Emilia was struck by her bright eyes, at the way she walked straight towards her with a big smile, hand outstretched. Emilia went to stand, placing her palms on the table to help the motion as her legs struggled to hold her, as she tried to remember exactly what she was supposed to be telling her. She was only seventy-five and yet her body and mind were both failing her at times. Some days it made her angry, and others she reminded herself of what she'd endured and knew it was hardly surprising that she'd aged so fast.

'Emilia? It's so lovely to meet you. Please, stay seated.'

The woman's voice was warm as she reached out to clasp Emilia's hand.

'It's lovely to meet you, too.' Emilia searched her mind for the woman's name, frustrated when she couldn't find it. 'Ahhh—'

'Hannah. Hannah Davies,' she said, taking the seat closest to Emilia and placing her bag on the table. 'You saw me on the documentary the other night, about Auschwitz?'

Hannah. Of course. Hannah the reporter. From the documentary. Emilia shut her eyes for a moment, taking a slow breath. Why was it that the past she'd tried so hard to forget came to her constantly and without warning, but the things she most wanted recollection of constantly evaded her? Ever since she'd lost her husband, it seemed as though the past was seeking her out, leaving her living in a world that had already been, which she knew must be difficult for her daughter. Lucy had just sent her children off to university, her house finally her own, and now she had her mother living with her.

'Would you mind if I used this?' Hannah asked, taking out a tape recorder and sliding it between them. 'I don't want to miss anything you have to say.'

'Of course,' Emilia replied, finding herself staring at the little machine capable of capturing her words.

'Your story, Emilia, it's one that I have waited many, many years to hear. There are so few people left who survived what you did, and my greatest fear is that stories like yours could be lost over the coming decades if they're not recorded,' Hannah said, smiling across the table at her, putting Emilia at ease. 'Whenever you'd like to stop, please just tell me. I'm in town for five days, so I'm hoping that's enough time for you to share your memories with me.'

Emilia nodded, looking up when Lucy came into the room carrying a tray of tea. It would be long enough, she'd make certain of it. Five days to tell her story, and then she would try to close that chapter once and for all in her mind.

'You know, I wasn't expecting to hear from anyone so soon after our documentary aired,' Hannah said. 'We've been searching for you for so long, and it appeared we were searching for a ghost. I'd almost given up hope of finding the connection.'

'These things, they're not something we wanted to talk about after,' Emilia said, watching as her daughter poured the tea, knowing that much of what she was going to share would come as a terrible shock to her only child. 'There was a sense of survivor's guilt, I suppose. Why were we spared when so many perished? It was a question I wrestled with for decades. I still do, I suppose.'

'Even after all this time?'

She paused. 'Yes. Even after all this time.'

There was silence as they all sipped their tea, before Hannah leaned forwards in her chair and smiled.

'May we begin?'

Emilia glanced at her daughter, almost wishing she wasn't in the room.

'Emilia, is it okay if we begin now?' Hannah asked.

She nodded, folded her shaking hands in her lap as she watched the tape recorder, the little red light showing it was working.

'Emilia, I understand you were a prisoner at Auschwitz-Birkenau Concentration Camp,' Hannah said, her voice soft, as if she were speaking to a child instead of a grown woman. *A survivor.* 'I'm particularly interested in how you became a midwife there, and the babies you saved. In how you survived such harrowing conditions for so long.'

Emilia took a deep, shaky breath as memories she'd vowed for so many years, so many *decades*, to never speak of, came flooding back to her.

'To understand how,' Emilia said, her eyes meeting Hannah's as she sat back in her chair, 'I need to take you back to the very beginning.'

CHAPTER THREE

EMILIA

POLAND, JULY 1942

At first, Emilia had been nervous riding past the patrol of German soldiers. They stared in a way that told everyone they were superior, or at least in their minds they were, but she no longer allowed herself to be intimidated by them. Most satisfying was giving them her sweetest grin while at the same time thinking what rotten pigs they were – if they were capable of reading minds, she'd not have made it past the first blockade. It was barely an act of defiance, but it made her feel better nonetheless, as if she were repenting for smiling at them in the first place.

As she approached the two soldiers, she lifted her fingers from her handlebar and waved, accompanying the action with a shy smile and a demure flash of her eyes. It worked, as it did every time, and they waved back and grinned, calling out something in their native tongue that she expected was a crude remark about her body. But Emilia didn't care; the only thing that mattered to her was riding safely past them each day so she could go about her work.

This part of her day wasn't likely to bring with it any risks. If the soldiers followed her, they'd see nothing more than a midwife going about her rounds, which made it easier for her to go undetected at other times. To them, she was a woman providing a service to the families who'd been allowed to stay in their homes and for now, that was permitted.

She kept pedalling as sweat formed across the back of her neck, relieved to have passed them. *Perhaps I'm more nervous than I want to admit.*

Soon, the house she was looking for came into sight, and she rode her bicycle directly to the door, propping it outside and taking the plums from her basket that she'd carefully wrapped before leaving home. She knocked softly on the door, not waiting to be invited in, and going immediately to the kitchen she placed the things she'd brought, her midwifery bag still slung over her shoulder.

'Hello?' she called out, quietly, not wanting to wake the baby if she was asleep.

'In here,' came a whisper.

Emilia followed the voice to one of the bedrooms, smiling when she saw that the baby was indeed sleeping, tucked up in her crib, but the mother was bleary eyed and looking as if she might cry.

'Come, let me make you a cup of tea,' Emilia said, guiding the woman from the door and gently pulling it shut behind them.

'She was awake all night, I don't know what I'm doing wrong.'

'You are doing *everything* right,' Emilia said, clasping her hands tightly. 'Babies can be hard to settle, and all we can do is love them and nurture them, it's as simple as that.'

The woman's eyes brightened and Emilia waited until she'd sat at the table before putting the water on to boil. While she waited she took out one of the bright yellow Mirabelle plums she'd brought, pleased she'd gone foraging for them when she saw the new mother's eyes light up.

'There's nothing easy about childbirth *or* having a new baby in the house. But you'll soon settle into motherhood,' Emilia said, sliding the plum to her as her own stomach grumbled. 'But for

13

now, we need to make sure you're strong, so that your milk comes in. As long as she's feeding, she'll be fine. *You'll* be fine.'

She stayed and chatted for a short time; it was something she loved doing. Assisting birth was one thing, but she'd learnt from her own mother as she'd accompanied her from house to house as a girl that the hardest time for some women were the days after delivery, learning to cope with being a mother for the first time. It was the part of the job she took the most pride in.

'I don't know how to thank you,' the woman said. 'Please, can we give you one of our hens, or—'

Emilia shook her head. 'I don't need anything. I wouldn't take it even if you insisted.' If she took every gift that families tried to thrust upon her, she'd have a backyard full of all matter of fowl and four-legged beasts, which would definitely put her on the Nazis' radar.

She rose and placed a kiss to the woman's head. 'While the baby sleeps this week, you sleep. You need to regain your strength. Childbirth takes a toll on the body at the best of times.'

There were more families to visit, some with children she'd helped deliver weeks earlier, and some women who were close to full term, and she left with a promise to return the following day. Every time she said it, part of her wondered if she might not make another day, that she might be stopped by a patrol when she least expected it and questioned, but she wasn't going to pass on her worries to anyone else. As far as they were concerned, her non-Jewish families at least, she was simply doing her job as she always had.

Emilia mounted her bicycle and pushed off, cycling slowly to the next house on her list as she lifted her face slightly to the sun and wished she'd brought some plums for herself.

Less than an hour later, Emilia found herself walking around the garden with a woman who'd already birthed three babies, and who had no intention of lying in bed waiting for the next to come. Her children were playing outside nearby, enjoying the sunshine and completely oblivious to their mother's pain.

'You don't need to stay,' the woman said, before letting out a hiss between her teeth. 'We both know this could go on for hours.'

Emilia laughed. 'Just as we both know how quickly this baby could arrive into the world! I'm not riding all the way home only to have to turn around and pedal back.' She linked their arms and held her firmly. 'Martha, I'm staying. You can't give birth on your own, and especially not with your children here and no one to look out for them.'

Martha sighed, before stopping and clutching Emilia's hand. They stood together for a moment, before the walking resumed. These were the easier labours, with experienced mothers who knew how to grit their teeth through each stage, keeping as busy as they could until they could stay on their feet no longer. Previously, Emilia might have left and come back later, regardless of what she'd just said, but Martha had lost her husband before she'd even found out she had another baby on the way. Which meant that she was all alone, and that wasn't something Emilia could stand.

'Sometimes I wonder why God chose to punish me like this,' Martha muttered, as the children ran around in front of them, their laughter making Emilia realise just how long it had been since she'd heard the sound of happiness. 'I don't even know how I'm going to put enough food on the table for these three, let alone another.'

Emilia gently rubbed her back as their walking slowed. She had a feeling this baby was going to arrive sooner rather than later. 'I hear that often these days,' she said. 'Many of the families I visit are questioning their faith, wondering why such horrors are happening.'

Martha looked her directly in the eye. 'Jewish families?'

Emilia cleared her throat and looked away. It didn't matter how well she knew someone or how kindly a family seemed, Emilia never disclosed the work she did. She couldn't; it wasn't only herself she'd be putting at risk.

'You just focus on birthing this baby,' Emilia said. 'And don't give up on your faith yet. I'd give it a little longer. We need to remember how full our lives once were, what it was like to live in peace. That's how we survive the dark times, by remembering the light.'

'If you were, though,' Martha said, 'helping them? I wouldn't say anything. It wasn't so long ago that—'

A groan escaped the other woman's lips and Emilia kept a tight hold of her arm, keeping her upright. The contraction had at least put an end to their conversation, for which she was most grateful.

'Come on, let's get you inside,' Emilia soothed, directing Martha towards the house. 'I'm going to put some water on to boil and get the towels ready.'

'Stay outside!' Martha called to the children. 'You can come in when you hear the baby cry, but not before!'

Emilia looked at the worried faces of the little children, the eldest barely six years old. It wasn't often she lost a mother during childbirth, but there was always a risk with any labour, and she did not want to be coming outside in a few hours' time with sombre news. These children had no one if they lost their mama, so that wasn't something she even wanted to consider.

'It's going to be all right,' Martha muttered.

Emilia clutched her arm and forced a smile, not sure if Martha was trying to reassure herself, or her midwife. Thankfully, less than forty minutes later, Emilia found herself holding a red-faced baby boy, whom his mother looked at with the most exasperated expression as if she couldn't believe she had another babe to care for.

——— ⁛⁘⁛ ———

It had already been a long day, but once Emilia finished work she always, without fail, rode the same path home. To anyone else, she hoped she appeared in no hurry, admiring the scenery as she carefully checked washing lines for signs that someone needed her help; someone she was strictly forbidden from assisting. When Germany invaded Poland almost three years earlier, they'd rounded up all the Jewish families and created ghettos for them, leaving them cut off from everyone else in the community. Their flags decorated Polish buildings, their boots clacked on the cobbles as they marched; it was no longer the Poland any of them knew or loved.

But no matter how badly Emilia had wanted to help those families, there was no way she was going to get past the guards at the ghettos to provide midwifery assistance – they'd rather the women there die in childbirth than receive help. But it hadn't taken long for her bravery to be noticed. A silent figure standing at her bedroom window one night had asked whether she truly wanted to help. Which was when Emilia had become aware of a number of Jews hidden not only in her village but everywhere throughout Poland, many of them families who desperately needed assistance – and not just her midwifery skills. Which was why she was riding past certain homes to check the washing they had on the line; a dirty rag hanging among clothes or sheets was her sign to visit. She would have felt a coward keeping her head down and enjoying her relative safety; if a woman was in need, then she refused to stay safe at home.

Emilia's breath caught in her throat as it always did when she realised her presence was required. It was the reason she kissed her father's cheek and held him so tightly in a long hug every morning before she left for work, the reason she counted her blessings every time she pushed her bicycle from the shed – because any day now, she could be caught, and she was under no illusions about what the Gestapo would do to her if she were. She'd witnessed their brutality first hand outside the butcher's shop only days earlier, seen the way they'd pulled Jews from their homes and treated them as animals some months before. She would not survive if they discovered her deception, of that she was certain.

She rode past the house and looked around, making sure no one was watching. Emilia glanced at all the windows, looking for prying eyes or curtains slightly parted, before eventually taking another road and circling back past the same way she'd come. The families she helped all knew the drill: they were to leave something around the back of their home for her to hide her bicycle beneath, and a rear door unlocked if they had one, so she could slip in without having to wait outside. The faster she disappeared inside a house, the less likely someone was to report her or even notice her whereabouts in the first place.

Today, everything went to plan, and for that she was grateful. Emilia dismounted and pulled a sheet from where it had been left, doing a hasty job of hiding her bicycle, before slipping silently into the house.

'Hello?' she called softly, padding quietly down the hall. She was about to call again, when someone said her name.

'Emilia?'

She followed the voice and found herself in the kitchen. Her heart sank. Standing in an old nightgown, her eyes as round as saucers, was the woman she'd been called for. But it wasn't just any woman; she'd delivered all this mother's babies, the eldest with her own mama when she was her assistant, barely capable of gathering enough towels let alone actually being helpful with the birth. She touched the locket at her neck as she thought of her mother, wishing she were here now. *I had to learn fast, Mama. If only you'd had longer to teach me. If only we'd had longer together.*

'Adela,' Emilia said, walking towards her with her arms outstretched, pushing away her own thoughts. 'It's almost time?'

Adela nodded as tears slid down her cheeks, and Emilia held her, embracing her for the longest of moments as they stood in the kitchen, the only noise the water boiling on the stove. Her shoulder was wet when Adela let go of her, her tears falling in fast succession down her cheeks.

'I couldn't leave her up there. It seemed so cruel.'

Emilia turned to the other woman in the kitchen, the one who'd bravely opened her home to the Jewish family they'd known all their lives. It wasn't just Emilia taking a risk today – they'd all be shot or rounded up if their deceit was discovered.

'Your husband?' Emilia asked.

'He's taken the children out. He promised they'd be gone for at least an hour.'

Emilia nodded. The children of the house had no idea there was a Jewish family living in the attic; it was a secret they'd all agreed must not be shared, not when children could so innocently say something that could lead to a discovery.

'I'm sorry,' Emilia said to Adela, 'but we need to go back up there, just in case.'

She placed her hand on Adela's swollen midsection, feeling how low the baby was at the same time as the woman's stomach went painfully hard. Emilia nodded and called over her shoulder as she led Adela away.

'I'll need water, towels and something to wrap the baby in,' she said. And on second thoughts: 'Perhaps something to bite down on might be helpful, too.' *She cannot make a sound. She will have to be brave beyond words to get through this labour.*

Adela gripped her hand tightly as they walked through the house together before they stopped at the wooden ladder that had been left propped in the hallway. She knew from visiting before that the family had taken away the built-in ladder from the ceiling, to make it less obvious that anyone could be up there. Instead, they kept an old, cobweb-covered wooden ladder outside, bringing it in at night only when they needed it. Adela and her husband were prisoners in the attic, trapped with no way to escape if there were ever a raid, but at least they were alive. For now.

'Come on, let's get you up there,' Emilia said, checking the ladder was sturdy before guiding her up, her foot on the lower rung.

Adela stopped, her hands resting on the timber as she groaned. The baby was coming soon, Emilia was certain of it. But it was the words whispered to her that she hadn't been expecting in that moment that caught her off guard.

'Have you heard?' Adela murmured. 'Has there been any word at all?'

Emilia shook her head, their eyes unblinking as they stared at one another. 'I'm sorry, but I haven't heard anything.' She paused, wishing she had some comfort to offer her, but she wasn't going to lie.

She glanced up and saw Adela's husband leaning through the hole, his arms outstretched as he waited to reach for his wife.

'What I can say is that no news is good news, in this case. If something had happened to their transport, I would have heard.' It was the truth, or at least it was the truth as Emilia imagined it. Surely someone would have got word to her if there had been a discovery? If they hadn't made it?

Adela stood still, as if digesting the information, before placing one foot and then the other on the ladder, managing to get almost to the top before pausing. Emilia blinked away tears as she watched her squeeze through the opening in the ceiling, hidden away as if she were a criminal. And unlike the last mother she'd attended, Adela desperately wanted the baby she was about to birth. Despite it all, despite the fear and the uncertainty, Adela was born to be a mother and Emilia could see how broken she was without her brood of children tucked to her side.

She placed a foot on the first rung on the ladder, forcing the memories away as she prepared to deliver Adela's fourth child, knowing that soon the young mother would be forced to give this little one up, too, no matter how much she yearned to keep it.

'Mama!' The little girl's cries almost broke Emilia's heart.

The two boys stood outside the house, stoic, despite being only a few years older than their sister. They were dressed beautifully, much-loved children with parents who adored them, parents who up until recently had been respected members of the community before they'd been hunted like unwanted animals when the Nazis had invaded.

Emilia took the girl's hand, holding firmly as she tried to pull away. Taking her from her mother wasn't something she wanted to do, but she'd been asked to keep them safe, and they didn't have much time if they were going to make it.

'Mama!' the girl whimpered, as her mother rushed to her, despite her husband trying to hold her back.

It was a scene like no other, and one that had Emilia grinding her teeth as she tried to remain outwardly impassive. She let go of the girl's hand and went to the boys instead, bending and placing a hand on each of their shoulders.

'I'm so proud of your bravery,' she said, hoping her touch felt as light and full of love as she intended. They carried nothing, wearing their best coats and extra socks, with food and some jewellery sewn into

their clothes. 'Can you each take your sister's hand, and remind her how important it is that we stay quiet?'

They nodded, the weight of the world on their shoulders as they did what she asked. Their mama pressed a kiss to each of their cheeks, her final, shuddering sob making all three children cry. But bless them, the boys stayed quiet, and they found a way to keep their sister silent too, as Emilia led them quietly through the woods, praying that they'd make it without being seen.

———— ❦ ————

It seemed as if there was no air left in the cramped attic. The little window was jammed shut, with black fabric taped across so as not to let out any light at night, and Emilia wished she could rip it away and find a way to open it. How Adela and her husband survived in the stuffy, small space was beyond Emilia. There was only room to straighten and stand in the very middle, where the ceiling was at its peak, and she noticed how stooped Adela's husband had become as he shuffled towards his new baby.

Emilia turned her back to give them a moment of privacy, embarrassed that she even had to be in such a small space with them when they'd already lost so much. Her eyes flickered to the mattress on the floor, still rumpled from when the children had been up there with them, the sheets no doubt still holding the scent of their warm little bodies. She could imagine Adela burying her face against the fabric, inhaling, praying for the day when they would be reunited. She looked at the single chair, the candle propped on an overturned apple box, a pile of books stacked neatly to the side. She imagined reading was one of the few enjoyable pastimes for the couple stranded there, along with the pile of cards that she discovered when she took a step forwards. She hoped that for a moment each day they were able to forget, to pretend that their life hadn't been stolen from them in one fell swoop.

It was hard to comprehend that they were the lucky ones.

'Thank you.'

She turned when Adela's husband spoke. His eyes were misty as he sat on their bed, or what counted as a bed, holding his newborn infant in his arms as his wife leaned against him. Her hair was still damp and curling slightly at her temple, and she appeared understandably exhausted, although the way she looked at her child told Emilia that she would do it all again if she had to.

Emilia sat in the chair, suddenly weary, the reality of what she was part of weighing heavily on her. She needed to consider her words.

'How long do we have?' Adela asked.

Emilia looked at her and then her husband, before fixing her gaze on the baby. Adela reached for him, taking him into her arms and letting the strap on her nightdress fall down, her breast exposed as she expertly guided the infant to feed. The simple action almost broke Emilia; her lower lip trembled as she watched the baby suckle, the bond between mother and child so immediate that it never failed to warm her heart.

'I will let them know that there is a baby to transport, if that's still what you want,' Emilia finally said. 'When I receive a message in reply, I'll send word.'

The husband stood, muttering something as he rubbed his eyes, going to the farthest corner of the attic despite how low it was. Emilia kept her gaze trained on Adela, wanting to be strong for her.

'Will it be days or weeks, do you think?'

Emilia swallowed. 'I honestly don't know. But if I had to guess?'

Adela's eyes widened, waiting for her to reply. Emilia shifted uncomfortably in her seat.

'Days.'

A sob from the man hunched in the corner almost broke Emilia's composure again, but when Adela didn't crumble, neither did she. It was her job to stay strong, to bring hope to the families she helped. She wasn't the one being forced to give up her child.

'Try to rest, and send word if you need me,' Emilia said, rising and going over to press a kiss to the top of Adela's head, before tapping three times on the floor.

She'd already stayed long enough. If she didn't make it home before curfew she'd be caught and questioned, and that wasn't something she wanted to risk. Especially not with tears gathered against her lashes and her hands trembling violently in a way they'd never done before.

CHAPTER FOUR

Emilia stepped inside and placed her bag and coat on the stand by the door. She was exhausted, the kind of bone-deep weariness that came not only from working all day and not sleeping enough, but also from worrying about the families in her care.

'Emilia?'

She was walking into the kitchen when she heard her father's call. He was seated at the table, his shoulders slouched in a way they never would have been before the war, before everything had slowly been taken from him.

'Sorry, *Tata*,' she said to him as she kissed his head and placed her hand on his shoulder. 'I didn't mean to be so late for dinner.'

He caught her wrist when she went to step away, holding it against his shoulder. 'Tell me where you've been, Emilia,' he said.

She sighed, standing still for a moment before retrieving her arm and going to the stove. She wasn't going to have this conversation – he knew precisely where she'd been, and it wasn't something she wanted to talk about. The less he knew, the better.

'I've been at work, delivering babies,' she said.

Emilia lifted the lid and looked at the contents of what was left for dinner. She'd prepared it early that morning, and it didn't seem any more appetising now than when it was cooked. Mind you, she'd never been partial to barley, and now it seemed to be the basis of every soup she made. It felt like barley and turnips were the only constants in her life since the war had begun, and she dreamed of a day when she could choose to eat neither.

'Emilia, you need to be more careful,' her father said, and as she filled her bowl, she found she had to bite her tongue to stop from snapping at him.

'I *am* being careful, *Tata*,' she said, unwrapping a loaf of bread and cutting a narrow slice for herself.

The silence between them was heavy, and after tidying up Emilia carried her soup and bread to the table and sat down, hoping the conversation was at an end. But the way he was looking at her, his eyes watery as he shook his head, told her it wasn't.

'Say it,' she said, angrily tearing off a piece of the bread and dunking it in the bowl first – anything to make it more palatable.

'I don't want you working with those families any more. It's time you stopped.'

Anger flared inside her and she gripped her spoon tightly. 'Would Mama have stopped? Would she have ignored those who needed her at a time such as this?'

She watched as her father dropped his head into his hands, guilt washing over her as she saw his pain. Before, she'd never have uttered a harsh word to him, but things had changed. She was no longer a girl who was prepared to blindly do what she was told.

'No,' he murmured. 'No, she wouldn't have, but your mother isn't here any more, Emilia. You're all I have, can't you see that? What would I do without you? What would I have to live for?'

Emilia set down the spoon she'd just picked up and levelled her gaze at him. She hated seeing him so upset – he was her father and she adored him – but she would not feel guilty for the work she was doing. 'I'm not all you have, *Tata*. Why is it acceptable for Staś to disappear and work with the resistance, but I cannot help those in need?'

He shook his head, his shoulders falling even further, and she immediately wished she hadn't mentioned her brother. Neither of them had seen or heard from Staś in well over a year, and after losing first his wife to illness, and then his son disappearing to fight for the Żegota resistance movement, she feared it was too much for her father to bear. But it wasn't enough reason for her to stop what she was doing.

'It is different, Emilia,' he finally said.

'Because I'm your daughter?' she asked, picking up her spoon and forcing herself to eat again. The only thing that made it palatable were the tiny pieces of potato floating in the liquid, and the odd morsel of meat. She'd stretched out a piece of pork to last them the week, but this was the end of it.

'Yes.'

She swallowed it, spoonful after spoonful, yet knowing it would do little for the gnawing hunger deep in her belly.

'How can I stop when there are families who need me?' she asked him. 'When there are babies and children who will face certain death if I don't help? How can you sit there and tell me to stop?'

He met her gaze, his eyes damp as he placed his hands on the table. 'Emilia, please. This is all I ask of you.'

'I cannot and *will not* stop when there's so much I can do! Please don't try to make me feel guilty for this, *Tata*. I don't want to drive a wedge between us, but I've made up my mind.'

The only indication that he'd heard her was the slightest nod of his head, and when she saw it, Emilia reached across the table and covered his hands with her own.

'I'm sorry, *Tata*, but I can't stand by and do nothing. You know I can't,' she whispered as her tears slowly fell. 'Saving these children, it's the only way I know how to help. It's the only thing I can do.'

'Your mother would have been so proud,' he said, before wiping his cheeks. 'I miss her so much.'

'So do I,' Emilia said with a sigh. 'I feel as if some days she's right there with me, as if she'll walk into the room and light it up with her smile, and when I'm delivering a baby I can hear her soothing words as she tells the mother how well she's done.'

Emilia glanced at the stove and imagined her mother standing there, singing quietly as she stirred something, the smell of which had always managed to permeate the entire house, wafting upstairs to her bedroom as a child.

'What I wouldn't give to eat her crayfish and sorrel soup,' she said. 'If I close my eyes, I can almost smell it.'

It was the first time in days she'd seen her father's eyes light up. 'Or her venison and mushrooms.' His lips smacked together. 'What feasts we once had.'

She smiled and blinked away tears. 'What feasts we once had, indeed. Those were the days, and I promise you, one day we will get our country back. This cannot go on forever, I refuse to believe it will. One day we will be honouring Mama by cooking her favourite recipes and sharing memories.' She squeezed her father's fingers in her own. 'We have to believe that, otherwise what hope do we have?'

Her father looked away, and she saw that she'd lost him once more to his thoughts. 'But I'll never get you back if they find out. If they come for you in the night.'

To that, Emilia didn't have an answer. And so she rose, rinsed out her bowl and quietly went to walk out of the kitchen, not wanting to imagine what it would be like to be dragged from her bed by the Gestapo in the dark of night. The thought alone sent a chill down her spine that she was certain she'd still be shivering from come morning.

'Emilia?'

His voice sounded hoarse. She turned to listen, studying her father's face and the pain that seemed permanently etched in the lines on his skin.

'Have you heard what's happening in Warsaw?' he asked. 'What they're doing to the Jews there, in the ghettos?'

Emilia's breath hissed sharply against her teeth as she shook her head.

'I've heard reports that they've rounded up thousands of them,' he said. 'They've begun loading them in freight cars at the station. I thought you'd want to know.'

'Bound for where?' she asked, her voice barely a whisper as she choked out the words.

'I don't think anyone knows,' he said, and she watched as he hunched over the table again. 'All I know is that they seem determined to get rid of them. Of every last one.'

As a child, her father had been strong and seemingly unflappable. He was a man who relished his role as caretaker of his family, who adored the way his wife was revered in their community for the work she did. Emilia could see that the pain of everything that had happened, of being unable to keep those he loved safe, had slowly broken her father into pieces, leaving only the shell behind.

'Everything will be all right, *Tata*,' she murmured, going to stand behind him and wrapping her arms around his shoulders as he stayed seated in his chair.

'No, *Kochanie*,' he whispered. 'No. It won't.'

--- ❧ ---

It had been over two weeks since she'd delivered Adela's baby, and still there had been no word. Emilia wished she could check on her daily, to ensure mother and child were doing well, but it was too dangerous for her to be seen there again, especially when the woman of the house wasn't pregnant. It would arouse too much suspicion.

But this morning, when she stepped outside and went to take her bicycle from the shed, she saw something that almost made her heart stop. On her seat was a small flower, pressed flat, as if it might have been flattened beneath her as she'd ridden home the previous day. Only Emilia knew that it was a sign – it was time to take Adela's baby to safety.

She knew little of the woman who arranged the transport, other than she was highly trusted among the Żegota resistance and was responsible for smuggling hundreds of children to safety. And now she was going to be meeting with her again.

Emilia looked around the shed, trying to see what had been disturbed, looking for the note that must have been left somewhere. If she didn't find it, she wouldn't know where to go, and then she'd be of no use to anyone.

She lifted two old flower pots and poked around in some of her father's old gardening tools, which were covered in cobwebs and didn't appear to have been touched. She sneezed from the dust, bending down low and moving old tins and a wooden box out of the way. It wasn't until she opened one of the tins and peered inside that she saw it – a small rolled up piece of paper with a tatty piece of string tied around it. She hastily opened it, reading the carefully printed words three times before ripping the paper into tiny pieces and taking them outside. Emilia looked around, stretching as if she was simply enjoying the morning sunshine, before nudging the dirt at the edge of their vegetable garden and sprinkling the paper there. She used her boot to cover it again, and then went to find the watering can. It contained a small amount of rain, and she used it to water the area she'd disturbed.

Satisfied there was no evidence left, Emilia returned to the shed for her bicycle and walked beside it to the gate before riding off to do her rounds. But as calm as she hoped she appeared, inside she was a bundle of twisting, gnarled nerves.

The hospital at five o'clock. It would be her most brazen attempt at smuggling a child out; in the past she'd spent hours walking through or hiding in forests, meeting in covert places that were less likely to arouse suspicion. But if she was told to meet at the hospital, then so be it. *I am merely a soldier following orders.* Or at least that's what she told herself.

—— ❦ ——

The day passed by in a blur of house visits, and Emilia knew she wasn't truly there for the women she spent time with. She went through the motions and did her job, but all she could think about was what came next, not to mention wishing that she could have forewarned Adela. She wasn't prepared to go there twice in one day, and Adela wouldn't want to risk the safe passage of her child either.

But now it was time. She arrived at the house much as she had the first time, only now there was no rag hanging on the line outside to invite her in. They'd known she'd come back, they all knew that the baby was only going to be in the house for a short time, but when she walked unannounced into the hallway she still felt like an intruder.

'Hello?' she called out, hoping she didn't startle anyone.

No one answered her, and when she walked through the house she couldn't hear any voices or movement. It was silent, despite the family hidden upstairs.

'Hello?' Emilia called out again, but still no one answered her.

She retraced her steps and went back outside, walking around the side of the house and looking out over the garden. That's when she saw the owners of the home, with two bowls placed beside them as they dug for vegetables, likely for that night's dinner. Emilia decided it was better they didn't see her, and so she hurried back and found the ladder, carrying it carefully inside and placing it beneath the attic door.

Once she was at the top, she tapped three times, waiting before hefting the panel across to reveal the attic. She took the final step up, her head emerging through the hole to find Adela's husband standing in front of his wife and child, a stick the only thing at his disposal to protect them. He wielded it in front of him, although as she raised her hands he slowly lowered it.

'I'm sorry I couldn't send word earlier,' she said, glancing behind him at Adela, who was rocking her baby, peppering his forehead with sweet kisses.

'It's today?' Adela murmured, as she stepped forwards.

'It is,' Emilia replied. 'I'm to be there by five o'clock, so we don't have long.'

Adela nodded, and Emilia cleared her throat and turned her back slightly. Last time she'd stood in the attic, she'd looked away to give the couple privacy in a joyous moment. Today, she was giving them a moment to say what might be their final goodbye.

She balled her hands and dug her nails into her palms, refusing to cry. These parents would at least have a chance to see their child, their *children*, again one day. So many had been rounded up and taken, those who were older or sick marched into the forest earlier in the occupation, their lives taken without a second thought. She had to remind herself that what she was doing was the best thing for everyone; the only chance to preserve the life of those who'd otherwise face certain death.

'Emilia,' Adela said, her arms empty when Emilia turned. She saw that the baby was now being cradled by his father. 'Would you ask for me, if my other children—'

'I will,' she promised. 'I'll find out anything I can.'

'There's only so long we can stay hidden here,' Adela's husband said. 'We'll need to move soon.'

'Where will you go?'

He passed her the baby, and she held him carefully, patient as Adela kissed his forehead one last time.

'We're looking at ways to escape. If you hear of anything, if there's any way you can help us get to safety too . . .'

Emilia nodded. 'I will do everything I can.' And she would. It wasn't a promise she made without meaning it; she would make enquiries and do whatever she could to save them, even if it meant moving them from house to house herself.

It was on the tip of her tongue to tell them they could go home with her, even for a short time, but she stopped herself from saying it. If her work was discovered, or her brother's work for the Żegota, her house would most definitely be searched, which would put this couple in even more danger.

So she said nothing as Adela stepped back and clung to her husband's side, her face gaunt while she studied her baby boy. Emilia carefully placed the infant in her sturdy leather bag, the one she carried every day and which would cause no suspicion, so long as she could keep the baby quiet.

She zipped it half shut, and placed it across her body, before giving Adela a long, hopeful look.

'I will do everything I can to transport your child to safety,' she told them. 'While he's in my care, I will think of him as my own.'

Adela smiled through her tears. 'I know you will, Emilia. I only wish I knew a way to repay you.'

Emilia just shook her head – as if she would accept anything from them, even if they could. Her mother had taught her the importance of helping others, of doing whatever one could to care for those around them, and it had stayed with her since she was a child. If her mama could see her now, she knew she'd simply nod and tell her that she was doing precisely what a good midwife was supposed to – keeping the children she delivered safe and well.

The house had been silent when Emilia arrived, but as she left, Adela's guttural cry was impossible not to hear. Although when the ceiling panel above her was pulled across, the noise became more muffled, and she hoped that soon the house would fall quiet again.

'Come on, little one,' Emilia murmured as she struggled with carrying the bag and the ladder. 'You just stay quiet, and everything will be fine. I promise.'

Emilia only hoped it was a promise she could keep.

'There she is!' a nurse exclaimed, rushing through the door to the hospital as if she'd been waiting all afternoon for Emilia to arrive. 'Quickly, we've been waiting for you!'

There were German soldiers nearby, and the hairs on the back of Emilia's neck rose as she got off her bicycle, careful to keep her balance as her bag lurched slightly to the side from the hidden weight. She froze, praying that the baby would remain silent, although there was such a commotion with the nurse grabbing hold of her and marching her into the hospital that she doubted anyone would have even noticed.

On the way, she'd sung under her breath, pedalling slowly as she tried to make it a comfortable trip, and she'd been lucky. If she'd been stopped, if soldiers had demanded that she open the bag . . . Emilia gulped, one arm around the thick leather as she let herself be led.

'Where's Irene?' she asked, referencing the woman she'd thought she would be meeting.

The other woman shook her head, tightening her fingers on Emilia's arm. 'Keep walking,' she whispered in her ear. 'You're

34

here as a midwife, I shall take your bag, and you're to simply do your job.'

Emilia wasn't entirely certain she understood, but she went along with it, not wanting to slow them down by asking questions.

'When we turn the corner, check all the women in the ward. Then there'll be a commotion when an ambulance arrives, and I want you to rush down with me and go inside once the doors open.'

Emilia didn't have time to answer before they swept around the corner and into the ward. She hesitated when her bag disappeared with the woman, but she knew she had to trust in the process, and she hurried towards the first expectant mother, praying that Adela's baby would be safe without her. She picked up the chart and said hello, her eyes darting around the room, wondering if anyone else was involved in their deceit. But all she could see were women in various stages of labour.

She'd barely made it to the third woman when a call came from the hallway.

'An ambulance has arrived! Where's the midwife?'

'I'm here!' Emilia cried, quickly running back the way she'd come and finding the same nurse there again, still holding her bag. She took it from her, immediately reaching her hand inside to check that Adela's precious bundle was still there. She was rewarded with tiny fingers clasping hers, and she managed to keep part of her hand inside the bag as she hurried along.

The ambulance had parked right beside the entrance, and when the rear doors opened, she saw Irene who ushered her in. The woman inside was in labour, her skin slick with sweat and her face contorted in pain, but they both ignored her as Emilia passed Irene the bag, watching as the baby was carefully taken out.

'Pull up the floor there,' Irene said.

Emilia dropped to her knees and took up the board that was covering the floor. She gasped when two little faces peered back at her, a boy of perhaps five and a girl a few years older. They blinked at her, their little fingers pressed to their lips, as if to tell her from where they lay, cramped and still, that she should be quiet.

'Quickly, pass them the baby,' Irene said. 'We don't have long.'

Emilia took the baby out of the bag, swaddled in a faded yellow blanket, his little face starting to screw up in a way that told her he was either hungry or about to start crying, or both. The little girl reached her arms out and settled the baby between herself and the boy, and within seconds Irene was covering them beneath the floor again, and then placing some towels and blankets down to disguise the board. Emilia prayed they'd be able to breathe, surprised the children weren't terrified down there. But then of course, she didn't know what terrors they'd been saved from.

'Take this one in,' Irene said. 'Shut the doors when you get out and bang your hand on the back twice. That's my signal to drive away. If anyone's watching, we don't want to draw attention by doing anything out of the ordinary.'

Emilia nodded, taking her bag back, which Irene had stuffed a towel inside to ensure it still looked full. She reached out to the labouring woman, soothing her and taking hold of her arm, wishing she'd known to bring a wheelchair down with her.

The woman stood, her breath coming in short pants, but before Emilia pushed the doors back open to get out, she turned to Irene.

'The children I brought to you, last time. Are they safe? Are they still in Poland?'

Irene pursed her lips, and for a moment Emilia thought she wasn't going to reply at all. 'They're alive, that's all you need to know.'

'Thank you.'

'Emilia?'

She turned.

'This may be our last chance to smuggle children to safety for a while, after what's happened in Warsaw. I'm taking these three to a local safe house tonight, but if there are any more babies or children . . .'

'You would need them before morning?'

Irene nodded. 'I would.'

'How would I get in touch with you?'

'I'll have someone watching you. He'll check your home before dawn, and if there are any children hidden with you, they will be the last ones we take.'

Emilia swallowed, thinking about hiding Jewish children in her own home, and how her father would react. But she would do it, of course she would do it. What choice did she have?

She nodded and stepped outside, acting as a crutch for the woman at her side. But they'd barely taken a few steps when words she'd long dreaded were barked at them.

'Halt!'

She froze, turning to see where the call had come from.

'*Halt.*' The word was repeated again, and two Gestapo men marched towards them.

Emilia stood tall. 'Sir, this woman is in great distress and about to have her baby at any moment. Please, could you give us some privacy?'

She received no reply, but one soldier stepped forwards and hooked his finger around the top of her bag, which was now unzipped. He looked at her as she held her composure, hoping he couldn't hear the rapid beat of her heart, and that the children inside the ambulance would miraculously be able to stay silent.

After he'd poked around in her things, he called out something she didn't understand, but she saw Irene appear in the open back of the ambulance, her palms facing out as she emerged.

They all stood as the soldier leaned in, the silence almost deafening. Thankfully the woman beside Emilia suddenly let out a guttural moan, which made both soldiers turn back to look at the women.

'Please, may I take her? Why are we being held?'

Irene glanced at her, but they quickly looked away from one another.

'Go,' he finally said, waving his hand.

Irene disappeared back into the ambulance and Emilia closed the doors and did the specified two bangs on the door to indicate they could leave. But once they were back inside the hospital, the soldiers finally out of eyesight, she collapsed against the wall.

Only the cries of the woman she'd been charged with caring for stopped her from sliding all the way to the floor.

If the children had been discovered, I'd either be dead or arrested by now, and Irene, too. Not to mention what could have happened to the children.

A rush of hot bile rose in Emilia's throat and she bent over, not able to stop being sick on her shoes.

CHAPTER FIVE

1943

Emilia snuggled deeper into her pillow, the covers pulled up tightly to her chin.

'Emilia!'

She heard her name and groaned, wriggling further down the bed. Surely it couldn't be morning already? She felt as if she'd only just closed her eyes.

'Emilia!'

This time her name was followed by a rough hand to her shoulder, shaking. She blinked and realised it was still pitch dark, and she sat bolt upright, seeing her father hovering beside her bed.

'*Tata?*' she said. 'What is it? What's wrong? Has something happened?' *Is it Staś?*

'Someone was here,' he whispered, placing the kerosene lamp he held on her bedside table. 'He was knocking on the door. He said you had to come, quickly.'

Emilia was fully awake now, and she swung her legs off the bed as her father sat down heavily beside her, his weight making the mattress sag. She'd always promised him that she wouldn't bring her work home, and now someone had been here?

'I'm sorry,' she said. 'It must be an emergency. Did he say where I was to go?'

'It was a man. All he said was that you would know what I meant by the name Talia.'

Talia. She hadn't expected her to give birth for another couple of weeks. 'It must have been her husband,' she murmured.

'Emilia, I'm sorry,' her father said, his hands folded in his lap. She yearned for the father she'd had before, the one who seemed frightened by nothing, and as she stared at him in the flickering candlelight, she realised that she might never see that man again.

'You have nothing to be sorry for, *Tata.*'

He took her hands in his, folding them together as he looked earnestly into her eyes. 'All your life, I've encouraged you to be true to yourself. To be brave and loving, to be like your mother.' He shook his head. 'But in my fear of losing you, I've tried to stop you from doing the things that have always made me so proud, and for that I am truly sorry. I hope you will forgive me.'

Emilia took her hands from his and instead opened her arms, holding on tightly to her father. 'I love you, *Tata.* I only wish things could have been different for us.' *I wish Mama was still here by your side.*

'So do I, my love. So do I.'

Her father stroked her shoulder and she smiled up at him, her eyes damp from unshed tears. Once he'd left the room she dressed quickly, fumbling for her bag and heading straight out of the door. If she was caught on her bicycle in the dark, she'd at least be able to say she was going about her work, but even the best planned excuse might not be enough to save her. *And that's without confessing that I'm going to attend a Jewish mother.*

Emilia pedalled fast, grateful for the wisp of cloud that moved to cover the moon. It left just enough light for her to cycle by, but she hoped it might mask her existence. She glanced over her shoulder, making her front wheel wobble, but she quickly corrected herself, trying to ignore the most overwhelming feeling that someone was watching her. It was perfectly normal, she was alone on the dark road, but still something didn't sit well in her stomach.

By the time she arrived at the house almost twenty minutes later, Emilia's pulse was racing and her skin was damp with sweat. But she didn't pause, going around the back to find a place for her bicycle before rushing into the house. Emilia had tapped on the door as she entered, and she was greeted in the hallway by a frantic-looking man, clutching his hat in his hand.

'Where is she?' Emilia asked.

He indicated that she should follow him, and they walked through the house to the back bedroom, where Talia was standing, holding on to the brass frame of the bed as she stood beside it.

'You don't want to go to the basement?' she asked Talia's husband as she set down her bag. 'You're certain we should be in here?'

'I'm not having her down there, not labouring.' The woman's voice wasn't Talia's; it was the woman of the house, who was also heavily pregnant and happened to be Talia's best friend since childhood.

Emilia went to her. 'Anna, how long has she been like this?'

'A few hours. We thought it was going to take some time, like you said, since it's her first. But something's not right.'

Emilia nodded and went to Talia, hearing her husband leave the room and shutting the door behind him. It was always easier when they didn't have menfolk in the way.

'Tell me what's wrong,' Emilia said gently, rubbing her back. 'Do you feel the urge to push?'

Talia was ashen white when she turned to her, her skin visibly damp, and Emilia didn't need to be told that something was wrong; she could see it for herself. 'Come on, let's get you on the bed so I can examine you.'

Emilia lifted Talia's nightdress as she gave a painful moan, touching her as gently as she could, before having to stifle a groan

41

herself. This was going to be a painful first labour. *Would Mama have known this earlier? Did I miss this last time when I was examining her?* There was nothing she could have done to change the fact, other than try some manipulations that may or may not have been successful, but at least she would have been able to prepare Talia.

'Talia, your baby is facing the wrong way, so this labour is going to be more difficult than I'd hoped.'

Talia's eyes widened, but Anna was by her side, stroking the hair from her forehead as Emilia spoke.

'Is the baby going to be all right?' Talia whispered.

'Your baby is going to be just fine,' Emilia assured her. 'The only trouble is that it's more difficult to birth a baby when they're posterior. It means that the baby's back is facing your back, so when you start pushing, it will be more painful than if he or she faced the other way.'

Talia looked terrified, and Emilia wasn't surprised.

'Many, many women have given birth this way,' she soothed. She gently examined her again, holding Talia's hand as a contraction tightened her body and made her cry out. 'I need you to imagine your baby in your arms, the way it will feel to hold your own child. Do you think you're having a boy or a girl?'

'A girl,' Talia cried.

'A sweet little girl, well, how about that?' Emilia smiled.

But in the back of her mind, all Emilia could think of was how to progress the labour more quickly. Since the Warsaw Uprising, her work had become even more dangerous, and if she was to get the baby to safety, she'd need the cover of darkness.

Emilia sat beside the bed and watched as Talia held her baby, cradling her to her breast. *A natural-born mother*, that's what her mama would have said if she was there, standing with a satisfied look on her face. *But it's different now, Mama. I can't smile, not when I know that they can't stay together, not when I know what might happen to them. All I can see is heartache.*

'You were right about her being a little girl,' Emilia said, reaching to gently stroke the top of the baby's head with the back of her fingers.

Talia looked up and smiled. 'As you were right about how painful it would be.'

Emilia grimaced. 'I wish there was more I could have done to ease your pain.'

Talia was looking at her baby again now, and Emilia shifted on the bed, trying to find the right words.

'I need to ask you something, Talia,' she said, looking up as Anna came back into the room. 'Do you remember what we spoke of, last time we met?'

Talia nodded, tears filling her eyes as she held her baby even closer.

'I can't guarantee we can smuggle your baby to safety, but I'm prepared to try.' Emilia paused as Anna sat on the other side of the bed. 'Do you understand what I'm trying to—'

'I won't let you give her up,' Anna interrupted. 'Can't we say that I had twins? Can't we find a way to keep her here, as my child? There must be something else we can do other than send her away? How will a baby this young even survive?'

Emilia looked between the two women. 'This is your decision, Talia. I suggest you discuss it with your husband while I pack my bag, but if I'm going to take her,' she hesitated, 'it will have to be soon.'

The truth was, it was almost impossible to smuggle anyone out of Poland any more, but she wasn't about to tell Talia that.

This was the best chance they had to keep their child alive. Perhaps their only chance.

It only took a short time before Talia called to her, her voice soft and echoing with emotion. Emilia went to her, her own tears flowing as she watched the new mother press a long, slow kiss to her baby's forehead, her fingers tangled with her newborn's, her breath shuddering from her lips.

'Take her,' Talia said, lifting her in her arms. 'Take her to safety, Emilia. Please.'

She looked first at Talia, and then at her husband, who'd come to sit in a chair beside the bed. A man broken if ever she'd seen one.

'You're certain?' she asked, tucking the baby into her arm.

'We are,' Talia said, as Anna walked from the room, crying. Emilia couldn't imagine what it must have felt like, the pain of knowing her best friend had to give up her baby when she would be allowed to keep hers.

'I promise you that I'll do everything I can to keep her safe.'

Talia touched her hand. 'I know you will. I trust you, Emilia. We both do.'

'There is a record kept of every baby, of every name,' Emilia said softly. 'If you survive the war, when this is all over—'

'She'll be able to find us,' Talia's husband said, his voice gruff in a way that a man's was when it was choked with emotion. 'Or we will be able to find her.'

Emilia didn't hesitate when they both nodded to her, taking her bag and looking inside. But the little girl was barely an hour old. Could she really place her in there and expect her to stay quiet? She looked up and saw a coat lying over a chair.

'Do you think I could take that?' she asked. 'That way I could keep her buttoned against my chest. I think it would be safer, and it would also keep her warm.'

Talia rose, wincing as she stood, before helping Emilia into the coat, carefully positioning the little girl against her, her hand lingering over her baby's soft little head.

'Her name is Eva,' Talia said, pressing her palm to Emilia's face, before whispering, '*Thank you.*'

Emilia stood for a moment, staring into Talia's eyes, wishing she could take some of her pain. But she knew the only way she could help was in leaving, and so she gathered her bag and walked away, through the house, following the steps she'd taken only hours earlier.

I will never get used to it. I will never, as long as I live, forget the cries of each mother as I took their child from them.

And as she cried, as her tears fell and were silently whipped from her face by the breeze, she rode back towards home, her suffering eased only by the warmth of the tiny body pressed firmly to hers beneath her borrowed coat.

The baby made a little bleating noise and Emilia started to sing, softly under her breath, in the hope that she might soothe the baby and also stop anyone from hearing her. Not that anyone should be out yet – the sky was barely beginning to lighten; everyone else was still asleep.

A noise startled her, and she wobbled on her bike while she tried to figure out what it was and where it had come from. Emilia glanced sideways, not seeing anything, but when she rounded the corner, her blood ran cold. There was a German patrol on the road, blocking her way, which meant she was going to have no other option than to stop.

She kept pedalling, still singing softly under her breath until she was closer and wishing she were nearer to home, as her eyes danced over the Gestapo men in their perfectly tailored jackets, belted at the waist with precision, their tall black boots making it impossible to mistake them for anyone else.

'Halt!'

It was the second time in two days that Emilia had heard the command, and this second one was far more terrifying than the first. She slowed, her boot skidding against the ground, stopping some distance from the two men. Against her better judgement, she glanced back over her shoulder, only to see three more Gestapo closing in on her, walking with a lazy, conceited gait. She had nowhere to go.

This is no random patrol. They knew I was going to be here. Someone has betrayed me.

She smiled despite her nerves, remembering how much they'd always liked her sweet smiles and waves in the past. Her only hope was to charm them, and she ran her fingers through her hair.

'Name?' one of the men barked.

'Emilia Bauchau,' she said, clearly, her voice ringing out in the early morning air. 'I am a midwife, just returned from delivering a baby.' She smiled as she reached into her bag, keeping her movements slow and steady, not wanting them to know how terrified she was. She'd always thought of them as predators, able to sniff out the weak and smell the fear of their prey, not hesitating to maim and kill those who dared to get in their way. 'Would you like to see my identity card?'

The men sneered and exchanged glances, as a pit developed in her stomach. She wrestled with her nerves, hoping they didn't see the shake of her hands. There was no way she was going to be able to use her feminine charms this time.

'I sincerely apologise for breaching curfew, but this was a medical—' She faltered as one of the men roughly grabbed her bag and emptied the contents on the ground in front of her. 'Emergency,' she said, as she looked at all her things strewn haphazardly at her feet. Thank goodness she hadn't put the baby in there, as she had the last.

Emilia tightly balled her hands, trying to stop from reaching for the little one, who so far had been miraculously quiet. She shut her eyes, imagining the infant suckling on her little fist as she nestled against her.

'Where have you been?'

She fixed her smile. 'Sir, I have been delivering a baby. I apologise for breaching curfew, but babies seldom work to a timeframe.' Emilia heard the tremble in her voice and knew they'd heard it too. How could they not have? 'Is there a problem?'

Emilia watched as the guard reached inside his jacket and produced a Strum cigarette, taking his time to light it, before offering one to his comrade. She held her tongue, wishing to reprimand him and remind him that his beloved Führer no longer permitted the Gestapo to smoke. When one was offered to her, she simply shook her head.

'I'm going to ask you one more time,' the same man said, as he blew cigarette smoke directly into her face. Emilia coughed, but she didn't turn away, holding his gaze, not wanting him to see her fear. 'Where have you been?'

So many desperate, pleading thoughts ran through Emilia's head in that moment, none of them helpful. She imagined falling to her knees and begging for forgiveness, or somehow mounting her bicycle and fleeing into the woods. But she knew that neither plan would change the outcome of her early morning interrogation – the Gestapo liked to hunt, and she'd watched them release their dogs on those who tried to run away before, followed by the sound of gunfire echoing through the trees.

I'm sorry, Tata. I'm so sorry to leave you alone. I'm so sorry I did this to you.

Someone was responsible for this. Someone had known where she was going, had followed her and tipped off the Gestapo, there was no other explanation. And now she was going to pay with her life.

'We know who you are, Miss Bauchau,' the other man said, who up until now had remained silent. 'If you want to live, I suggest you answer our question truthfully.'

Emilia shut her eyes. Nothing would make her talk, nothing would make her give up the families she'd fought so hard to protect. *Nothing.*

But as the baby moved against her, her heart began to pound. She'd made a promise to Talia, and now that promise was about to be broken.

CHAPTER SIX

Emilia didn't see the sudden movement until it was too late. The man who'd been speaking to her stood back, blowing another puff of smoke in her face, which meant she didn't notice the way his colleague moved. She shrieked when his fingers curled violently in her hair, dragging her off her bicycle. She kicked and flailed, her heels catching on the ground as she fought to keep her balance. She kept an arm around her middle, desperately trying to protect the baby, but he lifted her so hard by the hair she feared it would rip straight from her scalp.

Her luck had run out. She wasn't going to get the baby to safety. She wasn't going to make it home to her father.

It was over.

'Did you not understand the question?' he asked, his lips curling back into a snarl as he twisted her hair in his hand, making her yelp in pain. She gazed into winter-blue eyes, so cold she had to look away. 'Where have you been?'

She glanced at the pistol in his holster, his belt within reach if she tried hard enough, if she could just kick him and reach for it. As if reading her mind, he let go of her hair, kicking her as she fell backwards.

'No!' Emilia cried, her hands raised to protect the baby. She was scrambling to get back on her feet when the little girl finally cried, her little bleat impossible not to hear.

And that was when she saw both men smile.

'What do you have in there?' one asked, the men exchanging glances as they threw their cigarettes to the ground. One ground his beneath his shiny black boot, his eyebrows raised when he walked slowly towards her. She watched in terror.

'Get up.'

Emilia did as she was told, her arms wrapped protectively around herself now, around the child. There was no point in pretending otherwise, they knew there was something under her jacket. She trembled as she stood before them; a single tear escaped and ran slowly down her cheek.

I'm sorry, little one. I'm so sorry.

This time she saw the raised hand coming towards her, only it was followed by another, ripping her coat open, snatching her hand to stop her from catching the baby as the precious bundle tumbled from her coat to the ground.

'Look what we have here,' one of the men said, peering down at the now wailing baby, her cries filling the crisp morning air, her blanket fallen between them. She looked so helpless, her little body exposed to the elements instead of being cradled close.

'Please, I beg of you, please leave her alone,' Emilia said, her eyes darting between the men in front of her and the baby at her feet, wishing she could swaddle her tightly and at least hold her to her chest. She was barely hours old, she wouldn't survive for long without warmth and milk.

'Take it.' The order came as a bark. The Gestapo man who'd been behind her earlier came forwards and roughly picked up the child, as if he were collecting a thing rather than a living human being.

He took hold of Emilia by the collar as he hauled her up. This time she stayed on her feet as he marched, scrambling to keep up with him past her discarded bicycle.

It took only minutes for them to round the corner where Emilia had come from, and she saw more Gestapo waiting, two of them holding large, menacing attack dogs on thick leather leashes. Alsatians, capable of ripping her limb from limb should she even think of making a run for it.

Emilia quickly wiped her cheeks, not wanting anyone to see her tears. She'd always known this day could come, which meant she needed to be stronger, she needed to remember all the good she'd done. Someone had once said to her that the only sign of doing enough against Hitler and his tyranny was to be dead, because only then would one know they'd done everything they could, taken every risk possible to save another. Well, at least she could hold her head high.

When they finally stopped, Emilia was roughly pushed down to her knees, her hands cuffed behind her so tightly she could barely move her wrists. She looked at the houses before her, wondering where the traitor was, if they were watching, or if the person who'd disclosed her whereabouts was closer to her own home. She doubted she'd ever know, and there wasn't so much as a flicker of a curtain as she swayed, on her knees, trying to hold her chin high and not look at the rough way the baby was being held.

'Do you recognise any of these houses?'

She lifted her chin higher, her only mode of defiance. 'No.'

The smack of his fist hit her jaw so hard she fell backwards, the side of her head colliding with the dirt beneath her, her hands useless, restrained behind her. He hauled her straight back up by her hair, and when he stood she saw long strands around his fingers, ripped straight from her scalp.

She lifted her chin again, the pain in her jaw reverberating across every part of her face. She tried to open her mouth, and tasted blood.

'Have you been inside any of these houses tonight?'

He stared at her, and she saw his nostrils flare when she didn't answer him.

'Where are they hiding? Tell us where the Jews are.'

Emilia shut her eyes, not wanting to see the rise of his hand again, bracing herself for the impact to her face. But this blow came to her middle, the hard heel of his boot knocking the wind from her as she tumbled backwards, her insides exploding with a searing pain that continued to build. But this time she quickly righted herself, forcing herself back onto her knees, her fingers clenched together as she fought to be strong.

They cannot break my mind. I will never tell them. I will go to my grave before telling them where those families are.

'Get the baby,' he screamed, coming to stand so close to her that his spittle sprayed onto her face. She turned her head away, but he saw her defiance and took hold of her chin, tightly clenching it between his fingers and thumb as he forced her to look, made her stare at the baby. Arrows of pain anchored through her jaw when his hold tightened.

Blood trickled from some part of her face, she saw it when she looked down, the red staining the German's wrist.

'You're going to watch as I kill it,' he seethed. 'You'll know that child only died because you wouldn't open your mouth, *Jew lover*.'

No. 'No!' Emilia screamed as the baby was held out by her tiny little legs. The murderous creature disguised as a man used his other gun to take his pistol from his belt, the very same weapon that she wished she'd been brave enough to reach for when she had the chance.

'Please, *no!*'

52

The grip on Emilia's chin released and she tripped, her face contorted in horror as she saw Talia emerge from the house, wanting to scream to her that she needed to run. But the young mother, barely rested from childbirth, came hurrying in her nightgown, her bare feet sending dirt flying. She flung herself towards her baby, catching her just in time as she was carelessly dropped.

'Talia,' Emilia cried. 'You shouldn't have come out, you—'

'You promised me you'd keep her safe!' Talia screamed, hysterical as she fell to the ground around her baby, primitively trying to shield her. 'You promised me, Emilia. What have you done?'

I tried to save you all. I didn't speak because I wanted to spare your lives, to spare the lives of everyone here. I would have died for you, Talia. But of course she kept her words locked in her throat, not wanting to add to the pain no doubt rippling through Talia's body.

Emilia looked up then when the dogs started to bark again, when the men in their perfectly cut clothes marched towards the houses, the two women forgotten where they'd left them. She crawled on her knees now, to get closer to Talia. There was no chance they could escape, there was no saving children or trying to keep anyone from harm. It was over.

'What are they doing?' Talia cried, scooping little Eva up.

Emilia shuffled after her, struggling with her hands tied, wishing she could reach for her, to soothe her with her touch.

'Stop, Talia.'

'Why are they going in there? What are they going to do?'

What do you think they're going to do? How do you truly think this is going to end?

'It only takes one traitor,' she said, softly, as Talia finally stopped walking. Emilia stood beside her when the first door was kicked down. Screams echoed down the otherwise silent street, and her body started to tremble. 'That is all it takes, and then everyone connected with me, with you, with this street, will be hunted until every single person is caught. They won't stop until they get every last one now.' *So many families have risked so much, and for what? It's all over now, so many lives about to be extinguished in one heart-breaking raid.*

She wished it weren't true, wished that she could have somehow taken the fall and saved everyone else from the fate that was now theirs. But the moment Talia had run from the house, the moment she'd chosen to save her child, she'd also decided the fate of everyone else she loved.

Emilia refused to think about her father, about whether they'd already been for him, whether he was even still alive or whether he was lying, broken in their home. It was too painful to even consider.

'They won't hurt Anna, will they?' Talia whispered, turning to Emilia, her eyes wide and betraying her fear. 'What will they do with us? Will they let us stay together? Are they going to take us somewhere?'

Emilia leaned into her, both of them flinching when an elderly couple were thrown out of the door of their house with such force, there was no way they could have avoided broken bones. But it was the screams of children that Emilia knew she'd never be able to forget; much like the cries of mothers forced to give up their children, she knew they'd stay with her for an eternity, never able to escape even in slumber. She refused to turn away, watching the brutality, *needing* to see it.

Her wrists ached as she tried to move them, the metal cutting sharply into her skin, and when she moved her mouth her jaw spasmed in pain, already swelling, her head pounding from the blows she'd received.

'I'm scared, Emilia.' Talia pressed in tightly against her.

'So am I,' Emilia replied. 'But the only thing we can do is stay strong. We have to fight to stay alive, Talia. It's all we can do.'

But when more screams echoed out, cries of desperation as people were ripped from the homes around them, she wasn't convinced staying alive was even a possibility in the face of such brutality. Not any more.

She watched Talia cradling her baby, the precious, innocent little life unwittingly a casualty of war. *If I could give my life to save theirs, I'd do it in a heartbeat.*

CHAPTER SEVEN

When the cuffs were finally taken from her wrists, Emilia held her hands in front of her, gently massaging her raw skin as she was roughly shoved forwards. She couldn't look up, couldn't bear to see the faces of the people around her. People who had trusted her with the lives of their loved ones mixed with others she didn't know. Talia had stayed close to her as they were rounded into a large group, huddled together, some wearing barely more than a flimsy nightgown, others dressed in their outdoor clothes from head to toe, as if they'd perhaps gone to bed prepared for the worst.

She was one of the fortunate ones, wearing sturdy boots and a warm dress with a coat, although it now gaped at the front from being ripped open earlier. Emilia shrugged out of it, gently placing it around Talia's shoulders. Before, she couldn't help her, but now that her wrists were freed it felt only right to try to keep her warm. She'd just given birth – she should have been convalescing in her bed after such an arduous labour, not standing outside.

'Whose house is this?' one of the Germans shouted.

It was daylight now. The sun was obscured by clouds, and Emilia lifted her head to look at the house they were pointing at. It was the one Talia had been hidden in. She swallowed, glancing sideways and seeing the colour drain from Talia's cheeks.

'No,' Talia murmured.

Emilia took her hand, holding it tightly as the dogs began to bark again. 'Don't say a word. We must stay quiet.'

'Hers,' someone said.

Emilia pushed forwards a little, her hand falling from Talia's as she tried to see who it was, who'd betrayed Talia's friend so quickly, without a thought for what might happen to them.

'It was her house,' another person said. 'And his.'

Emilia shut her eyes when she saw an old woman lift her hand, her pointed finger shaking. She found Talia's hand again and linked their fingers, her body shaking as she heard the single fire of a gun. Clearly fear brought out the worst in some people.

A collective gasp rose from the group, and that was when Emilia saw, when everyone parted slightly, the fallen body of Anna's husband. But then something else caught her eye, a flash of white. A woman suddenly ran, her legs eating up the ground as she made for the wooded area nearby, clutching her rounded stomach, her white dress flowing behind her. She was making for the same treed area that Emilia had hidden in with children months earlier when she'd helped to smuggle them out.

This time, when she heard the crack of gunfire, she saw the figure fall. Anna slipped to the ground, the back of her blond head now matted with blood, her body crumpled. Unmoving.

'Let this be a lesson to all of you.'

Talia screamed and Emilia reached for her, holding her. The crowd erupted in cries and murmurs of pain, and they were all prodded and shouted at to move. Their captors laughed and joked, their weapons brandished as they kicked anyone who fell behind, their boots connecting with countless bodies.

But as they were marched forwards, their destination unknown, the worst part was hearing guns fired from behind them, her body shuddering at the unexpected blasts. It appeared that those who fell behind weren't given a second chance, but she never looked, not wanting to see if what she'd guessed was true.

'Where do you think they're taking us?' someone asked.

'Are we to walk all the way to the train station?'

'The train station? Are they transporting us somewhere?'

Emilia heard their questions, which echoed what was already going through her own mind. She knew about the places they took Jews and others who'd been helping them. But at that very moment, as they walked down the street, she saw a man standing alone, his hat clutched to his chest. She willed his eyes to find hers, seeking him out, and when he finally did she had to fight not to scream. It was the most painful moment she'd ever endured, more heart-wrenching even than when her mother had passed.

Tata. He'd seen her and he was alive. His face wasn't beaten. His eyes had met hers. He was safe.

Emilia kept watching him, lifting her fingers to her lips in a silent kiss even though it hurt her jaw terribly, until her head could turn no further; but her steps were lighter now, the pain inside her eased. They could do anything to her, all she cared about was that her father had been spared. For now at least.

She helped an older man nearby, catching his elbow when he stumbled, and she noticed that everyone was doing their best to help others now they'd seen what happened to the slowest of the group. It was only then that Emilia realised Talia's husband wasn't with them.

'Talia,' she whispered. 'Where is Luke?' He'd risked everything to come and find Emilia the night before, but now he was nowhere to be seen. Had he been part of the group? There had been so much commotion, but she couldn't recall seeing him.

Talia just shook her head, which made Emilia wonder if he'd managed to stay hidden. If they'd found him, surely they would have shot him to make an example of him?

Onwards they marched, and Emilia noticed that many of the people around her who were barefoot had begun to slow down. Talia's feet were visibly cut and blood had smeared across her skin, but when Emilia reached out to carry the baby for her, she refused, holding her tightly to her body. She only hoped that Talia wasn't also bleeding from her private parts. She'd had to stitch her after the traumatic labour, and she wasn't sure they would hold with such strenuous walking.

She'd heard rumours of Poles disappearing, being arrested and then forced to go to labour camps, but it wasn't until she saw the freight wagons with her own eyes that she understood what was to happen to them. They were the type of transport usually reserved for livestock or food supplies, but as they neared the railway line, Emilia could see that they weren't the only people who'd been rounded up in the night.

Groups of women and children were being corralled and forced into the carts. *Ten, fifteen, twenty, thirty . . . forty.* Emilia stopped counting. How were so many people being put into such a tiny space? It was as if it were an illusion and they would be walking out on the other side.

Eventually the door to the wagon in front of them was shut, and she could only imagine the terror of being plunged into darkness. There would be no light, no air, *nothing*.

'*Bewegung!*' a Gestapo man yelled. 'Move!'

They shuffled forwards, their group having become one now. No one fell, no one tripped, they just silently moved until they edged closer to the wagons. Emilia was still next to Talia, and she made sure to keep the new mother slightly in front of her, not wanting her to lag behind. She'd noticed the baby had barely made a sound since they'd started walking, but she was reluctant to say anything. What would she even do if anything was wrong? It wasn't as if she had medicine or other tools at her disposal, and Talia had just lost her best friend; she didn't need to know she might have lost her baby in the same night.

Something prodded into her back, the point jabbing into her spine. Emilia cried out and lunged forwards, almost knocking an older woman over with her sudden movement. But she soon forgot about that. Her throat went dry as she saw the number of people who were already crammed into the car when it was her turn to step in.

The hard thing jabbed her in the back again, and this time she turned, looking straight into the eyes of the Gestapo man standing behind her. He sneered and went to poke her again, but she was too quick this time, jumping to avoid the sharp pain before he could connect for a third jab.

Emilia's eyes began to water, the heat of so many bodies together almost too much to stand. She huddled even closer to the person next to her, to make room for others. Someone else pressed into her spine and another person brushed against her chest. She took a few deep, slow breaths, trying to calm herself when the dark wooden door slid shut, with only the barest amount of light coming through the small high window that was covered in timber slats. It was as if they were animals, shoved together without a thought, and it was an image she couldn't get out of her mind as she fought against tears and the darkest of thoughts her mind had ever been plagued with.

They stood like that, huddled and shivering, for what seemed like hours, but could easily have been minutes. Time stood still while the shouts continued outside, as their ears pricked and became more sensitive, their only sense that wasn't forcibly constrained. Emilia couldn't see, she couldn't feel anything other than the other bodies around her, so she listened carefully for a hint as to where they might be going, what their fate might be. Was she to be put to work in a labour camp or factory? That was where so many Jewish girls had been sent when Germany had first occupied parts of Europe, wasn't it?

'She's not moving, Emilia.' Talia suddenly interrupted her thoughts. 'Why isn't she moving?'

Emilia's hand found Talia's shoulder and she leaned into her for a moment. 'I'm sure she's just tired. Hold her close and sing to her.'

It was cruel, lying to her when she knew something was most definitely wrong, but in the dark, in a wagon full of perhaps seventy or even eighty people, what use was there in telling her that her baby might be gone? There wasn't even room to sit, let alone examine a child.

Suddenly there was a lurch that sent everyone scrambling to stay on their feet. The train came to life then, the reverberations coming through the wooden floor as some people tried to squat, their legs no doubt exhausted from the unexpected walk. And when they started to move, Talia began to sing, and it was almost as if she were singing for everyone, not just her child. Some joined in, others stayed silent, while many cried, softly as if they didn't want anyone to hear, but when done in tandem with so many others, it created a noise that Emilia knew would be unforgettable. It was the suffering of many, the pain of many, the understanding that everything they'd ever known, everything they'd once held dear, had been taken from them.

———— ⊱⋅⋆⋅⊰ ————

'Emilia, we need to be strong even when everything starts to go wrong.'

She turned her face to her mother, barely fifteen and yet already well acquainted with how babies were brought into the world, listening to her every word. She'd finished school now and she was to be her mother's shadow, learning from her so that one day she could assist the women of the town and carry on their family's tradition.

'How do you always know what to do though? What if you can't help them?'

Her mama touched her face, her fingers soft against her chin; she smiled down at her. 'Even in the darkest of moments, even when all seems lost, there's always something that can be done. These women in childbirth, they face a pain like no other, but no matter how traumatic their labour, we are there to soothe and calm them. And you will learn, as I did, how to help every woman in your care.'

Emilia listened, absorbing every word.

'By the time you're doing this on your own, you will know instinctively what to do, Emilia. Just like my mother taught me, I shall teach you everything you need to know, so that one day, when it is time, you will never doubt in your ability.'

'I've seen you though, Mama,' Emilia said. 'You know just what to say, what to do. It's like you were made for this work.'

'It comes with practice,' her mama replied with a smile. 'Now come with me, fetch those towels and hot water too, and remember, our words are powerful. What you say when you walk into that room will make all the difference to the woman lying there. You have the power to soothe her pain, simply by saying the right thing at the right time. Your words are the best tool you have.'

She followed her mother, her constant companion as she merrily talked about it being a beautiful day to bring a baby into the world, wondering how she'd ever live up to the woman whom everyone seemed to love.

Emilia wiped a tear as it escaped from her eye. Talia's gentle song stopped, the snuffle of tears the only thing she could hear as she held her mother in her mind.

'Shall we introduce ourselves?' Emilia said, raising her voice to be heard above the clatter of the car as it rattled along the track. 'My name is Emilia. I am a midwife.'

She was greeted with silence, before someone cleared their throat. There were so many people pressed together that she didn't know where the voice was coming from; she knew there was power in using one's voice, in uniting people in their darkest of moments. Today, she was going to remember her mother, and that meant following her advice on how to deal with the worst moments, the most painful moments, in a person's life.

'My name is Maja. I am a mother.'

Emilia breathed a sigh of relief, as murmurs started within the wagon. 'Maja, are your children with you?'

'Yes. My children are here with me.'

'My name is Jakub,' a man said. 'My wife is here with me.'

'I'm Elena.'

It's working. Mama, it's working. The power of saying the right words, of easing pain.

'We need to talk to one another, lean on one another,' Emilia said, after perhaps a dozen more people had called out their names. 'We can survive if we all stay together and take care of each other.'

A rumble of voices filled the carriage then, and Emilia turned to Talia, barely able to make out her face in the dark. 'Talia, may I hold your baby for a moment?'

She needed to see for herself, to know if there was any hope.

Emilia carefully reached for her, holding her close to her chest and turning her head to listen to her breath. It was impossible to hear anything over the rattle of the train tracks and the noise of people talking, and so she placed her fingers to feel for a pulse; for any sign of life. When she felt nothing, Emilia touched the infant's lips with the back of her fingers, hoping to feel her breath, for her mouth to move, *anything*.

She passed her back to Talia and then pressed a kiss to the new mother's hair.

'She's just sleeping?' Talia asked.

'She's just sleeping,' Emilia repeated, thankful no one could see the tears shining in her eyes. She'd never been a liar, but there was no way she was about to tell Talia that she feared her baby had already perished, not in these circumstances, not when she'd already lost so much in one night.

It seemed like they'd barely been moving for an hour when the cart suddenly lurched and came to an unexpected halt. *Are we already where we're supposed to be going?*

Emilia wished she knew German as shouts echoed out, but she couldn't understand what was happening.

'They're loading more people,' someone said.

'Does anyone know where they're taking us?'

Emilia shut her eyes and listened as all of the people around her fell silent, trying to think past the throbbing pain in her face, her jaw aching even in stillness. But they'd barely had time to gather their thoughts when their carriage rattled to life once more, to wherever their final destination might be. And as much as she would have liked to, she couldn't think of a single other thing to say to ease the worries of those around her. Or herself.

———— ⟡⟡ ————

When the train finally stopped, Emilia had a pit in the bottom of her stomach, a gnawing sensation similar to hunger, but much, much worse. They stood in silence; barely a cough or sniff rang out in the stale, tepid air, until there was a bang outside and the door rattled open.

The light that shone through almost blinded Emilia; it was such a stark contrast to the dark they'd been in, for so many hours, that it felt as if the brightness could cut straight through her.

'*Aus!*'

The shout startled Emilia as she stared past the people in front of her.

'Out, out, out!' came a shriek, clearly directed at them. Bodies started to shuffle forwards on legs that were tired and shaking from standing for so long.

Emilia's own legs ached, her muscles burning from all the hours on her feet. But she kept reminding herself how fortunate she was to have her warm boots when so many others were barefoot. Their toes must have been numb from the cold floor.

'Out!' came another shout, as Emilia stepped onto a platform and realised that theirs wasn't the only wagon being offloaded.

She stood on her tiptoes and tried to see where they were, to get some sense of what was happening, but all she could see were rows of lights, thousands of them in fact, in the most perfect symmetrical formation, and uniformed men with Alsatians on leashes. They were the SS; she'd heard about them and she knew they were recognisable by their all-black uniform, as fearsome in appearance as the animals they held. Emilia shuddered. She'd always loved dogs, but there was something about that particular breed, and what they'd been trained for terrified her.

That was when she noticed there were other people, many of them in the most curious striped pyjamas, their faces so gaunt they were almost painful to look at. One man moved past her and yelled to the crowd, urging them forwards. Some of them were barefoot, and it was then that she realised they couldn't be guards. *Are they prisoners here?*

'Keep moving!' the man yelled. 'Move!'

Someone protested, a man objecting to being shoved, and another man in the pyjamas leaned towards them, his face showing his terror.

'Please don't make us hurt you. Just do as we ask. *Please.*'

Emilia kept moving with the crowd, looking over her shoulder for Talia and wishing she'd stayed closer to her. *He spoke Polish. The man in the pyjamas spoke Polish.* Her heart began to pound as she realised that something was wrong, that the people doing the work for the SS were some of her own countrymen. Why were they helping the guards to hurt them? Did they fear for their own lives?

'Where are we?' she asked, when another man in stripes moved past her. 'Please, tell us where we are?'

'Auschwitz,' he said, without looking, without so much as breaking his stride.

Emilia stopped walking and exchanged glances with the woman beside her.

'What is Auschwitz?' she called out, hoping he would hear her. But in her heart, she knew. It was the place they took Jews and other political prisoners. It was the place from where no one ever came back.

But the man in the striped pyjamas was gone, swallowed by the endless swarm of humans filling a platform longer than any she'd ever seen before.

CHAPTER EIGHT

Auschwitz-Birkenau

Emilia tried to understand what was happening in front of her. She was so tired it was as if her very bones were aching from exhaustion, and she still wasn't certain how or why people were being separated into groups. Eventually it was her turn, and she looked over to see that Talia was also stepping forwards. She was still holding her baby, clutched to her like a child might cling to a much loved teddy bear. She heard Talia cry and wished she could comfort her, but she saw another woman amble closer to her and was relieved she wasn't alone.

The men standing in front of her were not in the SS uniform that she'd expected, although they held themselves with the same arrogance, peering down their noses at the people gathered before them. They wore white coats, marking them as doctors, or at least she presumed so, although she couldn't understand their involvement. They stalked up and down the lines of women, as if they were looking for something in particular.

'Age?'

Emilia cleared her throat. 'Twenty-two years.'

The doctor looked up and appeared to consider her. 'Health?'

'I'm in very good health,' she replied.

'No ailments?'

Emilia focused on the top of his head, wishing she were brave enough to tell him that it was none of his business. But when he glanced up at her again, she replied: 'None.'

The doctor stood then and took hold of her chin, roughly turning her head as he inspected her. He didn't ask her to open her mouth, instead roughly prying one of his fingers inside and forcing her jaw to work. In the commotion of what had happened she'd forgotten about her face and how it must look – the bruises would be purple and blue by now, and her jaw ached from having to open it. She resisted the urge to slap his hand away, to demand that he tell her exactly what he might be looking for.

'Occupation?' he asked, looking her up and down.

'Midwife,' she said.

He called something out and a doctor slightly taller than her walked over, his dark hair swept back off his face, a slight gap in his front teeth showing as he spoke. She didn't know what it was about him that was different from the others, but goose pimples rippled across her bare flesh as he stood before her.

'You're a midwife?'

'I am.'

'You have experience?' he asked, making her shudder as he slowly looked up and down her body, as if he were considering whether or not she was worthy of his attention. 'Do you have papers?'

Emilia lifted her chin. 'I am well experienced at birthing babies and tending to women, and I've also worked as a nurse.' She paused. 'I do not have my papers with me, they were in my bag when I was brought here and I wasn't permitted to bring it.' More like she was shoved so violently to the ground she couldn't have kept hold of it.

'Keep her,' he said as he walked away. 'She will be useful.'

The doctor who'd originally been questioning her nodded, before indicating with his thumb that she should go left. Emilia looked at the guards with their dogs; it was as if they were daring anyone not to follow orders, waiting to unleash them on the women. She lowered her gaze and went where she'd been told, watching as Talia was pointed in the opposite direction. Emilia noticed that the other group was full of mostly mothers, children and elderly people, by far the largest group of all, and guessed she'd been separated due to her work. There were only a handful of people who'd been ordered to the left with her, and as she considered who she was standing with, she realised they were all young, likely under thirty at most, and many of the women appeared strong. The men had been gathered separately, slightly further left, which indicated they were to stay separated by gender, and there were far more men being sent to the left side.

It took hours for the process to be completed, and the larger group were taken first, trudging away towards a big concrete building as the rest of them watched. She'd been terrified Talia's baby might be snatched from her arms by a doctor, but they hadn't seemed to care. Emilia stared after her, wishing she'd turn so she could wave to her, but no one looked back at those who were left, not even Talia. Her only hope was that they were being taken somewhere suitable, so they could rest after what they'd been through.

A young woman cried next to her and Emilia reached out her hand, linking their fingers as they were ordered to start walking. They were ushered into a different building and forced to stand in lines once again, as they had on the ramp, and although the line was much smaller, it still took just as long to make it to the front of the queue.

'Name?'

Emilia cleared her throat and considered the man seated at the table. He was wearing the pyjama outfit she'd seen people wearing earlier. 'Emilia Bauchau,' she said, realising that this was some sort of registration. She looked back over her shoulder, straining to see the other group.

'Address?'

She blinked back at him. She couldn't give him her address; what if they went looking for her father?

'Address!'

Emilia lifted her gaze and gave the address of a home close to hers that had long been abandoned.

She stood there and answered all manner of other questions, before eventually being passed a piece of paper. He gestured for her to walk on, and she looked down at the note, surprised when she saw not her name but a set of numbers. *63332*. She had no idea what that meant, and she kept staring at it, almost tripping on the concrete floor as she shuffled forwards.

As the women in front of her stepped aside, she found herself standing before two men, one holding a cloth and the other a metal instrument fixed to a piece of wood. The one with the instrument didn't look up, just held out his hand. She hesitated, before passing him the piece of paper, feeling as if she were giving him a receipt for an order, perhaps for a coat she'd come to collect.

'Left arm.'

'My arm? Why?' she asked.

She hesitated when he reached for her, and a guard took hold of her arm, roughly shoving up the sleeve of her jacket and slamming her arm down onto the table. Emilia trembled but kept her face turned away, the guard's spittle landing on her cheek, the smell of his breath making her stomach turn.

Something sharp stung her arm, and she winced as she looked down, the guard finally letting go of her and yelling at someone else, instead.

'Hold still, it won't hurt as much,' the man whispered as he marked her.

So Emilia stood, deadly still, afraid to move as a needle painfully etched her numbers into her skin. When he was finished the man with the cloth dipped it into green ink and then wiped it over her skin as she tried not to wince.

63332. The number was now needled into her skin, forever marking her, trickling with blood from the crude way it had been needled. She couldn't stop staring at it, at her arm that had barely been dusted by freckles.

Emilia pulled down the sleeve of her jacket, her hands shaking as she clutched it to her chest and followed the other women who were walking ahead of her. But a shout stopped them in their tracks, all looking around to see who was speaking.

'I am Commandant Rudolf Hoess, and I am in charge here. After you are processed, you will be taken to your new home, Auschwitz Two – Birkenau.' She finally saw him, standing high, perhaps on a table, his hair cut close at the sides and his head tilted upwards while he looked down on them. He was flanked by guards, and it struck her as ridiculous that an armed man needed guards to address a roomful of displaced people with no weapons at their disposal. 'You will not disobey the guards here at Auschwitz, because if you do, there will be consequences. Work hard, do as you are told, and you will go free. It is as simple as that.'

Emilia swallowed, looking away when a young woman tried to make a run for it, the commandant laughing as two of the guards tripped her up and began to beat her with the butts of their rifles. A tear escaped Emilia's eye, and then another; she fought to be brave in the face of such cruelty.

I don't believe him, Mama. I don't believe they will ever let us go free.

CHAPTER NINE

Emilia was used to nakedness. She was used to seeing women at what she'd once thought was their most vulnerable, but as she walked into the cold concrete chamber and saw the terror on the faces of those around her, she realised she had not. *This* was women at their most vulnerable. *This* was suffering unlike any she'd ever witnessed.

'Take off your clothes,' a guard shouted at them as they all stood in the centre of the room. When no one moved, he yelled, his eyes wide as he screamed. '*Ich sagte, zieh dich aus!*'

Emilia dropped her coat and slowly lifted her hands to undo her buttons. She hesitated when she reached the last one, not used to anyone seeing her undergarments. She looked around, shuddering as she realised how many guards were watching, all men, leering at the women stripping before them and making lewd gestures. There were more men in striped pyjamas too, standing there and facing them, although at least they had the decency to lower their gazes. Perhaps they too had gone through the humiliating ordeal.

'Hurry!' a guard yelled, at the same as Emilia was prodded sharply in the side. She hunched over, arms wrapped tightly around herself. *I can't do this. I can't take my clothes off. I can't. I won't.*

'Just do as they say,' someone whispered to her. 'The quicker we get undressed, the quicker it's over with.'

She looked sideways and saw a woman of perhaps the same age as her hurriedly stepping out of her skirt. Emilia leaned forwards, feeling sick when she realised that everyone else was now obeying the orders. If she refused, she would stand out from the group. She didn't wish for anyone to notice her.

Her skin broke out in goose pimples as she stripped down to her underwear. *Surely we don't have to take it all off? Please let me keep some of my dignity.* She'd never let anyone see her without her clothes on before, save for her mother when she was only a child.

But the barked order that followed sent a shudder through her. *This can't be happening to me.* But it was, and as the women all stood, completely naked, having placed their clothes neatly on the benches around them, they huddled closer, hands over breasts, legs tightly crossed, bodies rounded as if to try to hide their most intimate parts.

The people in pyjamas scurried in, taking the clothes as the women yelped and cried. Watching her clothes disappear, being ushered into another concrete room, Emilia had the most over-whelming feeling that any hope she'd been holding on to that things might not be as bad as they seemed, was gone. Incinerated as if it hadn't existed at all.

She looked up, her jaw thudding with pain, her nose crusted with dried blood, and watched as the leering guards all stepped back, disappearing into the shadows. It only took seconds for her to realise why.

Freezing cold water rained down on them as the guards laughed. Emilia screamed, so loudly that she even surprised her-self; her voice ricocheted out of her, from a place so deep inside that it sounded more like an animal howl. She hadn't even realised they'd walked into a shower block, the dim light making it almost impossible to know where they were being taken.

They will not take my dignity from me. I will survive this, whatever it is.

The water seemed endless, and when it finally stopped they all stood, shivering and chattering, arms once again wrapped tightly around their bodies as they were ordered to walk forwards, once more into the unknown. Emilia did as she was told, choosing to obey rather than rebel, knowing that now was not the time to be disobedient when she didn't have so much as the clothes on her back. And that's when it all suddenly made sense to her, why the people were wearing striped clothes, why they scurried around the guards as if they were scared of them.

They are prisoners here, just like we all are. Because there, folded on the benches that had once held their discarded clothes, were sets of striped tops and an assortment of other clothes. They were to wear the same clothes, to mark them as prisoners of this place they called Auschwitz. And to make it even worse, they were not allowed to dress yet. It appeared there was more degradation still to come.

'Keep moving,' a guard yelled. 'In lines!'

She fell into line behind the other women, wondering what was to happen to them now. What else could there be? But when she saw, when she realised what was about to happen, she knew it was the closest she'd come to breaking.

Her hair was her pride and joy. She wore her chestnut-brown locks just past her shoulders, glossy and dark; hair that her mother had loved to brush as they sat by the light of the fire, talking about their day as they sipped tea. Emilia lifted a hand and ran it gently through her hair, committing the feel of it to memory, telling herself that it was only hair. *I will grow it again. When I leave here, I will grow it long and never, ever let anyone cut it ever again.*

A tear slid from the corner of Emilia's eye as she sat down, roughly pushed into the chair as a fellow prisoner lifted the clippers. The metal tugged at her scalp as she twisted her fingers together,

her toes clenched when her hair fell in clumps onto her shoulders, sticking to her damp skin, hugging the sides of the chair. She couldn't bear to think how much of it was on the floor.

A dribble of blood trickled down her temple then, and Emilia raised her hand, feeling the rough stubble on her scalp as she wiped it away. But they weren't done with her yet. Another prisoner stood in front of her and roughly took hold of her chin, forcing her mouth open as he inspected her teeth. She was grateful when he moved on, but the woman next to her wasn't so fortunate, and Emilia cringed as the man produced pliers, her fingers tightly clenched as she listened to the woman scream. She could only guess they were looking for gold fillings, the only valuable thing one would find inside a mouth.

'Stand on there,' the prisoner said to her, pointing to the low table.

Emilia stared back at him, not certain what he meant. But when she looked across at another woman who'd come in just before her, her blood turned cold. *No. No, I can't do that.*

'Do it or they'll hurt both of us,' the man muttered. 'I am sorry.'

She knew she had no other choice, and Emilia forced her feet to move, using her hands to help her onto the table. She stood, biting hard on her lower lip as her pubic hair was shaved away, and then the hair on her legs, leaving her entire body bald, devoid of even the soft downy hair that had once covered her thighs.

'Move!' a guard yelled.

Emilia got down from the table and shuffled forwards again, unable to stop more tears as a guard reached for her bottom, shoving his fingers hard into her skin, another groping and squeezing her breast when she walked into the room containing the clothes they were to put on.

But when she saw that another girl had blood dripping down her legs, her heart broke. If there was any way to make what they'd just been through worse, it would be the humiliation of menstruating without any napkins to use. Emilia only hoped her monthly courses didn't start soon, too.

But it was what she saw just before she disappeared through the door that made her feel truly sick, that made her grateful for the bruises distorting her face, that told her that bleeding was nothing. A young woman, perhaps seventeen, was being forced to stand as a guard fondled her breasts and called out that her hair wasn't to be touched. *She is going to be used by him for her body, whether she wants him or not.* Emilia knew what these kinds of men wanted, and it was clear the men here would take it. They treated Jewish women and girls as if they were beneath them, but clearly the Nuremberg Race Laws weren't preventing these men from using their bodies.

They were directed to stand outside, still naked and now freshly shorn, bracing themselves against the wind that curled around them, unrelenting in its viciousness. But there was to be no reprieve, not yet.

'One at a time!' a guard yelled.

Dogs barked nearby, but Emilia refused to look. There was something even more terrifying about being naked, the idea of the dog's sharp teeth on her flesh enough to make her want to cry. But she didn't. She would not let anyone see her humiliation, *her mortification*, at what she was going through.

It wasn't until she'd shuffled further ahead in the line that she saw what they were doing. There was a large tub of water, filthy from all the women who'd been submerged already, and the cries were enough to tell Emilia that it wasn't simply water. When it was her turn she stepped forwards, moving quickly to avoid the stick that was waved at her, and the moment she put her foot in she understood the cries.

'All the way!'

She was barely standing with both feet in before something hard smacked down on her head, the pressure forcing her under.

The liquid stung; it ate like acid through her skin and burned her eyes, her scalp on fire. *They're trying to disinfect us as if we're a disease.*

When she got out, she resisted the urge to rub her eyes or her skin, knowing it might make the sting worse, as the cold wind stripped her skin of any last remaining reserve of body heat.

It was perhaps an hour, maybe longer, before they were finally marched back inside, to the relative warmth of the cold concrete building, ushered back to where they'd first undressed.

Emilia reached for a pile of clothes as fast as she could, quickly dressing, horrified that there was no underwear. Why couldn't they wear the underwear they'd arrived in? What purpose was there in depriving anyone of something so simple? They were issued only a skirt, blouse and headscarf, and Emilia gratefully put it over her bare scalp, wondering as she knotted it how it would stay in place without any hair. But she was dressed now, all she needed was to fumble through the shoes and try to find a pair that fitted her. She'd been so grateful for the boots she'd had and yearned for her warm, soft socks too, especially when she realised that the only shoes there had open toes. She wondered how anyone would avoid frostbite without socks to wear with them.

Emilia's thoughts caught in her throat as she walked alongside the other women. Everyone was silent; there wasn't so much as a murmur as they trudged out of the building. She looked at the fences with razor wire on top, at the SS guards with their rifles at the ready, in position as lookouts, and the never-ending huts dotted throughout the compound.

Faces peeked from the doors and watched them, sad, hollow-looking faces that seemed to be devoid of life, and it sent a shiver through Emilia. *What if I end up like that? What if this is where I am to live for the rest of my life?*

Would it even be a life worth living?

CHAPTER TEN

The walk seemed endless. Every step down the long dirt road made Emilia feel as if she would never be leaving, taking her further into the depths of something she didn't fully understand. It was like a wasteland dotted with buildings, an expanse of nothingness, not so much as a blade of grass covering the ground. But there was a woodland in the distance, dense trees that appeared to be birches.

As the light of the day began to fade, and rain started to gently fall, quickly soaking through the too-big shirt she now wore, Emilia looked at the rows of wooden buildings, built uniformly to her left. The razor-wire fences ran along the back of them, a wide road that they were walking on stretching far into the distance. And still the buildings continued. The thought sent a shudder through her, as she considered that there would be no way to flee whatever was planned for them.

'Here,' the guard finally said, stopping outside one of the barracks.

It was different from many of the ones they'd passed. This one was built of bricks, perhaps newer than the wooden structures in the other part of the camp, and nothing like the green ones they'd passed on the other side.

Emilia faced the open wooden door, waiting her turn as she was told to enter. She was the last to walk in and consequently received yet another shove from behind. If they kept doing it to her, she was certain she'd have an ugly purple welt on her back to match the ones on her face. Her feet were still reluctant to move, even as she risked another sharp prod.

But her mind quickly turned from her pain to the room she found herself standing in, on a dirt floor that added an earthy smell to the barracks. Eyes blinked back at her, the wooden bunks that stretched three high already full of women with such despair etched into their faces that Emilia had to look away. The smell of too many bodies was overpowering, and Emilia resisted the urge to take off her headscarf to cover her mouth. Was every block like this? Or had she been taken to the worst building in the camp?

'Hurry up!' someone yelled, a sharp female voice that sent a shiver through Emilia. When she looked, she saw the woman had a green inverted triangle pinned to her shirt, and she wondered what it signified, or why it was different from the red triangle she'd been given.

She was shoved in the side then, not by a guard but by other women, who were scrambling to find a place on one of the beds as even more women were ushered in from outside. The place was teaming with humans, crammed into a space that wasn't designed for even half that many people. The women already with their own space yelled and hissed at the newcomers, clearly not wanting to share their already tightly packed beds with another body. She didn't blame them. They appeared to be tucked together in groups, most likely to stave off the cold. How did anyone even climb to the highest bunk, which almost touched the ceiling?

There was no light, no heat, no beds – and only tiny windows that she was certain would barely let any light in come morning. The straw on the floor looked unfit for a pig to lie in, and Emilia's ankles immediately began to itch. By morning, she was going to be covered in red welts that she would be scratching for days.

'Listen to the *kapos*, they are in charge of you now,' a guard said, before turning to the door. 'They're free to do with you what they please, so do what they say.'

Emilia walked towards the back of the room, forcing herself to look openly at the eyes watching her, lifeless as if there was nobody home behind their stares. She climbed up to the second level, awkwardly, seeing a small area where she hoped she might fit. Each berth of triple bunk beds was occupied by five or six prisoners already.

'Find somewhere else,' someone said, as another woman stuck out her leg and kicked at Emilia's hand, almost making her fall back.

But Emilia fought for her space, shoving her bottom back so she could fit, her hands folded to make a pillow for herself as her body adjusted into the rough, straw-filled pillow beneath her. She could see there were some threadbare blankets, but they certainly weren't going to be shared with her. *I will not cry. I will not cry.* She needed to sleep, and in the morning, everything would seem better. Her mother had always said that dawn brought with it not only a new day, but a fresh perspective. But she wondered if even her darling mama could have found a way to stay positive in this hell.

——— ⟡ ———

Morning came faster than Emilia had expected. There was a sound of loud thumping, as the door to their barracks swung open, and a woman started to yell.

'*Zählappell! Zählappell!*'

Roll call, roll call. Someone climbed over her, and she curled into a ball as they passed, ending up being the last one down and receiving a smack with a whip or some such thing by the screaming woman. The *kapo*, that's what the guard had called the woman in charge. She was the one wearing the triangle.

Emilia had no concept of time, although she knew it was early. She sidled up to the woman beside her, hoping to receive a warmer reception from at least some of the women she was going to be sharing accommodation with. Everyone had the same look, a fierce yet desperate stare that told her they were trying to stay alive. The women who appeared to have been there the longest were in groups, clearly protective of one another and not pleased to see new arrivals.

'Do they wake us up at this time every day?' Emilia asked.

The woman barely looked at her, and Emilia tried not to be shocked by her bony wrist and arm as she lifted her hand to scratch her neck, which was covered in sores. Emilia also tried to ignore the pain building in her stomach, her bladder desperate to be relieved as she scratched at her own arms.

'We get up at 4.30 a.m. each day,' another woman murmured. 'Roll call is at 5.15 a.m. You're late, they will beat you. You don't do what you're told? They will beat you.'

Emilia squirmed. She didn't doubt it. The guards seemed to take pleasure in beating anyone, from what she'd seen. She followed behind the other women who were hurrying, discovering that there were facilities for washing, consisting of filthy dirty water she didn't dare to dip her fingers into. There was no toilet paper, no soap, *nothing*. She quickly relieved herself when she got the chance in one of the latrine buckets that was already nearly full, the smell almost unbearable. She didn't envy the person whose job it was to empty them, and hoped that as one of the newest arrivals, that duty wouldn't fall on her.

'Come on,' another woman said, her voice softer than those of the others she'd tried to speak to. 'Hurry and you won't be last in line for breakfast.'

Emilia trotted along beside her, grateful for someone to learn from. She had a feeling she would learn quickly not to misstep, if she wanted to avoid punishment.

'I'm Emilia,' she said as they walked.

'Lena,' the woman said. Her small smile took Emilia by surprise – it was the first she'd seen since she'd arrived.

'Do you have a job here? What are we expected to do all day?'

The woman stopped for a moment and stared at her. 'You truly don't know?'

Emilia shook her head. *Should I know?*

The woman began to walk again, slowly but steadily, and Emilia kept her pace, noticing for the first time that she had long hair beneath her headscarf. Another first – all the other women she'd seen had shaved heads, like her own. And this woman was pretty, with full lips and wide, bright eyes.

'They only keep the strong ones because they expect everyone here to work all day. They march almost everyone out for the day, and they work until their bodies give up, or they die.' She made a noise in her throat. 'We are the fortunate ones.'

Emilia tried to hide her shock. What did she mean, that they were the fortunate ones? 'It's like this every day?'

The woman nodded. But before Emilia could ask about where the other women who weren't strong went, wondering about Talia, they walked into a building and Lena disappeared into the mass of women. Emilia's stomach growled at the thought of breakfast. She lined up with the others and collected a cup, surprised she couldn't smell anything cooking. It took a long moment before she realised they were only being given liquid.

'We don't get food?' she asked.

Three women turned to look at her, their cheeks hollow, their eyes showing their pain, as something that someone announced was coffee was splashed into her cup, warm against her fingers. She watched as one of the women used her finger to scrub at her teeth, swishing the liquid around in her mouth before swallowing it. It certainly didn't look like coffee.

'Welcome to Auschwitz,' one of them muttered.

'It's like she expected a hotel.'

As Emilia lifted the cup to her lips, trying not to smell the foul liquid as she forced herself to sip, listening to the women sniping beside her, she found it impossible not to cry. *So much for being strong. One morning and I'm already falling to pieces. One morning and I already don't know how I'm going to survive.*

'Come on, let's get to roll call,' Lena said, reappearing beside her. 'And don't listen to them. They're always awful to the new arrivals.'

Emilia tried not to think about how bad lunch might be. 'Can I ask how long you've been here?'

Lena looked away. 'Long enough to lose almost all the other girls I arrived with.' She sighed. 'Drink it all up, you'll get used to it. The thirst is even worse than the hunger, and they don't give us any water.'

'Your family?' Emilia asked.

Lena's eyes brightened. 'Still safe, I hope.'

Shortly after, she found herself following Lena once again, all of the women forming a line as guards arrived and began to look at them all. One woman slipped over and was severely beaten for her misstep, and when Emilia went to help her, Lena reached out to stop her.

'Don't,' she whispered. 'It will only make it worse. For both of you. Whatever happens, you stay still.'

'But—'

'Don't.' The word was final. 'Follow the *kapos'* orders, don't do anything for anyone else, and you might live to see tomorrow. They will take any chance to be cruel, they don't need a reason, and no one will stop them. You need to make certain you're unseen, that you're just another number.'

She bit down hard on her lip.

'And stay still. One movement is all the excuse they need to beat you until you're broken.'

Against her better judgement, Emilia did as she'd been instructed and stood still, shivering as she tried not to look at the woman on the ground, or the guards, or anything else in the hell she'd been brought to. She could feel the *kapo* staring at her, wondered what she'd done to draw her attention, or if she'd noticed her initial reaction to help the woman. How were these *kapos* chosen, the fate of so many women in their hands? But it was the SS guard who was in charge now, slapping his stick against his boot, making her jump every time. As the roll call dragged on, she tried not to look or react without so much as a shiver, and only registered her number was being called when it was shrieked for the second time. She glanced down at her arm.

63332. Emilia looked up, terrified at what punishment might be served on her for her tardiness in replying, but instead the SS guard came closer, so close she could smell the sausages he'd eaten for breakfast, the second-hand aroma so putrid it made her shudder. But her body betrayed her, her stomach growling at the thought of actual food, even if it did smell revolting.

'You are the midwife?'

She nodded. 'Yes. I am.'

'Take the rest of them,' the guard said, pushing her forwards. 'I'll take this one.'

Emilia couldn't ignore the looks of the other women. They appeared angry with her and as they began to march in a slow, shuffling line, she realised that she'd avoided being put to work with them. Did they resent that she'd been singled out, that she wasn't going to do the same backbreaking labour as they would be forced to endure? Would it make them dislike her even more than they already seemed to? And then she noticed that a small group wearing red or white head scarfs hurried off without any guard to watch them, back towards the main entrance she'd walked through the day before. One of them lifted her hand ever so slightly, and Emilia realised it was Lena.

She didn't have time to look after them though, as she was ordered to walk quickly away from the barracks where she'd slept the night. It showed her how vast the camp was, how many buildings had been erected to house prisoners, and she tried to absorb it all, to figure out where she was as they walked along the long, dusty road, past endless wire fences that appeared substantial enough to keep dangerous beasts within.

'Block 25, the sick block,' the guard said as they walked. 'Block 23, over there, is the hospital block.'

She took in the numbers of the blocks and wondered what made the sick block different from the hospital block. Wouldn't they be one and the same?

'In here,' the guard said, shoving her towards a simple wooden hut, much smaller than the building she'd slept in.

She did as she was told, hope lifting as she wondered if she was to put her midwifery skills to use. If anyone could use her gentle hand and expertise, it would be the women living here. She couldn't imagine anyone would want to bring a child into the world inside the gates of Auschwitz. She expected they'd either arrived pregnant, or had been raped by the leering guards who'd seemed to greatly enjoy the spectacle of so many naked women huddled together.

It was the smell that first told Emilia that something wasn't right, as she stepped inside. She followed the guard into the primitive-looking hut, barely able to mask her surprise as she took in the two women standing in aprons, and three women in various stages of childbirth. The labouring women were lying on the floor or in the lowest bunk beds, their skirts pulled up to their waists, their cries muffled as they suffered on their own. When she stepped closer, squinting in the dim light, she saw that one mother was already holding her baby, clutched to her chest. Were the women in aprons midwives or nurses, or just female guards who had been brought in to assist?

It took all her willpower not to demand that birthing mothers be given fresh water; their lips were cracked and dry, their sunken eyes showing their desperation. Emilia noticed two buckets of filthy water near the door. She wasn't certain what they were for, but it most definitely wasn't for drinking.

The women in aprons glared at her. It was clear they were in charge, and they were making no effort to assist the mothers in their care, even with a guard standing in the room. She eyed the buckets again, confused, although something about the hut made the tiny hairs on the back of her neck stand on end.

'I have a new midwife for you,' the guard said, shoving Emilia forwards, as if offering her as a prize. She noticed that he kept his back slightly turned, and she guessed it was more to do with his being uncomfortable than trying to afford the labouring women any privacy. 'Put her to use however you want. The doctor thought she'd be helpful with so many pregnant wenches. We need them back to work straight after they labour, I don't want them in here more than a few hours.'

One of the midwives shrugged, the other grunted, roughly inspecting one of the women who was clearly in the midst of a painful contraction. Emilia knew her place was to stay quiet and learn, that the severity of not obeying any of the guards at the camp was surely death, but after dedicating her life to helping women and babies, it was almost impossible to stand by and not try to help. Where were the soothing cool cloths? Why was nothing being done to ease their pain?

The second the guard's back was turned, the midwife gave Emilia a long hard stare, before looking from the baby to one of the buckets. Emilia followed her gaze, as she slowly understood what she was telling her.

Surely not. I must be mistaken. I must . . .

The nurse just laughed grimly, and Emilia knew she wasn't mistaken at all.

'No!' Emilia cried, lunging for the baby. *Oh, surely not! Surely they cannot keep that water there for the reason I'm thinking of?*

The second midwife slapped Emilia away as she fought to reach the child, grabbing hold of her and trying to restrain her. The mother cried softly in the corner, too weak to rise, or perhaps simply resigned to the fate of the baby she'd just borne. Did she know what was to happen to him? Was she even aware? *How can they do this? How can such barbaric behaviour be happening here? Is it because the baby is a Jew, or do they do this to all babies born inside the camp? Is this why Lena said we're the fortunate ones?*

'Enough!' the guard barked from behind.

Emilia froze. A gulp of emotion, tears and hatred rose within her, like nothing she'd experienced before. If this was to be her life, then she wasn't certain she wanted to live it any more.

'Filthy Jews,' the midwife muttered as she stood over the mother and baby. But Emilia's eyes had landed on something else now, on a tiny body discarded in the corner, unmoving. She hadn't been wrong in her assumption, she knew that now without a doubt. This was a place of death. This was not the type of midwifery she wanted any part of. They clearly discarded the babies before hurriedly sending the women back to the fields to work.

Get out. I need to get out of here!

Emilia turned on her heel without thinking and ran, evading the guard as she slipped past him and pushed at the wooden door, falling onto the hard-packed ground where she vomited what little she had in her stomach, the memory of what she'd just witnessed making bile rise in her throat over and over again. She would run, as fast as she could, throw herself at the electric fence if she had to and end her miserable existence. But she would never, ever take part in the murdering of a child.

'Stop!' the guard who'd brought her to the hut yelled, his boots thundering towards her, towering over her as she tried to stand and scramble away from him.

She didn't see the rise of his boot, didn't have time to avoid it as he kicked her violently in the stomach, the air in her lungs expelling with a loud whoosh. But she wasn't going to give him a moment of satisfaction, wasn't going to let him see her cry, and so she forced herself up, straightening and staring defiantly at him despite the searing pain in her stomach, despite wanting nothing more than to curl into a ball and scream.

'I won't do it,' she said. He touched his hip, as if believing he could scare her by reaching for his gun or his stick. But she was stronger than that, she had to be, because no one was going to force her to do anything so cruel. To her, even being a bystander to such barbarity was as bad as doing the act herself. 'You may as well shoot me.'

Emilia trembled as he lifted his gun and aimed it at her head, but she kept her chin lifted, her eyes unblinking. If this was to be her last breath, her last stand, she wanted to be remembered for her defiance in the face of evil.

She listened to the click of his pistol and involuntarily shut her eyes.

CHAPTER ELEVEN

EMILIA

LONDON, 1995

TUESDAY

Emilia stared at the recorder as it clicked, making her jump, jolting her from her memories.

'Just one moment,' Hannah said, reaching into her bag and taking out another tape. Emilia watched as she carefully changed them over, scribbling a label on the tape that was now full of Emilia's story. The words had tumbled from her, as if she'd been waiting her entire life to tell them. Which in a way, she supposed she had.

Lucy leaned forwards, her eyes brimming with tears as she reached for her hand. 'Mum, all these years, I wish—'

'I should have told you,' Emilia said. She clutched her daughter's fingers, regretting every year she'd stayed silent when she saw the pain reflected in her daughter's face. Why had they thought it was a good idea to keep their past from their own family? From the people they were closest to? To tell their daughter that the war hadn't affected their families? But she knew, of course she knew. After surviving Auschwitz, after building a new life so far removed from what had happened to them, why would they ever want to relive it? Or at least that's what they'd told themselves. 'All these years, I didn't want to burden you; they were memories that were easier to bury than talk about. I didn't want you to know what I'd been through. I didn't want you to carry any of my pain, of knowing who I'd lost and what I'd suffered.' *I still don't. Even at seventy-five years of age, I still don't want to burden my daughter with my memories.*

Lucy nodded, her fingers still closed over hers as Hannah cleared her throat.

'And your memories, Mum, they seem so clear, so—'

Emilia nodded. 'The things I saw, the things I lived through, I would have done anything to forget them. And for a while, perhaps I did. Perhaps I did manage to forget the past as I made up for what I'd missed out on, but recently, ever since your father passed . . .'

Lucy's eyes were fixed on hers as her voice trailed away. 'Since he passed?' she asked, prompting her to continue.

'Since then,' she said, hearing the tremble in her voice, 'the past seems to have come racing back to me as fast as a train coming into the station. As if it happened only yesterday, as if those memories have been held in a vault in my mind, waiting to be unlocked.'

They sat in silence until Hannah cleared her throat and spoke softly.

'Emilia, would you like to take a break, or should we continue?'

'Mum?' Lucy asked. 'Shall I make another pot of tea? Or would you like to call it a day? You don't have to share anything more today, not if it's too painful.'

'Tea would be lovely, please,' Emilia said, missing her daughter's touch as she rose. 'And yes, we can continue. Now I've started, I think it's best if we keep going.'

Hannah smiled and pressed play on the recorder again, and Emilia realised how comfortable she felt with her. Or perhaps it was simply because she'd seen her on the television and it had made her feel as if she already knew her.

'Emilia, are you aware that during your time at Auschwitz, some babies survived and were given to German families? That not all the babies born there died?'

'Yes, I was,' she replied. 'They were the lucky ones, or so we told ourselves. Everything we did was to save those babies, from pain or harm. It was what kept us going.'

'When you say *we*,' Hannah asked, 'who are you referring to? Another midwife at the camp?'

'I mean Aleksy, of course,' Emilia said, as Lucy walked back into the room. 'If you want to know my story, then you have to understand his. Without him, I might never have lived past my first day at Auschwitz.'

CHAPTER TWELVE

ALEKSY

POLAND, 1941

'What will we do to stay safe, Aleksy? I can almost feel the Gestapo breathing down my neck sometimes, it's as if they're watching our every step.'

He reached for her hands, holding them tightly in his. Aleksy wanted to reassure her, to whisper soothing words to his wife that would stop her from worrying. But he wouldn't lie to her, and that stopped him from saying anything. How could he tell her that he'd keep her safe, when their village was occupied by the enemy? When he'd witnessed with his own eyes Jews being marched to a river only the week before last and commanded to swim, with most of them drowning before reaching the other side? It was a brutality, *a narcissism* that he simply couldn't fathom. And yet such despicable acts were happening all around them.

'I wish we could escape, Aleksy. I wish we could find some-where to disappear to, somewhere safer than here . . .'

'Natalia, you know I will do whatever I can to keep us safe, you have my word, but—' Did he tell her that nowhere in Europe was safe? That there was nowhere he could take her, even if he wanted to? That even if they made a run for the forest, they'd be found? He'd never felt more powerless, knowing there was nothing he could do as her husband to protect her.

He could see the tears gathered in her eyes as she looked bravely back at him. 'We can't protect ourselves from them, can we? Not if they come for us? Not if they decide to round us all up and take us away?'

They looked at one another for a long moment, before she buried herself against his chest, his arms instinctively going around her. They had their first baby, they'd only been married three years; it was supposed to be the happiest time of their life, and instead it had been the most fraught as he tried not only to keep his wife and young son safe, but his patients, too. He was thankful he'd made it home to her, when so many others hadn't, but there was still a sense of helplessness at not being able to guarantee the safety of his family.

'I've been working on something,' he eventually said, careful with his words and not wanting to worry her. 'Something that might help us all, help our entire village and all my patients, too.'

Natalia leaned back in his arms, wiping her cheeks with the back of her fingers. 'What is it?'

'I don't want to keep anything from you, but I'm not entirely certain myself how it's going to work,' he replied. 'I just need you to trust me, Natalia. I need you to trust me that I'm doing all I can, and that some things I may have to keep from you for your own safety. The less you know of what I'm doing, the better.'

She took his hands in hers and lifted them, pressing a kiss to his knuckles. 'I trust you, Aleksy. Of course I do.' She let out a long breath. 'I hate that you have the weight of so many on your shoulders, but I'm so fortunate. At least you get to come home to me at night.'

He sat with her for a moment longer before rising, hearing the baby cry from the other room and taking that as his cue to leave. 'I think someone is hungry,' he said, kissing the top of his wife's head before collecting his jacket. 'I'll see you after work and we can talk again then.'

She smiled her goodbye and he walked out of the door, looking up at the sky as the clouds parted and the sun shone through. He'd walked the same steps from his home to his office for almost a year now, and could find his way there with his eyes shut, but the one thing he'd never get used to were the Gestapo positioned on street corners, appearing in unexpected patrols, or their flags prominently displayed, waving high in the air. Just as Natalia did, he felt their presence with every step, had the most unnerving feeling that his every move was being monitored, lest he make a mistake. And a mistake with a Nazi could cost a man his life.

He'd heard stories of families in the village being rounded up before he arrived home, taken to God only knew where, and most of the men had been taken as slave labour by the Germans, working them to the bone as punishment simply for their ethnicity. It all made him even more uneasy about the future, and what could happen to him if he went through with his plan, if his deceit were discovered.

He unlocked the door to the Red Cross clinic and went through to his office. Previously, before the war, he'd had a nurse working with him who helped him during the day and greeted patients as they arrived, but now it was just him. Sometimes he tried to pretend he was building a normal life for himself and his family, but it was anything but normal; he was working for the Third Reich just like the labourers were, under orders to treat all patients working for the Nazis. Nothing seemed more important to Hitler than his work force, other than exterminating those he despised.

Aleksy looked through some notes he'd made the day before, and then took out his diary to see whom to expect. Many of the patients made appointments, grateful to have a doctor in the village again after so long without one, but some now arrived without warning. He looked up when he heard the door and saw one such man standing in the room by the reception desk.

He had his hat in hand, his big shoulders rounded as his eyes met Aleksy's.

'Leon,' he said, greeting the man by his first name, having known him since before the war. 'It's good to see you. How are you faring?'

Leon shook his head, and Aleksy ushered him into his office, worried by his silence. He was the type of man who would never usually come to visit a doctor without his wife insisting, so to see him in his rooms today was a surprise.

'Are you unwell?' Aleksy asked as he closed the door and went to his cabinet. 'Give me a moment to find your patient notes.'

'I'm not sick.' Leon's deep voice filled the room, and Aleksy stopped what he was doing and sat down in the chair across from him.

'Something is troubling you, then?' Aleksy asked. 'You know I treat anything you disclose to me in the strictest of confidence. You can trust me, Leon.'

'Even though you work for them?'

Aleksy fixed his gaze on the man, instinctively lowering his voice in case anyone was listening. 'My oath is to my profession, not to my master. We are all following orders to stay alive, but it doesn't mean I would ever betray a patient.'

There was a long moment of silence before Leon finally spoke, twisting his hat in his hands now. 'I was cutting wood this morning, trying to do what I could to prepare things for my wife. There's not a lot left, but I wanted to at least cut what there was.'

'You're home on leave?' Aleksy asked, knowing full well that Leon had been taken the previous year and forced to labour for the Germans in one of their quarries. 'How long do you have left?'

'They gave me two weeks,' he said. 'Two weeks to be with my family before reporting for work again.'

'I see. It must have been wonderful to be home with them again?'

Leon rubbed his eyes, his head hanging, his exhaustion evident, before he finally looked up at Aleksy again.

'Do you know how many men die doing the work I do? We work twelve-hour days, they barely feed us, and we have to carry hundred-pound blocks of granite on our backs. Men are crushed around me every day by falling rock or by being pushed by a guard off the edge of a cliff when they tire of us, when they're simply bored and want to have a laugh.'

Aleksy had no answer. But to be confronted by the reality of the other man's work made him realise how fortunate he was.

Leon stared at him. 'And then I come home to a wife so thin I can see her bones protruding, and children who cry every night not just for their father, but because they are so hungry it hurts. Because their bellies ache, their little arms and legs like twigs. There is nothing here for them, and there is nothing I can do if I have to go back.'

Aleksy listened, nodding, understanding. He had the same fears – imagining Natalia and his young son without him, left to fend for themselves – so it came as no surprise to hear Leon's concerns.

'You mentioned you were chopping wood this morning?' Aleksy said. 'Did something happen? Is that what brought you here to see me?'

Leon looked away then, out of the window as if his gaze were fixed on something far away. 'I looked at the axe, I held it in one hand, and I wondered if I could do it. If I could lift it and chop off my left hand, my left arm, hell, any part of my body that would stop me from being sent back.' The big, burly man seated across from him began to cry then, silently, tears running down his cheeks as he slumped, his head in his hands. 'I can't go back there. I won't. But unless I do something, they'll come for me. They'll hunt me down, or my family, and then they'll kill us. There's nowhere we can hide from them, there's nothing I can do.'

Aleksy leaned forwards, staring into Leon's eyes when the man finally lifted his head. 'You could kill yourself if you do something foolish like that, and then your wife would have no one. There is no way to do that safely, to ensure that you don't die.'

'At least I wouldn't be Hitler's slave,' he muttered, his head turned to the window again. 'At least I won't have to go back there.'

'Leon, do you trust me to help you?' Aleksy asked, rising and going into the adjoining room where he kept medicines and supplies. 'I know you don't want to die, that you want to be here for your family, but what if I had another way?'

Leon just grunted, but when Aleksy returned, he saw that he was watching him with interest. Aleksy held a syringe in his hand, and he sat down on the table, his own heart beating double time. He'd prepared this days ago, wondering if and when he'd use it, the samples hidden away in test tubes at the back of his supply cupboard.

'Roll up your sleeve.'

Leon did as he was told, and Aleksy prayed that what he was about to do would work. He'd been working on it for months now and trying to ascertain whether what he'd come up with was brilliant or foolish, but now seemed as good a time as any to try it.

'What happens in this room must remain a secret between the two of us. You cannot tell your wife or anyone else about what happened here, otherwise we could both face the firing squad.'

Leon nodded. 'Are you certain it will keep me from going back?'

'It will either give you a rash, an infection, or kill you,' Aleksy said, as he positioned the needle over the muscle in Leon's arm. 'Or it could save you. And if it saves you, it might also save every other person in this village.'

Leon looked away, his arm still outstretched, and Aleksy slid the needle carefully into place, having no idea whether his plan would even work. When he'd finished, as Leon was rolling down his sleeve, Aleksy returned to his chair. He was surprised not to be asked more, but Leon simply sat there.

'I want you to come back at the same time in two days. For this to work, I must take a blood sample to see the results of what I've done. Then, and only then, can I tell you what will keep you from leaving home again.' He paused. 'Do you promise me you'll come back?'

Leon stood, his shoulders a little straighter than when he'd first walked in. 'I'll come back.'

'Leon, before I came back here, I was a sergeant in our army. The Red Army opened fire on my battalion and most of the men I was with perished. I was taken prisoner when they found me alive, but by some miracle I managed to escape from the freight car, and made my way home,' he told him. 'I tell you this so you understand that I've seen the brutality of the Germans first hand, I know what they are capable of, of the fear they have instilled in so many. You can trust that I'm doing everything in my power to help.'

Leon stood and held out his hand, and Aleksy clasped it.

'Thank you, Doctor.'

Aleksy smiled. 'Thank you for trusting me.'

When Leon left, and after checking there was no one else waiting, Aleksy sat in his chair, his eyes closed as he ran through the decision he'd just made, and considered all the things that could go wrong. *But if I'm right* . . . if what he was trying to do was a success, then it wasn't just Leon he'd save from going back to the mines.

After a long day of treating men from the nearby steelworks, and seeing some other men who'd miraculously survived the labour camps and come back on leave, he went to do a house visit on his way home. Many of the locals were happy to have a doctor in their midst, but they saw visiting the Red Cross clinic as an act of desperation. It was always on the tip of his tongue to remind those patients that these were desperate times – they were all desperate by virtue of living under German occupation, after all – but he always managed to keep his thoughts to himself and simply get on with the business of treating people. Today, he'd heard that one of the mothers in the village had two sick children, and he'd decided to make a house call.

He knocked on the door, hoping he had the right house, and when a bleary, bloodshot eyed woman answered, he immediately knew he'd done the right thing.

'I'm Dr Aleksy Gorski,' he said, extending one hand to the woman as she held tightly to the door. 'I understand your children are unwell?'

She nodded, opening the door a little further. He dropped his hand when she didn't reach for it.

'I can't afford the doctor,' she said.

'I don't expect payment, so that won't be a problem,' he said. 'The only people who can afford to pay me are the Germans, and if I'm brutally honest with you, they're not my favourite patients.'

She smiled then, and when she stood back he followed her into the house. Like everyone's homes, black fabric covered the windows, and he wished he could tell her to rip it all down and fling all the windows and doors open. But of course he didn't, walking silently into one of the bedrooms, where he found two little children tucked up in bed, their faces flushed.

'How long have they been like this?' he asked, setting down his bag.

'Only a few days,' she said, wringing her hands as she stood over their beds. 'If it had gone on for longer than a week, I would have called for you, but—'

'You're doing the best you can under the circumstances,' he said quickly, taking out his stethoscope. 'We're living through trying times, but these children have a mother at home who loves them, so there will be no judgement from me.'

He listened to the raspy little breath of the first child, before putting his thermometer beneath her tongue to take her temperature. Then he turned to the other child and did the same.

'Will they recover?'

Aleksy smiled at her. 'They would become better much more quickly if we had access to nutritious food, but yes, they will recover. Their lungs are clear, which is always my primary concern.' He looked down at the two children, wishing he already knew the outcome of his little experiment. If it were safe, they would be ideal candidates for what he was planning, already with symptoms of an illness.

'What have you been doing for them, to soothe their ailments?' he asked.

'They've both complained of headaches, so I've been using cupping glasses, and cold cloths of course for the fever.'

He nodded and checked their temperatures. 'I'll leave behind some eucalyptus oil, which will be helpful to put on their pillows at night, and if you can keep them drinking as much water as possible, that will be helpful too.' He smiled at the mother; she looked as if she might collapse in front of him. 'How are you feeling? Do you have any ailments, other than exhaustion?'

She looked embarrassed, but he reached for her hand and held it for a moment. 'I too have a child, and I see the toll it takes on my wife, and yet we are luckier than most. In normal times, I would have had her bring you chicken broth for the children, but sadly that is no longer possible.'

Aleksy took out the little vial of eucalyptus oil from his bag and placed it on the table beside the bed, before packing up his things.

'If anything changes, please send for me. Otherwise I'd try to keep up their liquids as much as possible, even if it's just watery vegetable soup, and if by some miracle you can find honey, that might help too.'

The woman led him back through her home to the door, but when he reached it she asked him to wait and disappeared. She returned around the side of the house, a duck held firmly in her hands.

'Please, take this,' she said. 'As payment.'

Aleksy shook his head, placing a hand on her shoulder. 'You need that duck more than I do,' he said firmly. 'Now please, if you need me, call for me, and the same goes for any of the other families around here. Tell them that I expect nothing in return, I only want to help where I can.'

With that, he bade her farewell and began the long walk home, at least thankful he could stretch his legs and clear his head before seeing his wife. Because he couldn't stop thinking about Leon, and whether or not he might have killed the poor man.

———— ✑✣✑ ————

The next day, Aleksy was kept busy with a never-ending list of patients coming through his door. He tended everything from blistered, festering feet to broken bones, but still all he could think about was Leon and how he was faring. He was tempted to do a house visit just to check he wasn't suffering, but he also didn't want to draw any unwanted attention to the man.

He heard his door bang and looked up from his papers. 'The clinic is closed,' he called out. 'I'll be out in a moment if it's urgent.'

Aleksy put the papers he'd been looking at back in the file and sorted his patient notes before rising, although he stopped in his tracks when he saw a giant of a man filling the doorway. He was very tall, with wide shoulders, and he was dressed in civilian clothes, not a uniform, his coat as thick as a bear's skin. Something about him made Aleksy pause. The man seemed familiar.

'Can I help you?' he asked. He almost wished he had a weapon at his disposal as the man stared back at him.

'You are the doctor? Gorski?'

The man wasn't German. Aleksy relaxed a little. 'Yes, I am. Do you have an ailment I can assist you with?' He cleared his throat.

'You don't remember me?'

Aleksy considered him again, trying to place him. 'I—'

'The night we were ambushed,' he said. 'I thought everyone else had died.'

Suddenly he recalled the man, remembered seeing him on the morning they'd moved out with their unit, not knowing what the day might hold, all that time ago when they were still fighting the Nazis.

'I thought I was the only one.'

The man grunted. 'I crawled to a farmhouse in the dark and they kept me alive.'

Aleksy nodded, tears burning in his eyes as he remembered the day as if it were only yesterday, remembered the shouts of the men around him and the constant sound of firing.

'Do you know what men like me do? We are fighting for the cause.'

The resistance. Of course. 'Yes, I do.' Aleksy shifted uncomfortably, worried someone might hear them even though he knew he was being paranoid.

Aleksy collected the two glasses he kept in his office, pouring vodka into each. He didn't even know this man's name, but they'd once fought together, and that meant something. He passed him a glass.

'To surviving,' Aleksy said, before swallowing a large mouthful. 'What we survived, no man should have to endure.'

'To surviving.'

They stood for a long moment, finishing their drinks, before the other man set down his glass and cleared his throat.

'I've come here because we need a doctor, to tend to injured resistance members. There are many men fighting for us, but few with any medical experience.'

Aleksy hesitated, staring into the man's eyes.

'Will you help us?'

There were so many reasons he should have said no, but in the moment Aleksy knew only one answer could pass his lips. 'Yes. I will help you.'

'Good,' he said, holding out his hand. 'You may call me Captain.'

'Aleksy,' he said, clasping the captain's hand and hoping he hadn't just put his own life and his family's in danger.

'We will get word to you when we need you,' he said, turning to leave. 'I won't come here again; if we need you there will be a stone left near your front door. You're to come to the edge of the forest that night, and someone will be waiting to take you.'

'Not to my home,' Aleksy said. 'I don't want anyone coming to my home, I will not risk my family being part of this. It will have to be this door here.'

The man nodded.

'I will need to bring medical supplies whenever I'm called upon?' Aleksy asked.

'Yes.'

'Is there anything else you can tell me? About what I will be expected to do?'

'The less you know, the better.'

How ironic that I said almost those same words to Leon only yesterday.

The man left without another word, and Aleksy stood, looking after him, hoping that no one had seen him enter or exit the clinic. Only hours earlier he'd had a German officer sitting in his rooms; what would have happened if he'd still been there? If he and this Captain had crossed paths? It wasn't even worth thinking about.

Aleksy locked the door to prevent anyone else from entering and went to his supplies cupboard, reaching for the pouch he'd tucked at the very back of the shelf. He looked inside at the little pill, praying he never had to use it as he secured the pouch and put it into his top pocket.

A fellow colleague he knew had helped the resistance, and he'd told him he always carried a cyanide pill in his pocket, in case he was captured. They'd all heard the tales of torture exacted upon those who helped Jews or stepped out of line and rebelled in any way against the Nazis, and Aleksy knew that if faced with a fast death by pill, or a slow death at the hands of the enemy, he'd choose the pill every time.

The more difficult decision was whether to give one to his wife to keep on hand, as well. He pushed the thought away, not wanting to consider what danger she would be in if he were caught, for he knew that the enemy's cruelty knew no bounds, even where women and children were concerned.

Aleksy locked the supply cupboard and gathered his belongings, putting his bag over his shoulder before leaving the clinic and heading out on his evening rounds, the weight of the pill in his pocket as heavy as lead. He tried his hardest not to think about it.

Which proved impossible.

CHAPTER THIRTEEN

Aleksy had never felt so nervous before. Not when he'd run for his life from the freight train, or when his wife had been in the midst of labour. Five days ago, he'd sat across from Leon and taken a blood sample, telling him that he'd make a house call as soon as he received the result, before mailing off the sample. It was wartime protocol for all samples to be sent to Poland's Nazi-operated laboratory for testing, and he'd barely slept since, waiting for the result to arrive.

But after all these days, he'd received not a letter, but a telegram. He lifted it, his hand shaking. There were only six words on the page.

THE WEIL-FELIX TEST IS POSITIVE

Aleksy collapsed back into his chair, still holding the telegram, reading the words over and over again. It had worked. *His plan had worked!* The injection he'd given Leon, the substance he'd been researching for so long, had done exactly what he hoped it would. It had given his patient a false positive for typhus, which meant without a doubt that he'd saved the man's life. Best of all, having checked in on him daily, there was no sign he'd become infected or suffered any other side effects of the experiment.

He'd spent months preparing for this, for what might happen if he was ever able to produce such a result, and Aleksy quickly gathered his things, tucking the telegram into his leather satchel and hurrying from the clinic. He considered putting a note on the door, but decided he needed to move quickly and so simply locked it instead, spinning around and coming face to face with the same Nazi officer who'd come to him for treatment the previous week.

'Where are you going in such a hurry?' The officer's eyes narrowed, and placed his hand on his gun.

Aleksy froze. 'Sir, I have a confirmed case of typhus in the village. I have closed the clinic to attend a house call.'

He tried not to smile in satisfaction at the surprised look on the officer's face. 'Typhus, you say? Where is the proof?'

'If I may?' Aleksy asked, indicating his bag. He knew better than to reach for something without warning, lest he be shot.

The officer nodded.

Aleksy took out the telegram and held it for the officer to read. 'You will see, sir, that it is your own laboratory doctors who have confirmed the case. I sent them the blood sample not five days ago.'

'Typhus? There is typhus in the village?'

'Yes, sir. I have had reports of more patients being unwell, so I must act with haste to ensure it doesn't spread.' Aleksy tucked the telegram back into his bag. 'Did you need to see me urgently, sir, or shall I continue on? I can open up the clinic again for you?'

The officer barked at him to leave and Aleksy hurried off, a smile lurking as he started to realise that his plan was working. He wouldn't be surprised if half the Germans in the village were gone by nightfall, and the rest the following week once he obtained another one or two positive tests. He imagined they'd move on to the next closest village a couple of hours' walk from theirs, or perhaps they'd move even further away. So long as they left, he didn't particularly care where they went.

It only took him fifteen minutes to walk briskly to Leon's house, and when he arrived he found the man sitting in the sun, watching as his children played. If he were going with different news, it would have been a difficult call to make, but today he had a spring in his step as he called out to him.

'Leon!'

Leon looked up, his eyes widening. His wife appeared at the door then, and Aleksy could see how very thin she was, her eyes hollow, bony fingers clutching the door.

'Could we leave your children outside?' Aleksy asked. 'I need a moment with you both.'

Leon spoke to the children as his wife ushered Aleksy inside. He followed her, taking a seat at the table and shaking his head when she offered him tea.

'There's no one else in the house?' he asked, as Leon walked in and sat across from him, his wife hovering behind his chair.

'Just the two of us,' Leon said.

'I know this will come as a surprise to you both, but Leon just tested positive for typhus. I received a telegram not an hour ago, confirming the test result I completed last week, which means that he must now stay in quarantine at home.'

'Typhus?' his wife gasped.

Aleksy gave Leon a long look, knowing from the man's slight nod that he understood what he was telling him.

'I suspect you will be receiving a note shortly to request you stay at home and that you do not, under any circumstances, return to work,' Aleksy continued. 'Typhus is a highly infectious disease, and the Germans have a particular fear of it sweeping through their army.'

Leon's poor wife looked ready to faint, but Leon had started to smile, thumping his hand on the wooden table with a loud bang.

'I won't have to go back?' he asked. 'I can stay?'

'For as long as I can convince the Nazis that you have typhus, yes you can.'

'But he hasn't had symptoms, he hasn't—'

Aleksy watched as Leon rose and folded his wife in his arms, holding her tightly against his chest.

'It's best if you accept the diagnosis and don't ask any questions,' Aleksy said. 'For all of our sakes. And make sure to stay out of sight, especially for the next few weeks.'

He stood up to leave and Leon followed him, neither man speaking until they got to the door.

'The injection you gave me . . .'

Aleksy leaned in close and slapped him on the back, as one might congratulate someone who'd just won a hard-fought race. 'Has worked as I hoped it would. You don't actually have typhus, so please don't worry.' He lifted his hand to open the door, before looking back. 'You must never tell anyone the truth, including your wife, Leon. This must remain a secret between us, do you understand?'

'Yes, Doctor, I understand.'

As Aleksy walked away from the house, waving to the children still playing in the garden, he heard a shout from inside the house and couldn't help but smile. It wasn't the type of reaction he usually received from telling someone they had an infectious disease. He only hoped this was the start of something bigger, that it was a way he could keep those in his community safe. They were far enough from other villages that they could become entirely isolated from the horrors of Nazi occupation if his plan was a success; his biggest challenge would be to keep what was happening a secret.

Aleksy had walked for almost two hours to the nearest other village to visit his friend and fellow doctor, Marcin – someone he'd first encountered when he was doing his training many years earlier. They'd always stayed in touch, and months ago had theorised together that *Proteus* OX19, usually a tool to confirm typhus, could create a false positive when a patient's blood was exposed to it. If either of them was ever brave enough to inject it directly into a patient, that was. They'd had too many drinks and laughed at how brilliant it would be to deceive the Nazis and create an oasis of villages, returning them almost to pre-war times. Only Aleksy had gone home and thought of nothing else. Leon had come along at just the perfect moment.

Afterwards, he'd considered writing to his friend to share the news, but without a code he feared it could be intercepted. This was news that could change the lives of Marcin's patients too, as well as other villages around them if they were able to generate enough fear.

When he arrived at his home that Sunday afternoon, with no forewarning, sweaty and weary, Marcin received him with surprise.

'Aleksy? What brings you here?'

'I bring news, dear friend,' he replied. 'Although I fear without water I might perish before sharing it with you. I'm not used to such long walks.'

They both laughed and Aleksy clasped his hand before following his old friend inside, where they sat at the kitchen table. He gratefully gulped down the water given to him, grinning at Marcin when he finished.

'So, tell me the news,' Marcin asked. 'I take it you didn't walk this far just to drink putrid coffee with me and tell me how life under the occupation is treating you? Not to mention I've never seen you smile so much.'

'Coffee tastes so bad these days, I don't think it's worth drinking.' Aleksy reached into his bag and produced the telegram he'd carried ever since it had arrived. 'But I have something I very much think you'll be interested in. News that will change everything.'

Marcin took the paper, reaching for his glasses, but in seconds he'd taken them off and was staring at Aleksy again.

'This is what I think it is?' he asked.

'It is,' he said with a grin. 'It worked.'

'It worked?'

Aleksy laughed again and so did Marcin. 'It worked. I injected my first patient with the *Proteus* OX19, sent the sample away, and the test came back positive.'

Marcin stood. 'This calls for a celebration! I have a bottle of my favourite *wódka* tucked away for a special occasion.' He looked at Aleksy, shaking his head. 'You're certain it worked? Weren't you terrified of actually infecting him with the disease?'

'I promise you, it worked. Perhaps we're more clever than we thought? And no, I wasn't afraid. This man, he was prepared to take his own life he was so miserable. He was the perfect test subject,' Aleksy said, as Marcin poured him a glass and they raised them, touching the glasses together as they took a sip. 'But now we have to create a plan. I need to mimic the spread of an actual typhus outbreak among my patients if I truly want this to work, and we have to start the same spread here, in your village. I will keep brief records about each patient, stating that they are an epidemiological statistic which has been confirmed and registered by the German army, as well as stating how highly contagious it is, and that with each new case I'm concerned it may decimate our small town and those around us. Who knows how far it could have spread, if we're clever?'

Marcin nodded, his eyes bright as they spoke – perhaps the success of the plan they'd spent so long discussing had brought something to life within him. It was a miracle, or as close to a miracle as they were ever going to achieve.

'Yes, we will need to start a slow spread of the disease to make it believable, and most importantly we'll have to increase reported cases as winter sets in, and then ease them off again each spring. We need to plan this as carefully as possible.'

'I agree,' Aleksy said, taking another sip of his drink. 'I was thinking that anyone who presented with a fever or any red marks on their skin would receive an injection and subsequent blood test. If anyone was ever sent to check the patients, or our records, we would have justification for our diagnosis. We would need to give a reason for having taken the blood sample in the first place.'

'Aleksy, this could change everything.' Marcin poured them more of the clear liquid. 'If we can hold them off for long enough . . .'

'We could keep them away entirely,' Aleksy said. 'We may become the only villages not occupied. We may be able to keep everyone around us safe and free from participation in the war.'

'There's nothing the Nazis are more scared of than typhus. This is brilliant, absolutely brilliant!'

They grinned at each other across the table like a couple of children hatching a plan, before Marcin reached for the telegram again, as if he had to read it a second time to believe it. His friend was right, there *was* nothing the Nazis were more afraid of, knowing that it was a disease that could spread like wildfire through their army. It was also a disease they liked to insist was spread by Jews, and the last thing they'd want was it taking hold among their soldiers.

'Shall I wait a week before sending my first sample off?' he asked. 'I think it would be conceivable that it's already spread here, especially if you have another patient in the next few days?'

'I think that's a brilliant idea,' Aleksy said. 'But this stays between us?'

'Of course. We can't risk anyone else knowing what we've done, not when we don't know whom to trust.' Marcin looked at him across the table. 'We cannot even tell our wives, Aleksy. This must remain between you and me.'

'I agree.'

There were rumours of those among them who were conspiring with the Nazis – usually for the benefit of better treatment or better rations, and although Aleksy hated the thought, he knew it was likely true. He also knew that it was highly unlikely Leon would say anything, the man was too grateful to be allowed to stay home to let anyone in on their secret, but he chose not to disclose that to Marcin. But his own wife? Keeping it from her was going to be much harder – he usually shared everything with Natalia.

'To fooling the bastards,' Marcin said, holding up his drink.

'To fooling them,' Alex repeated, refusing to think about his wife or what would happen if his deceit was discovered. He was saving his village the only way he knew how, and all he could hope for was that somehow, they'd be able to hold the Germans off for long enough until the Allies had won.

Although some days he wondered if the rest of the world combined would ever be able to defeat the might of Hitler. If America didn't join the war, he feared that perhaps the reign of terror would never end.

'Marcin, in case we're ever found out,' he said, taking out the pill he'd placed in his pocket days earlier to show his friend, knowing now was as good a time as any to discuss it with him. 'If they ever see through the smoke and mirrors, if we're ever taken . . .'

Marcin's smile disappeared, and Aleksy watched as he downed the rest of his drink before nodding, his eyes turning as gloomy as the topic of conversation. 'I shall do the same. If they catch us . . .'

It appeared that neither of them was able to finish that particular sentence.

'Another drink?'

'Yes,' Aleksy said, putting the little pill back in his breast pocket and pushing away the sobering thought of Nazi capture. 'Please.' Anything to numb his mind from the circumstances that might lead him to knowingly swallow cyanide.

———— ⟶✦⟵ ————

When Aleksy arrived home that night, weary from so long on his feet, he was relieved he hadn't been stopped by the Gestapo. He wasn't certain if it was his imagination, but there seemed to have been fewer uniforms when he'd passed through the village than usual. He'd been prepared of course, with his telegram tucked safely in his bag and a story ready to share about needing to notify the nearest other doctor of the potential spread of disease, but it had turned out to be unnecessary. He wasn't, however, prepared for his wife's voice to cut through the darkness and make him feel like an intruder in his own home as he walked quietly through to their bedroom.

'Where have you been?'

He sat down on the bed, his body making the mattress sag in the corner.

'I've been so worried,' she said, before he could reply. 'I thought something had happened to you, that they'd found out about whatever it is you've been doing, that—'

'Shh, my love, there's nothing to worry about,' he said, reaching for his wife, hating the terror in her voice. 'I was visiting a colleague, you remember Marcin? We trained together many years ago.'

Even in the dark he could make out her face, his eyes adjusting as he stroked her hair and gently cupped her cheek.

'I know I said I understood, but I can't stand the not-knowing. I need you to tell me what you're doing.'

Aleksy took a deep breath, the truth on the tip of his tongue. But he'd told Marcin not to share what they were doing with any-one – could he then, in good conscience, immediately tell his wife? He could feel her waiting for his answer; they'd been married long enough that he understood her long pauses, the things that were unsaid.

'My love, there has been a confirmed case of typhus,' he said, carefully, considering his words.

'Typhus! Oh Aleksy, that's terrible.'

He kept his hand on her face, trying to think what he could say to reassure her and coming up with nothing.

'It's not so bad, the case is very mild, but I have had a con-firmed blood sample returned.'

'And it's confined to just the one case?'

'Well, yes and no. I have requested the man quarantine at his home, but this morning I visited a family to see two young children for the second time. I shall be returning the day after tomorrow to test them, also.'

'Why not test them today? Shouldn't you take the blood as soon as you suspect they may have it?'

He paused, dropping his hand to cover hers. 'Natalia, do you remember when I told you that I'd be doing things, that I may not always be able to share the truth with you?'

She was silent, but he knew that she understood.

'Then I know you'll understand when I say that there is no risk to me or to you from this typhus outbreak. However I do believe that the Nazis may leave our village, once there are enough cases to make them believe the disease is spreading.'

'When you say there is no risk to us, you mean from the virus?'

Aleksy swallowed. He knew what she was asking, and he didn't want to say more and betray Marcin. 'I don't believe there is any risk, my love. If there was, I'd be doing more to isolate you and Jan.'

'But the risk, if anyone finds out what you're doing, if they realise you've somehow deceived them, if that's what you're doing . . .'

He squeezed her hand. 'If I'm not taking any risks, then all I'm doing is sitting by and helping the enemy. I've come to understand that I don't have to be in a uniform to fight, Natalia. This, *this* is more lethal than all the bullets in the world. This means we can protect the lives of so many.'

He stood and undressed, before getting into bed beside his wife. She moved closer to him, her legs tentative against his until he reached out and folded her against his chest, his chin to the top of her head.

'I heard something dreadful today, it's why I was so worried about you.'

He pressed a kiss to her forehead. 'What was that, my love?'

'That there was a doctor in another town, found to be helping the resistance,' she whispered. 'They tortured him and then hanged him in the village square for all to see. I couldn't stop thinking that perhaps you'd been caught for doing something, too. That maybe your soft heart had made you take risks you wouldn't usually take.'

His jaw tightened as he listened to her words. So there had been a reason he was approached in his clinic the other day, only the captain hadn't thought to disclose what had happened to their last doctor. A shiver went through him, fear perhaps, but he ignored it. He'd sworn an oath when he'd become a doctor, and he would help anyone in need, no matter the risk. What kind of doctor would he be if he let the young men fighting for them, the men who were away from their families and living in the forests to fight a guerrilla war against the Nazis, suffer?

'Are you helping them, Aleksy?'

He wasn't going to lie to his wife, not about that. 'Would you be angry if I was?'

'Never angry, but I won't say I'm not afraid,' she said. 'Is there anything I can do, to help? Would I be less conspicuous if I were to assist them, as a nurse? Could I go undetected?'

Aleksy knew he was being hypocritical, when he was putting himself in danger without giving his wife a choice in the matter, but the very thought of her helping the resistance or doing anything else that could risk her life wasn't something he could allow. He needed to know she was safe. 'No, Natalia, the best thing you can do is stay home and look after Jan. Let me take the risk for both of us.'

She nestled closer just as the baby started to cry.

'I'll go to him,' he said, starting to push the covers off.

'No, he'll be hungry. I'll go.' She leaned over him and pressed a long, soft kiss to his lips, whispering as she hovered above him, before rising. 'I love you, Aleksy. You have such a big heart.'

'I love you, too,' he murmured, drawing her down for one more kiss.

He felt her absence when she left the bed, her warmth and weight no longer beside him, and he lay there and stared at the ceiling in the dark. His body was weary but his mind was alert, questioning, constantly making him wonder whether he'd done the right thing in starting the typhus outbreak.

Who would I be if I let everyone else suffer just to cocoon my family in safety? If I wasn't prepared to take a risk that could save the lives of so many, when so many of our men are dead, fighting or kept as prisoners of war?

He got out of bed, listening to the sound of his wife softly singing to their son, walking into the room and seeing her rocking him in her arms. She'd lit an oil lamp, which sent gentle shadows flickering around them, and he went to her, standing behind Natalia and wrapping his arms around both her and Jan. He nestled his face to her shoulder and they stood like that for a long moment, in the almost-dark, as he fought against the clouds of worry that were building in his mind.

If something happened to his family, he knew he'd never be able to forgive himself.

———— ⤸⤹ ————

It had been a little over three weeks since Aleksy had received the telegram. He stood outside his clinic and watched as the last of the Gestapo left the village, their perfectly polished boots marching them away, their flags taken down. It was something he'd dreamed of, but actually seeing them leave of their own accord was quite astonishing. It told him that he'd been right in taking the risk – soon they would all be able to frequent the places the Nazis had claimed for themselves, move freely without fear of curfew.

Since the first positive case, he'd created four more patients who had symptoms he could attribute to typhus, and when he'd received the most recent telegram confirming the diagnosis, it advised that the Nazis were effectively quarantining their village. None of the workers on leave would be expected to return, and the Nazis wouldn't be back until spring, which at least gave them a reprieve from occupation. But what had made him smile the most was hearing that his friend had also succeeded – theirs wasn't the only village to be deserted. They could blame the spread on so many things, a lack of soap for starters, but in the end it was the test results that spoke for themselves. The disease was present, at least based on the blood samples he was providing.

As he was about to turn away, a woman stepped out from the shadows, smiling as she walked past his door.

'Tonight, bring supplies for gunshot wounds and broken bones.' The words were said under her breath, her smile fixed as if she were exchanging greetings with an old friend.

'Where?' Aleksy asked, his voice low. 'I thought there was to be a stone left at the door? It's not safe for anyone to come near my clinic.'

'The brick house by the forest. Come after dark.'

Aleksy nodded and watched the woman go, wishing he could stop thinking about what his wife had said, about the doctor hanged for his work with the resistance. The pill in his pocket seemed to have its own pulse, which beat faster the more nervous he became.

'Sweetheart, is it time to go home?' said a soft voice from behind.

He'd almost forgotten Natalia was waiting for him. She'd been invaluable when he'd had to take blood tests for all the Germans before they were cleared to leave, and then today she'd come in to assist him with the backlog of patients needing treatment, leaving their son with their neighbour.

'One minute,' he said, taking his bag and beginning to fill it with what he might need.

But Natalia was one step ahead of him, poking her head in and searching his eyes. 'Is everything all right?'

'They have sent word,' he said.

'The resistance?' she asked, her face pale as she blinked back at him.

Aleksy nodded.

'Then tell me what you need and I'll help you find everything. We can work more quickly together.'

And just like that, he'd drawn his wife into his deception, despite having wished that she had no knowledge whatsoever of what he was involved in.

'They've gone, Aleksy, the Germans have gone,' she said, when they'd found what he needed and were about to head for home. 'Whatever you did, whatever plan you hatched, you've managed to rid our village of them once and for all, and I want to say thank you.' She touched his face. 'Without your bravery, who knows what could have happened next, how many more people could have been taken or killed?'

He locked the door and bent his arm so she could slip her hand through it, and he couldn't help but smile when they walked the entire way home without seeing one face that didn't belong in the village he so loved.

But what he did see were signs everywhere, signs that they were finally free of oppression, at least for the time being.

ACHTUNG! FLECKFIEBER!

Danger, typhus! They were the most poetic, satisfying words Aleksy had ever read. Somehow, in the middle of a war, he and Marcin had managed to create a fortress. He only hoped they could mimic an outbreak for long enough to keep everyone safe. Tomorrow, they were going to take a picnic, walking to a field by a lake, so they could dip their toes in the water and truly relax for the first time in what felt like forever.

'I love you,' Natalia said, resting her head against his shoulder, ambling in a way they never would have during the occupation.

He pressed a kiss to her head, slipping his arm around her waist. 'I love you, too.'

CHAPTER FOURTEEN

Two years later

Aleksy knew something was wrong the moment he touched the door to his clinic. It was ever so slightly ajar.

'Hello?' he called out, nudging it open with his foot.

He'd half expected there to be someone from the resistance, choosing to wait inside for him instead of risk being seen outside, despite his insistence that they not come to his place of work. Usually someone would be passing with a small parcel of food, thanking him for helping them with a medical ailment, and carefully hidden inside a piece of bread would be a tiny rolled up piece of paper, detailing what he might need to bring to treat someone. They had taken every precaution, careful about staying hidden, the chance of someone being eyes and ears for the Nazis a very real possibility. It was the reason Aleksy was so cautious with every aspect of his work, guarding his secret, meticulously documenting his typhus cases and reading everything about the disease he could to ensure the spread was mimicking a real one. Germany had some of the best doctors in the world, and he expected them to review the number of cases regularly to ensure his reporting was accurate.

What he hadn't been expecting, though, was a Nazi to be sitting in his office. His black boots were on Aleksy's desk, roughly pushed into some of his paperwork that he'd left out the night before, leaning back in his chair as if it were his own personal space. It was the officer he'd treated before the typhus outbreak, the one he'd almost run into the day he'd received the first confirmation telegram.

'Hello, Doctor.'

'Ahh, good morning,' Aleksy said, clearing his throat. He stood in the doorway, a stranger in his own workplace. 'I wasn't expecting you.'

I wasn't expecting any Germans, not in the midst of an ongoing outbreak.

He forced his shoulders down, relaxing his arms as he smiled. The Nazis were like predators, they stalked their prey, aware of every weakness, of every tell-tale sign.

'Join me for a drink.'

The man rose, crossing the room and reaching for a bottle of vodka that Aleksy kept there, roughly clanging two small glasses together. He'd obviously done a thorough inspection of the office already. Aleksy immediately ran through everything in his mind, certain the man couldn't have found anything to put him in the German's crosshairs.

'It's a little early in the morning for me, I have a full day of patients—'

'I insist.'

That was that, then. Aleksy set his bag down and took the glass when it was offered to him, the liquor sloshing up the sides. He nodded and took a sip, the vodka burning more than usual as it travelled down his throat.

'I've been sent to inspect your typhus patients. You might remember we were very comfortable in your pretty little village, before we had to leave in such an unpleasant hurry.'

'I, ah, wasn't aware you had medical training,' Aleksy said. 'But I'm very pleased someone has been sent, it's been exhausting managing this on my own, especially over the winter we just had.'

The knowing smile he received in return made it almost impossible to keep his composure. Aleksy squeezed his glass so tightly he feared it might shatter in his hand.

'It is quite convenient, this outbreak, no? Leaving you all here as if we don't occupy your pitiful country? You must have enjoyed these past two years.'

'Not at all,' Aleksy said carefully, taking another sip and watching his new friend pour himself another glass. He feared that a drunk Nazi could be far more dangerous, even more ruthless. 'We are down to only a small handful of cases now. I've been very careful to maintain strict quarantines for those infected.'

'And yet it continues to spread?' The German downed the rest of his drink and stood. 'Let me see your supplies.'

'My supplies?' Fear rose inside Aleksy. 'Are there any particular supplies you'd like to see? Bandages perhaps?'

'I should like very much to see what supplies you have left,' he said, kicking at one of the office chairs as he passed it. 'I expect you won't have used much, since there is no one here working for our fine country any more? No workers to treat?'

Aleksy took the key from his top drawer and, trying desperately to stop the shake of his hand, slid it into the keyhole and opened the door to the cupboard. 'Sir, if we were able to access vaccinations, or more medicine, even adequate supplies of soap, I believe I would have been able to stifle this outbreak months ago, if not a year ago. I have been diligent in my requests for appropriate supplies.'

'So it is our fault?'

Aleksy considered his next words carefully, unable to stop his eyes from falling to the gun at the man's hip.

'No sir, of course not. I'm merely giving you my medical opinion about my attempts to deal with the disease. As you know, it's highly infectious.'

He poked around while Aleksy watched. 'You know, there would be a much easier way to stop the outbreak.'

Aleksy paused, sweat beginning to form on his brow.

'A bullet for the sick, and then we could burn their homes down and the disease with it.'

There was no way to keep his face impassive, no way not to react, despite his best efforts. 'I think that would be a terrible waste of human life, and also of homes.'

The man's face had become florid, his cheeks prickled with dark pink blotches, and Aleksy watched as he reached for the bottle and took a swig before slamming it down.

'Take me to see these patients. I want to see one of them myself.' He took something from his pocket, which Aleksy could see was a list of names when it was passed to him. 'This man, at the top, take me to him. The Governor Oberleiter has told me to see these patients with my own eyes.'

Aleksy knew he had to play a part, that he had to keep his composure, pretend he was nothing more than a doctor doing his job. It didn't surprise him that they'd sent someone; he knew it would happen eventually, but he'd expected a doctor or even a team of German doctors, not a single Gestapo man.

'Of course, we may go to see him now. But I warn you, you are putting yourself at great risk.'

The man stopped, his boots squeaking against the floor.

'You must know how highly contagious this disease is? This patient, well, I'm sure you're familiar with the symptoms?'

The German's eyes narrowed and he swayed slightly on his feet. Clearly the liquor was starting to catch up with him. He regarded Aleksy for some moments before striding to the door.

'This isn't the last you'll see of us. You've been warned, Doctor. Next time, you won't be so lucky.'

When he left, the door banging closed behind him, Aleksy dropped into his chair, his legs no longer able to hold him.

What have I done? He would have to get word to Marcin, perhaps through the resistance. His friend needed to know that their secret could implode without warning. Two years of living without oppression, of basking in his wife's smiles, of not having to look over his shoulder to see who could be watching him.

He had the most overwhelming feeling that all of that was abruptly coming to an end.

———— ⨭⨪ ————

This time when they arrived, Aleksy was prepared. Not for the rumble of trucks and soldiers appearing in the village square, but certainly for his patients to be questioned and his diagnosis to be challenged.

'You are Dr Aleksy Gorski?'

Aleksy was outside his clinic, bag in hand as he waited to be summoned.

'Yes, that is correct.'

'It is good to make your acquaintance in person,' the man said, his white coat clearly marking him as a man of medicine. 'I am Dr Richard Herbold, we have exchanged letters about your typhus outbreak.'

They'd sent the Nazi chief of medicine from the local steelworks. Aleksy knew this man would not be easy to fool.

'Dr Herbold, it's my pleasure to meet you,' he said, shaking the man's hand. 'I expect you would like to look through my notes or perhaps visit some of my patients?'

'I think we should begin with seeing the patients,' he said, his tone cool as he appeared to consider Aleksy.

'As you wish. Please, follow me.' He would take him first to an elderly man with a terrible cough and red rashes on his face from the cupping his wife insisted on doing each day, and then another younger man who was his most recently confirmed case and was suffering from terrible fevers. He was convinced he would be able to fool even the most senior of doctors with their symptoms.

'You're not concerned about my examining them? As I said in my letters, I am surprised by how few deaths you've reported. We usually find the cases of typhus at the steelworks are almost always fatal, yet you've been remarkably lucky.'

'Perhaps it's due to my patients being in their own home, and being tended to by a family member?' Aleksy said. 'Or perhaps, as I tell many of my patients every time I see them, it is simply the grace of God.'

'There have been suggestions,' Dr Herbold said, 'that you could have one patient with typhus, and be taking his blood each time to create positive test results.'

Aleksy frowned. 'That is most certainly not the case, and I invite you to take your own blood samples while you're here. My patients have largely been blessed with more minor symptoms than I might have expected during an outbreak, but I can assure you that your testing will provide the same results as mine.'

That, at the very least, he was confident of. What he wasn't sure of was how those results would be scrutinised, whether the Nazi doctors would realise that something had created the false results. He'd never expected to have to keep the hoax going for so long; he'd never thought the war would rage on with no hint of ending year after year.

But so long as his work for the resistance went undetected, so long as no one knew that he was using supplies to aid the very men who were causing havoc for the German army, then he should be safe. Only last night he'd crouched in the dark, a single torch his only source of light, and taken a bullet out of a young, feverish underground soldier. He'd gratefully received medicine to help with the infection, biting down on a stick as Aleksy had sewn up the wound. It was difficult work, in the most trying of circumstances, but the joy it brought him to know that he was doing something to help his fellow countryman made it worth it.

'Doctor, you do know the repercussions for lying to us, don't you? For deceiving our Führer?'

'Of course. And when you see these patients and do your own testing, you will be reassured that I've done nothing of the sort. I would encourage you to do blood tests, and I would be grateful for your assistance in dealing with this outbreak.'

Aleksy thought of his friend Marcin and wondered whether he was to receive the same interrogation, hoping that he'd kept his records as meticulously as they'd both planned. 'Please, come this way,' he said as they arrived at the first patient's house. 'And I do apologise, soap is very hard to find, so my patients aren't the cleanest. Perhaps allowing us more rations might help to clear up this outbreak?'

He laid eyes on the man they'd come to see, and he was pleased to hear him cough, and see the familiar blotches on his face from his wife's insistent cupping practices.

If anything, he hoped that this inspection would at least keep them safe for another few months. After that, he knew he'd have no option but to bring his fake epidemic to an end.

Since the last visit, Aleksy hadn't heard anything from Dr Herbold. It had been more than a fortnight, and within that time he'd written to Marcin and told him that he was pleased to not have any new cases of typhus to report, and that he hoped their epidemic might be coming to an end. He was certain his friend would be able to understand the hidden meaning.

Thankfully there had been no more visits from his Gestapo friend either, although he had had the loveliest visit from Natalia and little Jan earlier that day. While food was scarce, and Natalia had become worryingly thin, they were managing to supplement their rations from their vegetable garden, which she spent hours tending to each day. Today she'd surprised him with a little picnic. They'd taken it to a nearby field and spent half an hour sitting in the sun, making the most of their little lunch. Jan had toddled about, making them laugh as he plucked at grass and spun around until he fell. His pudgy hands were warm and soft in Aleksy's while they'd slowly walked back to the clinic. He'd thought about them all day, eager to return home and see his son before he went to bed.

He locked the door to his clinic and looked about, surprised how quiet the streets were. He'd been busy all afternoon, holed away in his office either seeing patients or working on his typhus notes, going through everything to ensure it was meticulous.

'Dr Gorski!'

The shout made him turn, a young man running down the street, his arms raised high as he waved them.

'Aleksy Gorski!'

The man shouted again, and Aleksy's blood ran cold. It was a young man he'd treated barely two weeks ago, removing a bullet from deep in his thigh. None of the resistance members ever came so openly into town, preferring to stay hidden in the forests that stretched between the villages.

'Doctor,' he said, breathless when he reached Aleksy, his tattered clothes hanging off his lean frame. 'Doctor, you are on the Gestapo's hit list. They've already taken your friend, Marcin.'

'You know Marcin?' Aleksy asked, gripping his bag as he stared at the young man. 'You're certain they've taken him?'

'He's been helping us, the same way you have.'

Aleksy touched his pocket, felt the pill he'd hidden there. Had Marcin chosen to end things of his own accord, or would he wait for a Nazi bullet?

'You have to go. They know you've been helping us. Someone has betrayed us.'

So it wasn't the phoney typhus epidemic that had caught up with him, it was his work with members of the underground. His hands began to shake.

'Where do I go?' he asked. 'What do I do?'

The young man shook his head. 'Run.'

The moment the word had left his mouth he turned on his heel, sprinting back down the road. He'd risked his life to warn Aleksy, and for that he would be eternally grateful. Aleksy dropped his bag, unbuttoning his jacket as he began to run as fast as he could.

Natalia. I have to get to Natalia before they find me. I have to make sure she's safe. If the Gestapo couldn't find him, he knew that it was his family they'd go looking for next.

Terror rose in his throat like a lump of food he couldn't swallow, his legs trembling as he forced them to go faster and faster and ran as if his life depended upon it. Because it did; without his family, he had no life. Without his family, he didn't want to live.

The road seemed to go on forever, the longest journey of his life. He finally rounded the corner and slowed down, half expecting the Gestapo to have already surrounded his house. His breath rasped as he leaned against a tree, fingers scraping against the rough bark. But there wasn't a sound coming from his house.

Natalia would usually be in the garden at this time of day, picking something for dinner or letting Jan play before dinnertime, and it made the hairs prick on the back of his neck when he realised how unusual it was not to hear anything. But then perhaps they were sitting in the kitchen, she singing and talking to their son as she tried to coax vegetables into him, blissfully unaware of what was unfolding.

Aleksy walked slowly to the door, careful with each footstep not to make a sound, his breath loud to his own ears. He turned the handle, letting himself in and walking silently towards the kitchen.

It took all his effort not to scream, to not bellow with despair as his worst nightmare came true. His wife's eyes met his, her beautiful face mangled and bleeding, her eye swollen shut. He heard his son cry; his heart ripped from his chest at the desperation in his wail. How long had they been like this? How long had they waited for him to return?

'Good evening, Doctor,' said a voice from the shadows. 'I trust you didn't expect to see me again so soon?'

CHAPTER FIFTEEN

'Please,' Aleksy begged, his hands raised as he walked into the kitchen. He stared at his wife and silently pleaded for her forgiveness. *What have I done? What have I done!* 'Take me, but leave my wife. She has nothing to do with this. Please, can't you let her go?'

His answer was silence. Deadly, all-consuming silence.

Aleksy's heart was pounding. He edged closer, seeing that their Gestapo visitor appeared to be alone. He needed to find a way to distract him, to do something, *anything*, to save Natalia. To get to Jan and scoop him into his arms, and then run just like he'd been told to do – run and never look back.

'Please, I beg you, let her go.'

The sound of footsteps behind him, his wife's eyes widening in terror, made him stagger. When he heard his son scream, saw two more Gestapo behind him, he dropped to his knees.

'I will do anything, *anything* you ask of me,' he cried. 'I have served as a loyal doctor, I have done nothing other than care for my patients.'

'Ahh, but that is not true, is it, Doctor?' The heavy boot steps of the Gestapo man sounded out in his kitchen, echoing around him. He came closer, using his gun to lift Aleksy's chin. 'It seems you've been very busy doing all sorts of work that you shouldn't have been.'

He shut his eyes, trembling as he kept his head lifted, feeling the hard butt of the gun against his skin.

'I am a doctor for the Red Cross. I am bound to help anyone who comes into my clinic, and that is all I am guilty of.'

'And your little typhus ruse?' The gun pressed hard into his jaw now. 'We have no evidence, but I will find out, one way or another.'

'Your own doctor took blood samples when he came. Did they not come back positive? Did he not see my patients with his own eyes? I have done nothing, *nothing*!'

The Gestapo man shrugged as Aleksy looked up at him. His son wailed even louder and his wife sobbed, her cries breaking pieces of his heart as he listened to her pain. It was then that he realised her hands were bound, tied tightly so as to give her no chance to escape or defend herself.

'Shoot them,' said the man standing over Aleksy. 'But this one we keep. This one will be useful.'

'No!' Aleksy screamed, as a boot connected with his chest and he slammed hard against the wall. He was on his knees, crawling towards his wife, his nails against the floorboards when a deafening crack sounded out in the small room.

His wife slumped forwards, a trickle of red from her temple. He grabbed for her hands, untying them, his arms around her as she fell against him.

Aleksy knew she was gone by the way her body moved, the way her forehead bumped against his shoulder. He sobbed as he spun around, let Natalia go and frantically reached for his son, staring into his beautiful, wide brown eyes, trying to tell him everything would be all right, trying to tell him that he loved him, that his father would do anything he could to save him.

What he didn't see was the rifle coming towards him, smacking him clean across the forehead at the same time as he heard another crack, another explosion that may as well have been aimed at his heart.

— ❧ —

Aleksy had no concept of how long he had lain on the ground, unconscious. When he woke, his head was pounding, and when he raised his hand he felt a hard lump there, sticky blood matted against his cheek and neck.

And that's when it all came back to him, when he realised that it wasn't his blood, but his wife's, from when he'd cradled her. Before . . . He cried out as he sat up and saw his little boy's fallen body, as still as Natalia's, killed and abandoned as if their lives meant nothing, in the blink of an eye.

'He's awake,' someone said. 'Take him.'

They had to haul Aleksy to his feet, pushing him, kicking and prodding him to keep him moving while he tried desperately to resist, to scramble back to those he loved, ready to take the pill he'd saved so he could join them. He inhaled the faint smell of Natalia's cooking as they dragged him down the hall, past a photo of their wedding day in the hallway and the open door to his son's room. He could almost see him in his cot, smiling as they readied him for bed, always wanting another story, always reaching his little arms up to loop them around his mama's neck for another bedtime cuddle.

He was shoved forwards, out of the door, away from his family. He wished they'd just shot him too, that they'd taken his life in the kitchen and let him stay with them instead of enduring the torture of being left behind.

Aleksy collapsed then, his legs buckling. He dropped to his knees, the pain of every step too much to endure. He couldn't cry, the emotion caught in his chest, choking him, almost making it impossible to breathe. How could he live without them?

But still they didn't shoot him, even though he prayed for his life to end.

Someone hauled him to his feet by his collar, and he stumbled forwards once more, hearing the men joke and laugh. Cigarette smoke blew past him, curling into the air, and the wind took it away; life somehow continued as normal despite the atrocity that had happened in his own home, that had ripped apart his very existence.

And still they made him walk, down the dusty road, his head hanging as they joined others; more helpless people who fell into step beside and around him. Aleksy didn't look up, didn't want to see who else they had, what other families had been destroyed with out warning. For he knew that everyone would have lost someone, everyone around him would be mourning their own painstaking loss just as he was.

He thought of Marcin and his family, wondered if they'd had time to escape or if they had suffered the same fate, at the hands of such brutes, who snuffed out lives as easily as they might a cigarette.

They walked endlessly, the only noise the shuffle of feet and the cries of those who'd lost someone, but most walked in silence. He eventually touched his hand to his pocket, knowing the choice he had, knowing what he could do if he so chose, but he didn't reach for the pill. He wouldn't take it, but he wouldn't discard it either, not yet. Not when he might come across someone else who needed it, someone he could help.

When he looked up, they'd arrived at the train station. The signs that had so alarmingly declared their typhus outbreak had disappeared, abandoned on the ground for soldiers to trample. But what scared him most weren't the soldiers and Gestapo, but the wagons that were waiting at the station, at the humans who were being forced inside them, packed like sardines from the looks of it. Many of the people were barefoot, barely wearing enough clothes, but no one cared. They were beaten, yelled at, *laughed* at, as if their suffering was nothing more than a cruel game.

Aleksy looked around then, took stock of what was happening as he was prodded sharply, finally stepping towards the closest cattle cart. The line of them seemed to stretch on endlessly and when he looked up at it, he saw the noticed affixed to the side. *Eight horses.* This was a wagon designed to transport animals around Europe, not humans, and he watched as those in front of him helped to hoist others aboard. The people with luggage clutched handles, desperate to keep hold of their only remaining possessions. It took minutes to load them, for the door to be closed, leaving them in almost-darkness, the stench of too many bodies overwhelming in such a cramped, airless place. He touched a hand to his throat, wondering how he could continue breathing, where they were going and what his fate would be now that everything had been taken from him.

'Please, can someone help?' somebody cried. 'I think my daughter has broken her leg. Please.'

Aleksy breathed deeply, filled his lungs with the stale air and cleared his throat. If it was to be his penance to live, then he would dedicate his life to saving others, to doing anything he could to ease the suffering of those around him. It was the one gift he had left, and as he silently mourned his family, their memories together etched into his very existence, he lifted his head and dedicated himself to service.

'I'm a doctor,' he said, quietly. 'I will help you.'

The train shuddered to life and then started to roll forwards, making them all wobble and crash together on unsteady feet. He squeezed his way past all the bodies and found a father in the corner, his daughter folded in his arms.

'You can help us?'

He blinked away his tears. 'I can try.'

'Is that you, Dr Gorski?' someone asked. 'Where is your family? What happened?'

He silently reached for the girl, knowing that no matter how many times he was asked that question, he would never, ever be capable of answering it. But when someone began to sing, and others joined in, their soft voices united inside the rattling cart, tears began to stream down Aleksy's cheeks.

The words of their national anthem had never seemed so true.

Poland has not yet perished,
So long as we still live.
What the foreign force has taken from us,
We shall with sabre retrieve.

Aleksy did his best to treat the girl by using a splint and bandage from his bag.

'Dr Gorski,' someone else said in a hoarse voice.

He felt his way towards the voice, pushing past the tightly packed people around him.

'Are you injured?'

The woman cried, and as he leaned closer to her, she gripped his shoulder. 'I'm all that's left,' she whispered. 'My family, they're gone, and I've hurt my arm badly.'

'What can I do for you?'

'The pain is too great, I can't go on.'

Aleksy held her as she sobbed, trying to hold in his own emotion, knowing it was the woman's arm she was talking about, but instead sensing the pain in her heart. He felt his pocket, touched the pill there and knew what he had to do.

'If the pain is truly too great, if you decide you cannot face another day, this will give you a choice,' he said. 'You can end your own life in an instant with this.'

She went still in his arms, and when she took the pill from him, he closed his fingers around hers.

'Please take your time to think about this,' he said, and they never said another word as they tried to stay upright, the carriage violently lurching and making it almost impossible to stand.

———— ❦ ————

By the time their train stopped, Aleksy had cried so many tears in the dark that his eyes felt as if they might not open again, they were so swollen and dry. The wagon they'd been piled in was fetid; everyone, including him, had vomited from the swaying motion, some had had to relieve their bowels, and others were simply sweating profusely and were adding to the unpleasant aroma. His own skin was sticky, his clothes damp against him. At one point, he'd fixated on a gap between the wooden slats of the cart and seen a glimpse of the countryside passing them by, as the train rattled along at speed. He was fairly certain the extreme motion was due to the fact there were humans on board, and not the heavier cattle or horses that were usually transported.

Many of the people around him were shivering violently, and Aleksy knew it could be as much from shock as the cold, although it was starting to feel frigid inside. He straightened when the train finally slowed and eventually stopped, waiting with everyone else to see where they were, their breaths held collectively.

There were shouts outside in German, and Aleksy strained his ears to listen to what they were saying. But then, without warning, the door to their cart was flung open, and bright lights shone at them, blinding after so long in the dark. He held up his hand, shielding his eyes as those around him cried and murmured; someone yelled and the distinct sound of a whip cracking alerted them to the fact that they were expected to obey. He glanced at the woman he'd stood beside all those hours in the dark; he knew she wasn't stepping off that carriage, and he reached for her hand to give it one final squeeze.

'*Raus! Raus!*'

The crowd shuffled forwards, and Aleksy moved with them, thankful they were moving instead of standing in the wagon. In there, he hadn't been able to stop reliving the last time he'd seen his wife; held his son. Having something to do was a small reprieve from the memories he would be forced to endure for the rest of his life.

He barely noticed what was happening, where he was, or what was going on around him. He trudged on, step after step. They were processed like prisoners, as if they were guilty of some terrible crime, even though he knew many of those around him would be Jews, persecuted for no reason other than their religion, or non-Jews like him who'd simply tried to help others. The only thing he noticed, as he lifted his head to stare at the sky, was a cast-iron arch that was flanked on each side by barbed wire.

Arbeit Macht Frei.

He translated it in his mind, realised that it said 'work will make you free', and wondered what that even meant. Was this the labour he'd heard of young Polish and Slovakian people doing? Was he destined to do back-breaking work for the Germans, as Leon had once done, when he'd come to Aleksy and pleaded for help?

On they walked, into a concrete building that was even colder than the outside air. He stripped off his clothes when he was ordered to, lifted his head and shivered as he was blasted with cold water, as his head was shaved, as his mouth was inspected, dressed in clothes that weren't his own when he was directed towards them.

'Name?'

Aleksy blinked, staring at the moving mouth of the person seated before him. Someone prodded at him, and he tried to focus on what was being said.

'Name?' the man asked again, and Aleksy saw that he winced when a guard stepped closer, as if he were scared of what was to come.

'Aleksy Gorski.'

He answered some more questions, his mouth so dry he could barely force his tongue to move around the words.

'Occupation?'

'Doctor.'

It was all recorded and eventually he was given a card and told to move into another line. The shuffle continued, until he came to another man, this one seated not with a pen, but a crude-looking needle.

'Arm,' the man said, pointing to his left arm.

Aleksy rolled up his sleeve, wincing when the needle started to move against his skin, not realising until the green ink was being rubbed over the wound that he was being tattooed with the same number on his card.

'Halt.'

He looked up from his newly inked marking.

'You are the doctor, Gorski?'

Aleksy nodded.

'You are qualified?'

He cleared his throat, staring at the man in his perfectly starched uniform, who looked so like the man who'd taken the life of his wife. Of his beautiful Natalia.

'Yes,' he said. 'I am a Red Cross doctor, and before the war I worked for a hospital in Warsaw, as an obstetrician.'

'Then you will come with me.'

Aleksy glanced at the tattooist, but his face was impassive. He didn't give anything away, didn't give Aleksy a hint as to whether he should be fearful or not.

They walked back through the building where he'd been processed, to an area where men in white coats were examining young women. Aleksy looked away, seeing how embarrassed they were. Only teenagers and they were being poked and prodded, naked in front of men who seemed to be enjoying their discomfort at being scrutinised. He noticed that one of the women was visibly pregnant, her stomach swollen, which made the situation all the more appalling.

'This is the doctor?' The man who turned carried himself as if he were in charge, his walk confident as he strode towards Aleksy, a chart in his hand. 'You are Dr Aleksy Gorski? The Polish doctor?'

'Yes,' Aleksy said.

'I have heard all about your typhus outbreak. It seems my colleagues believed you were fooling them, until they examined your patients with their own eyes.'

Aleksy stayed still, silently swallowing as he stood to attention.

'My name is Dr Josef Mengele, and I am an SS physician,' he said, glancing at his notes. 'I see that you were an obstetrician, before the war? Is that correct?'

'That is correct,' Aleksy said, his eyes flitting back to the young women who were finally being allowed to put their clothes back on.

'You will appreciate my fascination with pregnant women, then,' he said, smiling. 'These women are all pregnant, and I'm going to monitor them. Perhaps perform some experiments to see how miraculous the human body is.'

Aleksy felt colour rise in his face, anger at the way this doctor was smiling, at the way he was looking at the women.

'You are to report to the hospital block in the morning,' Mengele said, turning his back on the women who huddled together. 'We are now allowing prisoner doctors to treat other prisoners, and I shall expect you to report for work each day as required.'

'I will be a doctor here?'

'Yes. You will be,' he replied. 'And with that will come extra rations and the benefit of no hard labour. You will likely be the envy of your fellow prisoners.'

So I am a prisoner now. A prisoner with a number tattooed on my arm, marked until the day I die.

'Dr Mengele, the people here,' Aleksy asked, needing to know. 'They are mostly Jews?'

He blinked back at him. 'You have a problem treating Jews?'

Aleksy shook his head. 'No,' he said, carefully considering his words. 'I will treat all patients, regardless of their ethnicity or religion. I only wanted to know what this place was, if this is where so many Jews have been taken over the years?'

'This is Auschwitz,' Dr Mengele said. 'Those in the camp are useful to us for the work they can do, and those that are not useful? Well, they go elsewhere.'

Aleksy stood there until a guard came and shoved him forwards, and they retraced their footsteps. He wasn't certain he wanted to know where *elsewhere* was.

CHAPTER SIXTEEN

Auschwitz-Birkenau

'This is it?'

Aleksy stood in the room. It looked like the block he'd been assigned to live in, only worse, if that were even possible. He'd lain awake the entire previous night, trying not to scratch from the filthy straw he'd been forced to lie on, trying to tell himself that he'd have never forgiven himself if his wife had had to suffer through the indignities of being a prisoner. But then of course he'd remembered her final moments, what had happened in their home, and wonder if he could truly believe that she would choose death over survival. No matter how horrendous it was.

'This is Block 23. Dr Mengele will be over to see you himself later today.'

The guard speaking to him looked disinterested, and Aleksy wondered what he was even supposed to do.

There was nothing he could see in the way of supplies; no bandages, no medicines, no blankets. Nothing. He heard a cough and squinted, walking towards the far corner of the room. There was a woman there, an emaciated, coughing, feverish-looking woman.

'There is someone in here!'

The guard stared at him as if he were insane. 'It is a hospital.'

Aleksy turned around. He knew he might be beaten for it, but he had to ask for supplies. What could he do if there was nothing to treat his patients with? And why was he the only doctor?

'I will need supplies,' he said. 'Blankets, clean water, food, bandages, and a selection of medicines for treatment.'

The guard laughed. 'Patients receive less food than the others. They are lazy bastards who aren't working, they don't need feeding.'

Aleksy swallowed, keeping his anger from showing. It would do him no good, not here. 'There are other hospitals here?' he asked. 'At Auschwitz?'

The guard shrugged. 'You ask too many questions.'

With that, Aleksy was left standing in the room, the door banging shut behind him. He immediately followed the guard's footsteps and opened the door, letting in some light, and more importantly fresh air. There was a little sun peeking through the clouds, and he wanted to make the most of it.

'It's so cold in here,' the woman said, huddled against the wall in the corner.

'Opening the door won't let the heat out,' he said. 'There's none in here to begin with.'

He looked at the stove, knowing what a difference it would make if he *could* heat the room. But it wasn't just patients who were suffering, he'd seen the faces and sunken bodies of those in his block, knew that everyone at the camp was suffering from lack of facilities.

He approached the woman, noted the way her bone-thin arms wrapped around herself. He reached for her hand, placing it on the bed as he took her pulse, trying not to shudder as he saw the tiny red welts all over her skin, indicative of the bugs and lice living in the straw-filled sacks. Aleksy smiled and checked her eyes, the inside of her mouth and throat, and carefully listened to her breath, wishing he had his medicine bag with him.

'I think you are suffering from pneumonia,' Aleksy said, as the woman's breath wheezed in and out. *There is so much I could do for you, to save your life, if you'd come to my clinic.*

Aleksy stood then, smiling down at his first patient. 'Try to rest.'

'Thank you,' she said.

He paused, looking down at her, before lowering to his haunches. 'I will do my best to help you. Can you tell me your name?'

'Joanka,' she murmured. 'My name is Joanka.'

Aleksy nodded, patting her hand. 'Joanka, I am Aleksy.'

The woman started to say something, but her cough rattled her chest and put an end to their conversation. So Aleksy did the only thing he could do to improve the quality of the block he'd been put in charge of, standing up and using a thick wad of hay to try to sweep the floors, his back protesting at being bent over for so long, before taking all the straw-filled pillows from the bunks. He took each one outside and beat it with his fist, over and over, trying to rid them of lice and get rid of as much dust as he could. Then he left them in the daylight, hoping the sunshine might help.

He turned to go back into the block, feeling dizzy from all the work he'd been doing without any sustenance.

'Why are the pillows outside? Do you not want them?'

The voice behind him made Aleksy turn. There was something about the man that made him uncomfortable, that caught him entirely off guard. He stood back to let him pass.

'It appears the block is full of lice, and I thought the bedding could do with some air,' Aleksy said.

'Good.'

He waited, his breath catching slightly, not able to make this Dr Mengele out.

'Sir, you are in charge here, of the patient care?'

'Of all the hospitals and infirmaries here at Auschwitz-Birkenau, yes. Over in the main camp, we have a contagious diseases block as well as a block for surgical.' He smirked. 'Perhaps I should have sent you there?'

So there are other hospitals.

'I'd simply like to know more about your hospital facilities. About what you might expect me to do and how I can be of assistance.'

Dr Mengele strode towards Aleksy, seemingly ignoring the patient in the corner. 'You are pleasing to me because you're not a Jew, and I'm impressed with your work. Your colleagues speak highly of you.'

Aleksy knew nothing about what colleagues he might have spoken to, but he hadn't seen Marcin arrive, and he was too afraid to ask after him.

'My job is to treat only Jewish patients here though?' Aleksy asked.

'I would like you to treat all patients and get them back to work as quickly as possible. We are losing too much of our workforce.'

He wished he were brave enough to tell him that as doctors, they both knew no one could thrive in such conditions, let alone recuperate from illness. But he held his tongue.

'Are there supplies I may have access to? To ensure I can treat these patients adequately for you?'

'I shall see what I can find,' he said, seeming to study Aleksy. He almost felt as if it were some sort of test, as if he were perhaps being set up to fail.

'I would be appreciative of whatever you can spare,' he said, before adding, 'to ensure they are back to work as quickly as possible.'

Mengele stayed silent for a long moment, as if deep in thought, before turning on his heel and striding towards the door. But when he got there, he turned.

'I would like you to report every pregnant woman to me directly,' he said. 'Take down their number and ensure to alert me immediately.'

Aleksy nodded. 'You will treat them yourself?'

Mengele smiled. 'I shall personally check them and have them moved to another camp, where they will receive better nutrition and servings of milk. You can help me spread the word that any pregnant woman should come forward, so we can care for them. They will trust you.'

'Yes, sir.'

Aleksy didn't believe for a second that he'd show the women kindness. All of the women he'd seen so far, other than the ones who'd arrived on the train with him, looked like walking skeletons. He doubted many of them could even become pregnant, certainly not after being at the camp for more than a few months, unless they were receiving extra rations.

'I have a special interest in pregnant women, and twins. I'm sure you can understand that, being an obstetrician? There is something so fascinating about the female body, wouldn't you agree?'

Aleksy forced himself to nod, bile rising at the doctor's words, and when Mengele finally left there was a weak voice from the back of the block. Clearly his one patient had purposely kept quiet while the SS doctor was in the room.

'You know, the sickest ones go straight to the concrete building, the one out there.'

Aleksy looked to see where the woman was pointing and stood at the door, seeing smoke billow from the chimney.

'What is in there?' he asked.

The woman coughed before answering. 'I don't know. But no one ever comes out. They call it the chimney.'

———— ⁂ ————

Aleksy trod the same path from his barracks to the makeshift hospital straight after breakfast. He looked down at his hands as he walked, noticing how much they had changed in the months that he'd been in the camp. Before they had been smooth and firm, his nails neatly trimmed, and now they looked more bone than flesh, his nails bitten short, and his skin chapped red from the cold.

Auschwitz was like nothing he'd ever imagined in his life before, and every day he woke, he wondered if it was penance for what he'd done. But then he'd listen to the stories of others as he tried his best to assist them with their troubles, and realise that he was no different from anyone else. They were all either there because of their religion or for working against the Third Reich, and he knew in his heart that all he'd done was fight to help others. For that, surely, God wouldn't seek to punish him.

He stepped into the block then and looked around. Every morning he felt the same – a sense of helplessness that there was so little he could do – but he also knew that sometimes, his best was enough. That a rest for the day and some kind words could do wonders for a person in pain, and he was relieved to see everyone had survived the night.

'Anastasia,' he said, as he saw a young pregnant woman moving around the other patients. 'How many times do I have to tell you to rest?'

She smiled as she passed him, touching his shoulder. It stopped him in his tracks, the gentle touch of a woman, her fingers brushing against him as his wife might have done if he'd passed her in the hallway.

Anastasia was a Roma, and he'd discovered she was pregnant when he'd been moved into one of the blocks in their section. They had welcomed him in a way he hadn't expected, many of the people there in family groups, and he'd immediately warmed to Anastasia when she'd spoken to him one day. But when he'd overheard her sister urging her to tell their *kapo* she was pregnant, he'd taken her aside. His thoughts about Mengele had been correct, confirmed when he'd heard horror stories about the experiments he was doing on pregnant women, of the terror they were subjected to. But most horrifying of all had been seeing the women walk to that building with his own eyes, and he shuddered as the memory came back to him, of the day he'd realised what it all meant, what that place was for.

She looked at him, her baby cradled to her chest. And he'd known. There was no special camp, there were no extra rations or milk. The woman looked like a walking skeleton, and her eyes . . . They'd told him that whatever had happened to her, it had taken the life from her. Dr Mengele had done something with her, but he certainly hadn't helped her.

And then he'd stood, helplessly, his hands hanging by his sides as he'd watched from the other side of the wire fence, as she and other women were walked to the building. The building that no one ever returned from. The place they called the chimney. It was then that he'd realised what the plumes of smoke signalled. Why no one ever came back.

'Aleksy, come back to me,' Anastasia said, her voice kindly as he blinked at her. 'We can't think about them. We can't think about what we've lost, we can only think of our survival.'

He nodded. But even if he didn't think about the past, his mind turned to how he would keep her safe. How would he stop her baby from being taken? From both of them being taken? There was only so long her pregnancy would go unnoticed, and then he would be questioned, too.

'I don't know how long I can keep you here,' he said. 'I don't want you catching anything from those that are unwell, but you know I'll do anything I can to help you.'

'I think the *kapo* knows I'm not sick enough to be here.'

'You let me worry about the *kapo*,' Aleksy said, smiling at the young woman who was older than her years. 'I shall send you back tonight and say that you're to come here immediately if you become ill again.'

Anastasia patted his hand and he did his rounds, listening to everyone's ailments. Sometimes he found that it was as much help letting his patients be heard as treating them, making them feel like people rather than numbers.

'Anyway, I have good news today,' he said, unwrapping a little package that he'd kept in his pocket all night. 'It seems the *kapos* like me treating their ailments, and they have given me some extra food.'

The room went silent, and Aleksy found himself dividing two sausages into ten pieces, one for each of his patients, and one for himself. Although when he went to Anastasia, he gave her two. When she looked to question him, he merely shook his head and closed her fingers around the extra piece.

He hadn't been able to save his wife, but he was determined to save this young patient, even though his stomach twisted with pain at seeing food and not being able to consume it himself. And even though he wondered how a baby would ever survive the conditions at Auschwitz, he hoped he could save her. Mothers had been banned from feeding their babies, not permitted to do anything that could stop them from working, and that meant it wasn't only the babies Aleksy was concerned about. If you didn't work, you didn't survive.

The words he'd read as he'd first walked into the camp said 'Work will set you free', but he thought it would have been much more appropriate to simply state: *Work or you won't live to see another day.*

They didn't want to *keep* the prisoners at the sprawling camp alive, they wanted them to die.

Aleksy had come to realise that life at Auschwitz was an exercise in routine, as well as brutality. They were woken at the same time each day; they stood in the cold for roll call at the same time, and they were fed the same slop at every meal, if he could even bring himself to think of them as meals. And another unfortunate part of his daily or weekly routine was seeing his patients, those deemed too weak to survive, taken from his care and wheeled or marched to the building from where no one returned.

He'd asked questions, quietly figuring out the comings and goings of the camp, and the more he found out, the more he understood that SS Dr Mengele was not to be trusted under any circumstances. But what he'd also learnt was how fortunate he was not to be sent out on agricultural detail or other back-breaking work that most others in the camp had to do. The lucky ones, those who had somehow found favour with the *kapos*, were put on detail cleaning the blocks, serving the coffee and bread, and working in the office. But for most, the work was beyond anything they could have ever imagined, made worse by the fact they were barely being kept alive with the meagre rations they were permitted each day.

Aleksy smiled at the faces looking back at him. The one tool he had at his disposal was the power to order rest, and he did it as often as he was able. There were no special ointments for blisters other than some salve when he was lucky, and medicine was almost impossible to procure, but the patients in his care could rest, and for that he was grateful.

The one thing he had been given was a knife, and although it wasn't much, it was his most valuable possession, and he took it to bed with him each night in case it was stolen. He kept it sharp, able to slice off dead skin or open infections, and use as a blade to remove hair if necessary. The women hated keeping their heads bald, but it did help with the lice, which seemed to invade every pillow, every piece of hay, and every body.

Someone came through the door then, a *kapo* helping to prop up a woman who was bleeding. Aleksy rushed forwards and caught her before she fell, half carrying her to the closest empty bunk bed. He mainly treated women, which was unusual as men and women were strictly separated in the camp in their quarters. He'd been a red-cheeked young man when he'd started out as an obstetrician, but it hadn't taken long for him to become comfortable around women, and that only increased after marrying Natalia.

'What happened?' he asked. 'Where is the blood coming from?'

The woman held out her foot, wincing as he touched it, his hands carefully moving over the rough skin. Her feet were a mess, her toes black, filthy as all of their feet were. And there was a big gash that curved over her foot and up her leg.

Aleksy took a deep breath and went to retrieve his things. He had a needle, and the only thread that he'd procured was from the edges of blankets – those patients who weren't sick enough to be unconscious often helped him, and he had a small pile of thread with which to stitch the young woman's wound.

'I'm afraid this is going to hurt,' he said. They weren't words he'd have uttered before the camp, always prepared with whatever he needed to prevent his patients' suffering, but here, they were necessary. 'I suggest trying to think of something pleasant from home, somewhere to take your mind, and I promise to work as quickly as possible.'

The door banged open then, but Aleksy didn't look up, determined to clean the woman's wound quickly, dabbing the small amount of water he'd been permitted against her skin, the needle between his teeth as he prepared to begin stitching.

'Come with me.'

The words were sharp, a command that he chose to ignore. He kept stitching, pulling the needle through the skin, trying to do it as quickly as possible. Aleksy did glance at his patient though, relieved to see that her eyes were shut. She'd passed out from the pain.

'Now.'

Something sharp prodded against his back, bumping him and making him push harder than he wanted beneath the woman's skin. He quickly finished what he was doing before standing.

'I have been told to work here as a doctor, that these women are my patients,' Aleksy said. 'I am following orders.'

The guard stared at him. 'New orders are that women doctors will treat women. You won't be coming back to treat these flea-infested wretches again.'

Aleksy didn't react to his deliberately hurtful words, wishing the women behind him hadn't had to hear it. But the truth was they would have heard much worse during their incarceration.

'Where am I to go?' he asked, desperately hoping he wasn't being put on agricultural detail. So many of his patients were rural girls who'd volunteered to do agricultural work, thinking they'd be farming or harvesting, but the reality of working back-breaking land and spreading cow manure by hand, with no way to wash afterwards, had told him the work was as bad as in the quarries.

'There's been a typhus outbreak,' the guard said, pointing towards the door. 'I hear that's your speciality, and we have a new infectious diseases block.'

Aleksy glanced at his knife, wondering if he should leave it for the next doctor, but decided against it. It was one of the only tools at his disposal, after all.

'So I'm to care for those patients instead?'

The guard grunted and Aleksy followed him, looking over his shoulder one last time to see the patients he was leaving behind, seeing some of them sitting on the edge of the bunks, crushing lice between their fingernails. He knew that only the ones with minor injuries or illnesses would make it, but it hadn't stopped him from trying.

The infectious diseases block at Auschwitz was like nothing Aleksy had ever witnessed before, although he was immensely grateful for the other prisoner-doctors who'd already begun to set up Block 24. Where they couldn't have rooms they had the area segregated by condition, which meant they kept diarrhoea patients well away from those who weren't suffering from that yet, and the same for those with coughs.

'Thank you,' he said on his second day to a nurse, who had just completed the arduous task of sweeping the dirt floor and then emptying the latrine buckets.

She smiled and nodded. They were all grateful to one another, especially the patients. Without their prisoner-doctors, they all knew what would have happened to them; they would have been left to die.

'Doctor, come and see what they're doing in the women's camp.'

They were alone in the hospital, the guards didn't bother to stand watch over them any more, and Aleksy followed two of the nurses outside, not certain what he was going to be looking at.

'What is it?' he asked, as he followed the nurses closer to the wire fence.

She adjusted her scarf on her head. 'I heard some of the guards have caught typhus.'

Aleksy's eyebrows shot up. It didn't surprise him. The conditions were so unhygienic, and the guards were around them all day. Lice were everywhere, there were as many resident rats as humans, and everyone was filthy – they had no proper facilities to wash in.

Women were standing, naked, at least fifty of them, huddled outside the hospital barracks that he'd once been put in charge of. Their spindly arms were wrapped around their bodies as other prisoners appeared to go inside, carrying buckets.

'What are they doing to them?' one nurse asked.

He shook his head, wishing he could do something to help them, to shake some common sense into the guards. But of course they didn't care about common sense, because their efforts were not designed to save those in their care.

'They're washing them,' he said, as he watched the first woman step into a tub. 'I'd say it's full of disinfectant.' He could also see that their heads had been freshly shaved. 'They've realised it's the lice that's spreading the typhus. They didn't care before, so you must be right about the guards contracting it. I think they're trying to kill the insects.'

Woman after woman went into the water as guards stood by, at a distance. Eventually they had all bathed, and now they were huddled once more, only this time they were dripping wet. If they weren't already sick, they were at risk now, their skinny bodies berated by the wind. It appeared their clothes were also being washed, and they were given back to them dripping wet.

The women were eventually pointed back in the direction of the barracks.

'You know, back in my village,' one of the nurses said, her gaze fixed on the group of women, 'I had someone ask me why we couldn't see the horns on the Jewish children. They actually believed that they had horns hidden in their hair.'

'It's hard to believe how many people were willing to believe the lies they were fed,' Aleksy replied, turning away, not wanting to watch any more.

He went back inside to the relative warmth, looking around at the patients in their care. They were all doing their best, but every new patient who was sent to them expected more, or at least for the 'hospital' to resemble one from their previous life, before the camp.

'Get everyone up!' The shout came before the door banged open, and Aleksy shut his eyes for a moment, wondering what they were to be subjected to. Was it their turn to go in the bath?

'Under whose orders?' he asked when he turned, seeing the terrified stares of the two nurses working alongside him.

'Get out!' the guard yelled, ignoring him. 'Get them all out!'

Aleksy knew better than to ask questions. They started to get their patients to their feet, all of them, from those with suspected pneumonia and pleurisy, to those with stomach ailments and fevers. Some had to leave the urine-soaked rags behind that had been resting across their skin – there was no cold water to use, and it was often the only thing the doctors could suggest to help bring a fever down.

'Clothes off!'

His shoulders slumped as he repeated the order to his patients, as the nurses helped them out of their ragged clothes as efficiently as they could. But it was when the order came for the hospital staff to undress that the tears began. His nurses held their heads high, cheeks wet from the humiliation of it all, as they were forced to leave their patients behind and march out with no clothes on.

'Where are you taking us?' he asked. 'What have we done?'

'We're disinfecting everything,' the guard said. 'Including you.'

'And our patients?'

Another guard grunted. 'Block 25.'

The nurse ahead of him cried out, but before the guard could use his stick on her, Aleksy stumbled, making certain it was he instead of she who received the sharp welt across his skin.

Block 25. His footsteps were heavy as he trudged to wherever they were being taken. What was happening to them might be humiliating and dehumanising, but at least they were alive. For now. But no one ever came back from Block 25, the building he and the other doctors and nurses were expected to haul dying patients to on a daily basis. Mind you, they could just as easily perish without being sent there, or be killed for looking at a guard the wrong way. Aleksy knew his life meant nothing more than any other prisoner's; to the guards, they were all simply numbers.

He thought of Anastasia, wondered how she was, whether she was close to having her baby. And he wondered just how long he was going to be able to treat patients, knowing that no matter what he did, no matter how much he tried to save them, no matter how hard he fought . . . it was almost impossible to keep any of them alive.

Natalia. He was doing this for Natalia, he had to, because otherwise what had it all been for? She would want him to keep fighting, to keep doing everything in his power to save even one life, to keep even one person alive to return to their family once this horrible ordeal was over. But it would have been so much easier to join the never-ending list of people who threw themselves against the wire to put an end to their misery once and for all.

In the beginning, he'd wondered how they could do it, thought it such a waste of a human life. But that was before he'd understood the hell of Auschwitz, and how much easier it was to face death than fight every waking hour, every minute of every day, to stay alive.

CHAPTER SEVENTEEN

Four months later

The woman was slumped against the wall, her baby clutched to her chest without so much as a towel to wrap him in. Never, in all his years of being a doctor had Aleksy felt so helpless. Before, he'd always found a way to ease his patients' suffering, but if the past months had taught him anything, it was that there was no hope in Auschwitz, only death. It was all around him, seeking him out, taunting him, reminding him that no matter how skilled or determined he might be, he was almost useless without medicine and other supplies.

He excused himself, doubting the mother even heard him as she shivered with fever, and walked to the door. The barracks were cramped, filthy despite his best efforts, and unbearably damp, with rats often scuttling over his feet; it was the worst place for an infant to be welcomed into the world, and Aleksy had the most overwhelming feeling that the walls were closing in on him. He was still working in the infectious diseases block, and delivering a baby wasn't something he'd expected to be doing there; it simply seemed too cruel for a woman so sick to have to give birth.

He desperately needed fresh air, although as soon as he stepped out, the cold wind whipped straight through him, making him double over, his thin shirt doing nothing to shield him from the conditions. But it was still better than being inside.

It should have been a joyous occasion, welcoming a child safely into the world, but as he leaned against the side of the block and looked at the building in the distance, the one sending plumes of smoke and pieces of ash into the air, death was the only thing he could think of. He turned his head away and shut his eyes, remembering home, remembering what life had been like before he'd been stolen from his village and sent into the darkness that was the camp. He ground his teeth together as he thought of home; every time he tried to find a happy memory, it was tainted with his final day, his final moment before he was dragged away.

Aleksy slouched forwards, his shoulders hunched to protect him from the wind.

What he would have given for a cigarette. He'd dreamed of food for weeks, and still did, but it was a cigarette he most craved at the end of the day. If there had been a guard close by, he wouldn't have been above begging for one, although he doubted his grovelling would have helped his cause.

A noise made Aleksy open his eyes, and he pushed away from the wall as he watched a woman stumble from the nearby hut. She fell and crawled forwards on the dirt, and he noticed that her hair was freshly shaved as her headscarf slipped back, but she didn't make it far before a guard ran out and viciously kicked her. Aleksy grimaced as he watched the guard's heavy boot connect with her stomach, sending her flying, but despite the brutality he found it impossible to look away as she defiantly stood and faced the guard. There was something about her, something that held his attention despite the cold gnawing at his skin. Or perhaps it was simply that he hadn't seen anyone for so long with any fight left in them, and he found himself drawn to her, to the type of energy he'd once possessed.

He edged forwards, flexing his fingers and then curling them into tight balls. He watched as the woman rose after being kicked again, despite what must have been overwhelming pain, her eyes still wide and defiant as she stared back at the guard. Anywhere else, Aleksy would have admired her bravery, but here, bravery only resulted in one thing: death. As such, he found himself hoping that she submitted soon.

'I won't do it,' she said, loud enough for Aleksy to hear. 'Shoot me! I'm not going back in there.'

Studying the feisty young woman, Aleksy realised what she was protesting about. *She's seen what they're doing in there, to those babies.* He'd heard of the horrors of the German midwives and what they did to Jewish infants, which told him that she'd likely witnessed it with her own eyes. He'd have found it just as impossible to digest himself.

'You follow orders, or you're dead.'

Aleksy watched in horror as the guard lifted his gun. The woman's eyes widened and then shut, as if she'd decided that she was indeed prepared to die instead of following whatever unfathomable orders she'd been given. But even as she stood there, he noticed that her body never trembled, never betraying a hint of just how scared she must be, her chin jutted high. He recognised that look; it was a look the new prisoners had, before they'd witnessed the terrors of life in the camp.

'Stop!' Aleksy hurried forwards, holding up his hands as if he were a criminal. He couldn't stand by and watch her be shot; he didn't need another woman's murder haunting his memories. 'Please, is she a nurse?'

The woman turned, her ink-dark eyes meeting his.

'I am a midwife,' she said, and he exhaled as he heard her accent. She was Polish, like him.

The guard fixed his gaze on Aleksy, and he kept his hands raised, not wanting to give him a reason to turn the gun on him instead. He'd seen men and women killed for sport, bored guards deciding to play target practice, and he wasn't about to give him any reason to shoot.

'Please,' he said, his voice low as he slowly lifted his gaze to meet the guard's eyes. 'I'm a doctor, I am from Block 24.' He paused. 'Dr Mengele needs me back in the hospital and I've been tasked with finding a nurse to assist me. A midwife would be even more helpful, and I'm certain he would be pleased to fill the position.'

Aleksy found himself holding his breath as he slowly lowered his hands, hoping that the mention of the head doctor's name would save both of them, despite the order being a lie. The wind had turned his fingers to ice, the winter weather almost impossible to stand in the flimsy shirts they'd been issued, while he waited for the guard to make a decision.

'Take her,' the guard said, shrugging. He lowered his gun, using it instead to shove the woman forwards, the butt pointed into the small of her back. 'But if she doesn't do what she's told?' He grinned and lifted his gun again, grunting as he reached out with his other hand to grope the woman's bottom. Aleksy looked away, hating that he was powerless to do anything about the man's behaviour. But for now, he'd saved her, and that was what mattered.

He waited until the guard had started to walk away before hurrying over and grabbing hold of the woman's arm. She resisted, trying to tug it away, but he held firm, even when she refused to move, her nostrils flaring as she glared at him.

'Come with me,' he said. 'I won't hurt you, but we need to get inside.'

Still, she didn't move.

'Do you know what they're doing in there? Are they truly so barbaric as to drown newly born babies?' she hissed.

'I believe you are right, although I haven't witnessed it myself.'

'So they are murderers?'

He sighed, letting go of her arm and tucking his hands under his armpits instead in an attempt to stay warm. 'What's your name?'

She lifted her chin. 'Emilia Bauchau.'

'Well, Emilia Bauchau, my name is Aleksy Gorski.'

'I won't kill babies,' she said, stepping away from him, as if she had a choice in what she could do next. As if *any* of them had a choice in anything any more.

'I swore an oath when I became a doctor to do no harm to my patients, and while they are under my care, I will do everything I can to keep them alive.' Aleksy gave her a long, steady look that he hoped might reassure her. 'There will be no murdering of babies in my block, of that I can assure you.' He didn't tell her that the fate they suffered for the hours or weeks they managed to live might be worse than being killed in the first place.

She wrapped her arms around herself while a strong gust of wind circled them, a moment of vulnerability, and blinked back at him.

Aleksy spoke more softly this time. 'If you want to live, Emilia, I suggest you come with me.'

They walked to Block 24. He followed her gaze to the building he'd been staring at earlier, the chimney still filling the air with smoke, ash fluttering so close to them now that a piece landed on Aleksy's shoulder.

'What is that?' she asked.

Aleksy let out a breath and took her arm, more gently this time, and steered her towards the entrance. She didn't need to know, not yet.

As he opened the door, Emilia turned her face up to him, seeming to study his eyes, and he found himself aching to lift his hand and touch her cheek. He knew she was waiting for an answer, but he wouldn't give her one today.

'What happened?' he asked instead, looking at the ugly purple bruises that ran across one side of her face. 'Who did this to you?'

'The same kind of man who kicked me outside just now.'

He would have offered to examine her, to treat her even, but what was the use with no medicine at his disposal? He didn't have so much as boiled water and a clean towel. It appeared the moment had passed, anyway, as she stepped away from him.

'The baby over there. Will he stay with his mother?'

He ushered her inside and shut the door as she rushed past him and towards the mother and infant in the far corner.

'He will, for now at least,' he said, following her. 'Although that doesn't mean they will stay alive. Not once they leave this block.'

Emilia turned and looked back at him, and it struck him how pretty she was. Even with her hair shaved, there was a strength and beauty about her face, her dark eyes framed by even darker lashes.

'And the Jewish babies?' she whispered. 'The ones next door? They're all killed like that, in the water?' She made a choking sound in her throat as if she could barely expel the words. 'Straight after birth?'

Aleksy met her gaze. He wasn't ready to talk about the babies in the next hut, or their mothers, who were forced to endure labour only to be taken to the building of no return the very next day.

'You ask too many questions, Emilia,' he said, knowing how weary he sounded.

He half expected her to be indignant at his choice of words, but she surprised him by reaching for his hand.

'Thank you, Aleksy,' she murmured. 'I should have said it before, but thank you for saving my life out there. I will not forget your kindness.'

'You're welcome.'

She hesitated, opening her mouth and then shutting it again, before finally speaking. 'He would have shot me, wouldn't he? It wasn't an idle threat?'

'Yes, Emilia,' Aleksy said. 'He would have shot you, without a doubt.' *People are killed here every day for simply existing, they don't hesitate to kill.* She'd figure it out soon enough – he didn't want to be the one to explain the crushing truth of life in Auschwitz to her. Emilia still had hope; a woman still with one foot in the past, not yet surrendered to life as a prisoner, the light still shining in her eyes.

Emilia nodded, and as he watched she let go of his fingers and dropped to her knees to check on the mother lying before them. It had been a risk deciding to help her, but he could see that it had been a worthy one.

Aleksy saw the way her hands moved expertly over the infant, whispering to the mother as she reassured her that all would be well, that any pain she had would soon begin to ease. Emilia was what this woman needed, and likely what any other pregnant women in the camp needed, too.

'We can help these women, can't we? There must be a way?'

He nodded, although in fairness he wasn't certain whether they *could* help them. But for the first time in months, he felt a lightness inside him, that perhaps he'd found someone to work alongside who could offer real hope to those who needed it.

'Aleksy, this is no place for delivering babies.'

He laughed and looked around at the squalid block. He couldn't remember the last time he'd truly smiled, but it was impossible not to see the humour in her words. 'I'm well aware of the unsuitability.'

'Well, we need to tidy it up and get rid of the vermin, for a start,' she said, standing with her hands on her hips as she surveyed the room. 'It's unsanitary and entirely—'

'Unsuitable,' he said for her, shaking his head. 'I agree.'

'And this here, is there ever firewood for it?' Emilia stood in the centre of the room, inspecting the stove.

'Rarely,' he said. 'Keeping us warm isn't a priority for the Third Reich.'

'Well, it shall be perfectly suitable for birthing,' she said. 'The height is appropriate and the lighting is dim enough to afford some degree of privacy.'

She moved with the energy of someone who hadn't starved for months on end, and he found himself drawn to her strength. Before Auschwitz, if he hadn't lost the only two people he loved in the world, he might have approached the block with the same sense of purpose. But he'd been here too long now, had seen too much death and suffering to even believe he could make a difference any more.

'Well?' she asked. 'What do you think?'

Aleksy smiled again 'I think, Emilia Bauchau, that I'm very happy I met you today, but I must tell you that this is the infectious diseases block.'

'We're going to save babies here, Aleksy, and their mothers too,' she said, looking around perhaps a little more cautiously than before, as if only just realising that there were other patients filling the bunks around them. 'I won't be told to do otherwise.'

She didn't have to tell him twice, for he didn't doubt her for a second.

CHAPTER EIGHTEEN

EMILIA

LONDON, 1995

WEDNESDAY

Emilia had barely slept; she'd sat in the kitchen until daybreak, her tea long-cold, waiting until it was finally time for Hannah to arrive. She'd written herself a note, to remind herself that Hannah was coming back, but she needn't have; Hannah had occupied her thoughts ever since their meeting the day before.

Lucy had constantly asked questions over dinner, curious about her mother's secret life, and if Emilia was honest with herself, that was the reason she'd been unable to sleep. Her daughter had been blissfully unaware of what her mother had survived, not knowing the death and suffering that had tainted the early years of her life, and in a way she'd wished she'd chosen instead to write a memoir of sorts that she could have left behind. Something Lucy could have read once her mother had passed.

If only she'd thought of that sooner.

Now, she was back sitting at the kitchen table, and Emilia turned to face Hannah. It was the same as the day before; her settling herself across from Emilia, taking out her recorder and then giving Emilia the warmest of smiles as if to tell her she was ready to listen, that she could trust Hannah.

Now she'd started talking, Emilia knew she would tell her story until the very end, but it didn't make finding the words any easier. She pressed her fist to her chest, rubbing there, as if she could ease the pain that had begun to flare.

'Emilia, are you ready?'

She nodded, dropping her hand, her fingers worrying a rough edge of wood on the table as she lifted her gaze to meet Hannah's.

'The babies that I asked you about yesterday, the ones who were fortunate enough to survive, I understand those that were allowed to live in the camp were tattooed on the thigh soon after birth, prisoners of Auschwitz, as their mothers were.'

Emilia held her breath. She knew the question that would follow, because it was something she'd thought about so often, even all these years later.

'But it's also rumoured that some babies, the ones who were taken from the camp and given to German families, were marked in some way, in secret, so that one day they might be able to find their birth mothers, if they both survived.' Hannah paused. 'Do you know anything about those markings?'

Emilia continued to trace her fingers over the rough piece of wood on the table as she shut her eyes, vividly recalling the tiny green marks on the infants' skin.

'We knew we had to find a way to mark them, just in case, otherwise how else would they ever be reunited with their mothers if they both survived? Everything we did there, we did to save the lives of mothers and babies. We did everything we could, we risked our lives because that's what we felt was our calling, it was the one thing we could do.'

'You were personally involved in marking them? You and Aleksy?'

Emilia met Hannah's gaze, surprised to see tears shining in the other woman's eyes. She watched her for a long moment, before finally looking away.

'It wasn't just us,' she replied. 'It was Lena, too.'

CHAPTER NINETEEN

EMILIA

AUSCHWITZ-BIRKENAU, 1943

It had only been days, but already she felt as if she'd been at the camp for months. She'd become used to the gnawing hunger that was so fierce it was sometimes hard to think past, the constant worry of memories, and the permanent brutality of those chosen to guard them. But what she hadn't become used to was the helplessness she felt when it came to treating other women for their ailments and pregnancies. Assisting their labours was one thing, but knowing they had little hope of survival was something else entirely.

She noticed Lena walk in, and as she smiled at her, the other women around her stopped talking. It appeared they were all staring at Lena.

'How did you get the *kapo* to like you so much, Lena?' one of the women said, as Emilia sat on the edge of the top bunk, looking down. 'We want to know what you have to do to get chosen for Canada.'

Lena looked up at her. Emilia had no idea what they were even talking about, but she did know they were being cruel with their words, there was no doubt about that.

'I think she's doing more than making friends with the *kapo*,' someone else sniped. 'It's the SS who decide who gets those roles.'

'What yummy food did you have for dinner, Lena? Does your master feed you well?'

The women laughed and Emilia immediately shifted over and made space for her, holding out her hand to help her up. She hated seeing the tears in Lena's eyes, the way she wrapped her arms around herself and looked away, shunned by those around her, especially after she'd been so kind to Emilia when she'd arrived. She could see the women were mostly kind to one another, that they were all looking out for each other as best they could, their hostility for the newcomers, and Lena.

'Going up to eat the extra food you have hidden?'

'That's enough!' Emilia cried, keeping hold of Lena's hand. 'We're all being kept here against our will, it's the least we can do to all be kind to one another.'

Lena's eyes widened, as if she couldn't believe someone had stood up for her.

'Thank you,' she whispered, tucking closer to Emilia.

The women were muttering to one another, and Emilia took the opportunity to turn to Lena. 'What's Canada?' she asked in a low voice. 'I don't even understand what they're talking about.'

'Canada is where they keep all the confiscated clothing and personal belongings they've taken from the prisoners,' Lena said, turning slightly to face her.

'I didn't know they did that.' Of course it seemed obvious now that Lena said it, because surely not everyone came here with only the clothes on their back. 'But why Canada? Why do they call it that?'

Lena smiled, and for a moment Emilia could almost imagine that they weren't in the camp, that they were simply two women talking at the end of the day. 'Canada is free, a place of peace and riches, or at least it was when we all came here,' Lena replied.

'What do you do with all the clothes and possessions?' They certainly weren't giving the items to anyone at the camp. 'Is it all given to the guards?'

'It's all sent to Germany. We have to sort through it all and put it in boxes. The trains that bring prisoners in are often reloaded later with all their belongings. Fur coats, jewellery, boots, everything is sent away to Berlin.'

Anger prickled Emilia's skin. 'It's not enough to take women from their families and treat them like criminals, they have to take their belongings, too?' It made her so angry. Those women in her barracks, they could have a chance at surviving if they'd been allowed their warm coats or boots.

'You seem surprised,' Lena said, twisting a lock of hair around her finger, making Emilia yearn for her own long hair. 'You didn't have anything special taken from you?'

Emilia shook her head, the day she was taken coming back to her. It was the memory of her father that hurt the most, seeing him standing there, watching her as she was marched away from him. She'd tried so hard to banish it from her mind, but it was easier said than done.

'I was, well, I was taken from the street. I didn't have anything,' she said. 'Other than the clothes I was wearing at the time.' She supposed her sturdy boots and warm coat had ended up in this place called Canada.

'You were arrested?' someone else asked, telling Emilia that others were listening.

Emilia nodded, surprised at the question. No one had seemed interested in speaking to her before. 'Yes. I'm a midwife, and I was caught delivering babies and, well, smuggling them to safety.'

There was silence, and she wondered if she shouldn't have been so honest about her story, especially after how cruel they'd been to Lena. But weren't they all here because of either what they'd done or who they were? She didn't feel she had anything to hide.

'You were delivering *Jewish* babies?'

Emilia cleared her throat. 'Yes. I was.'

There was silence again, and a movement across from her. One of the women lifted her head, staring at Emilia, her expression no longer so unfriendly.

'I'm impressed,' said another voice.

'Don't be nice to her, she's as bad as the other one,' someone sniped. 'Didn't you see her taken out of roll call? She probably didn't save Jewish babies at all.'

'I'd say they both get ten times the food we do,' another woman grumbled.

Emilia knew the other woman was referring to Lena again, and she instinctively shuffled closer to her. They could say what they wanted to her, but she had an overwhelming desire to protect the younger woman.

'Do you think you'd be able to get us sanitary napkins?' someone else asked, in a much more friendly voice. 'Since you're in the hospital?'

'I honestly don't know. I can try.'

'Most of us don't need them any more, anyway,' someone muttered.

'Why?' came a shy, quieter voice. 'Why have most of us stopped bleeding?'

Emilia looked at the faces around her, the bald-headed women with eyes that seemed too big for them, all waiting for her to reply. There were hundreds in their block, packed into the space, but it was just the dozens of women around her who seemed to be listening.

'Well, in times of great stress or when our bodies are being starved, we can stop menstruating,' she explained. 'After a few months of being here, I'd expect almost all of us to stop bleeding.'

'Will it ever come back?'

Emilia sat for a moment, considering her words.

'If we survive,' someone else said. 'First they take away what it means to be a woman, and then they let us die. They don't want us to live.'

After a long pause, Emilia began to speak again. 'If we survive this place, there is every chance we could begin to menstruate again. Sometimes the damage can be too great, sometimes our bodies don't recover, but it all depends on how long we're here.'

She knew the question hanging, unspoken, in the air. It was only so long before it was asked.

'Many of you will be wondering if you'll be able to have children, and the answer is that I hope so. A woman's body is nothing short of extraordinary.'

'I've heard that if we get pregnant here, they look after us,' someone said quietly from the bottom bunk.

'I'll find out everything I can,' Emilia said. 'But if any of you find yourselves needing my help, please come to me. I can examine you here without anyone else knowing, we don't even need to go to the hospital.'

Some of the women began whispering to one another, and Emilia settled in close to Lena. Sharing body heat was one of the few things they could do for each another.

'It's because they all have to work outside and we get to stay warm,' Lena said, her voice low. 'It's why they're so cruel.'

'Is that why they seem to dislike me, too? They think I'm getting special treatment and getting to stay inside out of the cold? That we're getting more food?'

Lena nodded.

Emilia understood now; it was why they'd been so unkind to her as soon as she had been taken from roll call that very first day, and it was certainly why they disliked Lena so much. Although she suspected Lena's hair was also part of it.

'Did you mean what you said? That you'd help anyone who came to you?'

'I don't have much in the way of resources, but yes, I will do anything to help any of the women here.'

'Thank you,' Lena murmured. 'For sticking up for me before. I haven't had a true friend to count on for a very long time.'

'Perhaps we can promise to always stick up for one another. It might make life here a little more bearable?'

'I'd like that.'

Lena's smile was sweet, making her look more of a girl than a woman, and she wondered then how old she was, and how old she'd been when she'd arrived at the camp. But before she could ask, the second gong for the night sounded out, and the bunks around her went silent. And for the first time, Emilia went to sleep without feeling completely alone. She didn't need much, she was determined to survive no matter the conditions, but Lena, tucked close, gave her hope that she might at least have made a friend.

It was times like this that made her miss her mother all the more, even though she'd been gone for almost four years. Sometimes it only felt like yesterday.

'Mama, how will I know that it's time for the baby to come out?'

Her mother smiled at her, in that knowing way that was understanding yet amused.

'My darling, you will get a feel for these things. The more babies you birth, the more you will know what to do.'

'It seems such a responsibility though. How will these women trust me when I haven't even had a baby of my own?'

'Come here,' her mother said, kissing her head and wrapping her in her arms. 'You worry too much, my love. And remember that I became a midwife long before I gave birth to you or your brother.'

Emilia sighed, inhaling the floral fragrance that always clung to her mother's skin and clothes. She knew that it was a scent she'd never forget for as long as she lived.

'But in answer to your question, labour becomes something instinctual. Most women can feel when it's time to push, and you should encourage them to wait until then. Their bodies will guide them; it's your job to make sure they're listening to what it's telling them.'

She followed her mother into the house, listening to her sing-song voice as she called out to the woman they were visiting; always cheerful, always making everyone feel at ease.

Emilia tried to absorb everything, hoped that one day she would fall into her mother's footsteps and become half the midwife she was.

'Are you ever scared?' Emilia whispered as she hurried along beside her down the hall.

Her mother stopped. 'Often, my darling. I'm scared with every birth, scared that something out of my control might happen. But the greatest art of being a midwife is making everyone believe that nothing will go wrong.'

Emilia hovered behind her, watching as she swept into the bedroom and took charge, pulling the heavy drapes and lighting the oil lamp, before plumping up the cushions behind the soon-to-be-mother lying on the bed.

Her mother turned then and gave her a little smile. It felt conspiratorial, as if they were holding a secret between them.

───── ❧ ～❧ ─────

There was a knock at the door to Block 23, and Emilia opened it cautiously, not certain whom to expect. She knew for sure it wouldn't be the SS or a *kapo*, for they would simply throw the door open and march inside, but her trembling fear immediately turned to pleasure when she set eyes upon a familiar face.

'Aleksy! What are you doing here?'

'May I come in?' he asked.

Emilia stood back and gestured for him to enter. When she'd met him on her very first day at the camp, she'd thought they'd be working together all the time, but instead she'd ended up being assigned to female patients in the main hospital block, and he was nearby in the infectious diseases block. But because he was the only obstetrician at Birkenau, he was permitted to attend to non-Jewish pregnant women if they needed him.

'How are you, Emilia?' he asked, and she watched as he glanced around the room. 'You are learning to adapt to the conditions?'

She nodded, toying with the edge of her rough cotton shirt. It was the first time since she'd arrived that she'd been so conscious of her appearance, which was silly of course, they all looked the same after all. It was as if in cutting away their hair the guards had *wanted* to make them feel less like women.

'I feel hopeless every day, and wish I could return home for my bag, so I had everything I needed at my fingertips,' she confessed. 'I wish we had hot water at our disposal, even cold water would be a blessing at this point, and some clean towels, tea for after the birth.' She had tears in her eyes, but she forced a wry smile. 'Should I continue?'

Aleksy gave her a small, understanding smile that told her he knew exactly what she was trying to say. 'The things we once took for granted seem like such luxuries now, don't they?'

She sighed, before sitting down on one of the empty bunks. 'They do.'

Aleksy followed her lead, keeping some space between them. Space wasn't something she was used to any more – usually when she was sitting or lying on a bunk there were people crammed all around her, leaving barely enough room to stretch out a leg or turn over.

'My mother once told me that the most important thing is making everyone else believe that you are in control, that nothing will go wrong. I remember her words so clearly it's as if she is standing beside me sometimes, encouraging me, reminding me.'

'Your mother was a midwife, too?'

Emilia smiled as she thought of her, almost able to smell her familiar perfume. 'She was. Everything I know, I learnt from her.'

'These women here, they're very fortunate to have you. I can see the compassion you have for those in your care.'

'Sadly, I don't think that my compassion is enough to save them, though,' she said.

They sat in silence for a long moment, Aleksy staring at the ground, or perhaps his feet, she wasn't certain which.

'Emilia, there are things happening here, things that are difficult to comprehend,' he said, looking up at her with such sadness in his eyes that she wished she knew how to comfort him. 'I see your smile, the way you approach your work here in such primitive conditions, and it breaks my heart to tell you what I've discovered.'

She swallowed, carefully folding her hands together, bracing herself for whatever he was about to share.

'You can tell me,' she said. 'Is it about my patients? The women I treat?'

His breath shuddered from him, reminding her of that first time they'd met, when he'd risked his neck to save hers.

'I suspected that something wasn't right, after I sent the pregnant women to Dr Mengele, and the women who willingly went to him when they found out what he was offering.' He shook his head. 'Emilia, they didn't survive.'

'None of them? They haven't been transferred to another camp, perhaps?'

'They want us all to die, Emilia. This is not a place we're supposed to survive, especially not the Jews.' He cleared his throat and looked away again. 'He's doing all sorts of things to these women, experiments it seems, and only yesterday I was told of his fascination for babies with any abnormalities. Offering the milk and extra food was simply a ruse to get pregnant women to come forward.'

She went still, her stomach twisting as she digested his words, shuddering while the enormity of what he was telling her truly sank in. Aleksy took her hand and she let him, taking comfort in his touch as he squeezed her fingers.

'Aleksy, where do the children go when they arrive? Why are there hardly any children here in the camp?'

It was a question Emilia had been wanting to ask for days, not understanding where the women and children were sent, why they were separated and not processed in the same way the single women and men were. What happened to the women after they gave birth? Where did they go when they were released from her care?

Aleksy sighed. 'I've been waiting for you to ask me that question.'

'You have?' She looked over at him. 'Then will you tell me the answer?'

'There is a building they're taken to, herded into in the hundreds or even thousands. All of the mothers, children and elderly.'

'But they said the families were being taken to a different camp,' she said, feeling in her bones that what he was about to tell her was going to shock her. 'They said they would be going somewhere better than here.'

'Emilia, they use a type of gas to kill them all,' Aleksy said. 'That's why they don't process them, they take them there and they never return.'

'No,' she gasped, staring into his eyes and wishing she didn't see the truth shining back at her. '*No.*'

He shook his head, but it was such a small movement she would have missed it if she wasn't watching him so closely.

'You think this is what they are doing to the women with babies? After they give birth?'

'One of my nurses, she said that her husband has got word to her, that he has to take the bodies and put them in the crematorium. He's told her there are thousands every week, sometimes every day. It's why the chimney is always smoking.'

Emilia leaned over, the small amount of food in her stomach rising violently, as she thought about the ash that so often fell through the air around them. Aleksy's hand was warm against her arm, comforting as he kept his palm to her skin.

'I'm sorry. I only wanted you to know the truth, so you could spread word through the women's blocks. They mustn't come forward if they're pregnant, they should tell you in confidence.'

She wiped her mouth. The murder of women and children? The hot sensation in her throat rose again, threatening to choke her, while she thought of all those families who'd arrived the day she had, of all the children, of all the pregnant women.

'Thank you,' she managed. 'You're right, I need to know the truth to better understand the situation we're in.'

'Is it true that you worked with the resistance?' he asked, standing now as if to leave.

She nodded. 'Yes. It is.' Emilia wasn't even surprised he knew, or perhaps he'd simply guessed why a non-Jewish woman had been sent to Auschwitz.

'Then I take it we both know how to help those in need without being discovered.'

Emilia blinked up at him. 'You aided the resistance, too?'

Aleksy sighed. 'I did. And for a long time, it seemed I would never get caught.' They watched one another for a long moment, both lost in their own thoughts. She had so much she wanted to ask him, but she held her tongue. It could all wait for another day.

'Will I see you again soon?' Emilia asked. Aleksy had finally turned to go, a wintry blast of cold air coming through the door.

'You will,' he replied, before stepping out into the cold.

It was on her walk back to the barracks, weary, her feet heavy, that Emilia heard someone scurrying after her and realised she was being followed. She turned, arms around herself, ready to withstand the blows of a guard berating her for not moving quickly enough, but instead she found a woman. It was Lena.

Emilia admired her long strands of hair that were visible beneath the white head scarf. That alone made her stand out from most of the other prisoners, as did the fact they were both returning at a different time from the women with the outside work.

'Why do some of the women wear white head scarfs and the others red? Is there a reason?'

'White means you sort through the coats, red is for everything else. But it's the white most people want, because most people have food or money sewn into their coats. They thought their coats were the one thing that wouldn't be taken from them, because no one ever thought they'd have to remove them.'

Emilia nodded. If there was anything more barbaric than being rounded up in the first place, it was being stripped naked and having your coat taken from you in the middle of winter.

'Put out your hand.'

Emilia glanced at Lena before holding out her hand, seeing Lena's almost childlike grin when she did so.

Lena placed something in her palm, closing her fingers around it, and when Emilia looked down she realised it was a piece of bread.

'How did you get this?'

'It's one of the reasons all the girls want to work in Canada,' Lena said. 'We find food and jewellery sewn into pockets. Sometimes there's lots of food in the suitcases, which we smuggle out or eat when no one's looking, and sometimes we can take something little, like underwear, because we can hide it under our clothes. There's a black market for jewellery, especially if you can get close to any of the workers they send in, the ones working on the new buildings. They'll always swap food and medicine for jewellery.'

Emilia looked down and for the first time noticed Lena wore boots, whereas so many of the women wore open-toe-style clogs that were entirely inappropriate for the weather and the work they did. No wonder so many of them disliked the girl.

'Thank you,' Emilia said, tucking her hands under her armpits to keep them warm, the bread firmly concealed in her palm. It would double her ration for the day, of which she was beyond grateful. 'This means so much to me. Truly it does.' But it was the mention of medicine that had piqued her interest.

'I have barely any friends,' Lena said as they neared the bunks. 'If the girls were nicer to me, I'd share the food I found with them. But they've always hated me.'

Emilia wasn't surprised Lena didn't want to share with them, although that might have made them warm to her. She suspected that many of the other women had formed very close relationships, but there was certainly a divide between those who were seen to have the easier jobs and those working outside. 'You could? But what would happen if you were found out?'

Lena shrugged. 'They won't catch me.'

Emilia knew there was always a chance of being caught, she'd learnt that the night she'd been arrested. No matter how careful a person was, they could always be caught.

'I can get you more. If that's what you want.'

Emilia leaned in closer to her. 'It's not for me, it's for the women I'm treating. The ones who are giving birth,' she whispered. 'A little extra food might give them the strength they need.' She didn't think about the ones who were sent straight to the gas, couldn't stand to even consider that some of the women didn't last one day.

Lena's face lit up, reminding Emilia of a child once more. 'You would actually give it to them?'

Emilia smiled. 'Of course I would. There's so little I can do for them, but if I could feed them, it might save them.'

'I can do that. I can help you.'

Emilia took Lena's hand, holding it tightly in her own. She reminded her of Talia, whom she hadn't seen since they'd arrived and been sent in separate directions. She swallowed, knowing now what had likely happened to her, why they hadn't bothered to take her cold baby from her arms.

'If we can find someone we trust, someone who could trade things for us, do you truly think we might be able to obtain medicine for me? Lena, this could save so many lives, if you're willing to help?' She couldn't wait to tell Aleksy of her plan, that there might be something more she could do. 'And perhaps you could smuggle out some clothes that we could tear into rags? That would help so many of the newer women arriving, for them to use when they bleed.'

Lena's eyes were wide as she listened. 'I wish I'd thought of that before.'

'I don't want you taking risks though. You need to be careful in what you take, make sure that no one suspects what you're doing.'

Lena's smile was contagious. 'I'm good at stealing, the guards will never suspect a thing. I've been doing it right under their noses for months.' Her smiled faded then. 'But what the women said last night, about me doing something to get my job? They were right.'

'Whatever you have done or have to do here, no one else has the right to judge you.'

Lena reached for her arm and stopped her from walking. 'Don't you want to know, though? What I've had to do?'

Emilia put her hand over Lena's. 'Did you do it to survive? To make life a little easier for yourself here?'

Lena gripped Emilia's arm more tightly.

'We are all doing our best to survive here, Lena, and you've been here longer than many, from what I can gather. That's all I have to know.'

'Thank you,' Lena said, her head dropping to Emilia's shoulder. 'You're the first person to say anything like that to me.'

They walked in silence for a bit, before Lena finally spoke again.

'A friend of mine, one of the only girls left from my village, she needs your help,' Lena said. 'If I traded you some things, would you be able to stop her from being pregnant?'

A shiver ran through Emilia as she listened to Lena's words. 'She wants to end her pregnancy?'

Lena nodded, and Emilia digested what she'd asked. It wasn't something she'd done before when a woman was obviously pregnant, but in the earlier stages. Her mother had taught her about root bark teas and other herbal remedies that could do such a thing, but she didn't have access to anything like that inside the camp, or even a way to trade for such items. But now that she thought about it, perhaps helping women to end their pregnancies was the one thing she could do to keep them safe.

'Lena, the best thing to do is for you to bring her to me. I will see what I can do.' *I need to talk to Aleksy. He will know how to do such a thing.* 'But you don't need to trade me anything, I'll help anyone who needs me.'

'We don't have to work on Sundays, so I'll bring her to see you. She was moved into a nicer block, with her own space.'

'She was? Why?'

'She's one of the tattooists.'

Lena smiled and adjusted the white head scarf on her head, and if they'd had longer to talk, Emilia would have asked her more about how her friend had become the tattooist. But it was what she'd asked her that kept running through her mind, and what Aleksy had told her earlier in the day. Ending a pregnancy could save the life of a woman in Auschwitz.

'Emilia, I have to do things. With one of the SS men.' Lena looked away, clearing her throat. 'My friend, she does, too. It's why she's pregnant.'

Emilia reached for Lena's hand. She tried to restrain the anger rising inside of her. 'Does he hurt you? This SS man of yours?'

Lena's eyes were as wide as saucers, and they were brimming with tears. 'Sometimes. But sometimes he's nice to me.'

Emilia nodded and kept a firm grip on Lena's hand. 'Promise me you'll come to me if he hurts you?'

Lena just squeezed Emilia's hand in reply, and Emilia took that as confirmation. She couldn't stop the brute from hurting her, but she could tend to her afterwards.

When they walked into their block, some of the women had already returned from their back-breaking work in the fields, shivering and wet. Emilia understood now why they disliked her, and why they hated Lena; deep down she knew she'd have likely felt the same in their position. What they endured every day had turned them against those they perceived to have it easy, and maybe they needed someone to hate. But she knew that these women were all mothers, sisters and daughters; she knew that if they'd crossed paths outside of the camp, under normal circumstances, any of them could have become her friend.

When Emilia looked over at Lena, who was huddled on her bunk now, she knew that whatever the SS guard was doing to her, it would be horrendous. No amount of extra food or small luxuries could ever be worth what she was forced to do. Everyone was making a sacrifice, doing things they'd never imagined in the lives they'd led before, in order to stay alive.

CHAPTER TWENTY

LENA

Lena brushed her fingers against the fur coat, smiling at the softness on her skin. She took a moment to press it to her cheek while no one was watching, before finally putting the coat down to search the pockets. It was exquisite, and she knew instinctively that she'd find something inside. In the pocket was a photo, and she stared at it, searching the faces and wishing she could reunite it with the person who'd worn it here. But although the pockets were otherwise empty, she expertly searched the lining and found what she was looking for. *Here it is.*

She picked at the thread, careful not to react when she found a diamond ring and notes of money tightly folded. The other girls would be clambering over her if they knew what she'd found, so she began to quietly sing under her breath, expertly sliding the ring into her brassiere. She searched the pocket again, her rough nails snagging on the fabric, and was rewarded with a few loose diamonds, which she also tucked into her underwear. She was fortunate to even have undergarments, but almost all the girls working in Canada did, it was one of the perks of being able to take the odd thing for themselves that no one would notice.

She would keep the loose diamonds for herself, in case she needed to trade them for something, and the ring she would give to Becker. She tried not to think about what might happen if he came looking for her that day.

Sometimes he was gentle with her when he touched her, but other times she knew it was going to be different. He'd walk in with his nostrils slightly flared, his eyes narrowed, and if she didn't have something of value to give him . . . Lena looked out of the window, watching the latest new arrivals, mainly older people who were stooped over as they walked, peppered with a handful of mothers and children. She quickly diverted her gaze, not wanting to think about where they were going. It was worse than thinking about Becker's imminent arrival. She hadn't seen him for six days, which meant he would be coming for her soon. He never left her for longer than a week.

Lena went back to her sorting, checking and then folding jackets, setting some little things aside like underwear that she would try to smuggle out later. She wanted to give Emilia a few luxuries where she could, especially after she'd been so nice to her. It had been a long time since she'd had a friend in her block, and even longer since she'd had her sister. Since Emilia had arrived, it was the first time she'd had someone looking out for her.

She gripped the jacket in her hands more tightly, trying to push the thoughts away, not wanting to remember what it was like to have her sister at her side, because the memories were more painful than the reality of living without her.

'She's over there.'

Lena startled, as nausea rose in her stomach. It was him. She could feel it in her bones that Becker was there. Martin Becker, a man she was sometimes scared of, and other times outright terrified of.

She instinctively looked up when she heard someone coming closer, and then he appeared around the corner of the door. His blue eyes were bright, and when he saw her she noticed the way his lips turned up ever so slightly at the corners.

He's not going to hurt me today. She could tell he was in a pleasant mood, which meant he'd want her body, but his hands wouldn't leave marks from their encounter. Her hands began to shake, regardless, at the thought of what she was about to endure.

'Come with me,' he said.

'Yes, *Untersturmführer* Becker,' she replied.

She set down the jacket she was sorting, knowing that he expected her to follow his command immediately. She'd made the mistake once of finishing what she was doing before going with him, and it wasn't a mistake she'd make again. She instinctively touched her abdomen and remembered the ugly purple bruise he'd left there.

Lena didn't look at the other women in the room as she passed them, her head bowed. They moved through another cabin, until they were eventually alone. They were surrounded by boxes, all ready to be sent to Berlin. Becker closed the door and when he turned back to her, he loosened the top button of his shirt and smiled at her. She immediately reached into her brasserie as he came towards her, trying to tell herself that he was handsome, that it could be someone so much worse touching her body, doing things to her that haunted her every time she shut her eyes.

'Lena,' he said, smiling as he lifted his hand to touch her face, his blue eyes bright.

She fought not to flinch, eventually relaxing into his touch. When she produced the diamond ring though, his hand fell away. She'd also found a sapphire ring a couple of days earlier, but his eyes widened so much at the diamond, she decided not to show him the ring or the other diamonds. She would save those until next time, in case she didn't find anything else valuable between now and then.

'I've missed you,' she said, as she always did, forcing herself to play a part. 'It's good to see you.'

'I have been on holiday,' he said, smiling, and slipped the ring inside his jacket pocket. 'I was rewarded for catching those prisoners who escaped into the woods last week.'

She forced another smile and nodded as he began to undo his belt. Her pulse started to race and she reminded herself to breathe. So he'd been one of the SS men who'd hunted down and shot the women who'd been so close to leaving Auschwitz behind; and he'd been handsomely rewarded for his cruelty. She'd heard their screams as the dogs had been sent to chase them.

'I've been enjoying our famous SS resort, Solahütte, near the Sola River. It was quite extraordinary.' He grinned, looking particularly pleased with himself. 'You wouldn't believe how close it is to here. It was the most wonderful weekend away.'

'I'm pleased you enjoyed it.' Lena stiffened when he reached for her; it was almost impossible not to. How could he go about his life so normally, while she and so many others lived in hell?

'You know I will look after you here, don't you Lena? I won't let anyone else touch you.'

'I know.' Her voice was barely more than a whisper. *But you will keep touching me. I don't have a choice in that.*

'You're special, Lena. Pretty girls are always special, you deserve to keep your beautiful hair. I would hate to see your head bald, like all those other ugly women.'

She nodded and lifted her chin when he spoke, knowing that he liked her to look him in the eyes when they were together, but hating the way he took off her head scarf and wrapped her hair around his wrist. But instead of thinking about what he was going to do to her, about what was to come next, she thought of the food he would give her afterwards and remembered that it was only because of him that she'd been chosen to work in Canada. It was only because of him that she hadn't yet starved to death, that she'd been able to keep the long hair that he was tugging. It was because of him that she was one of the only Slovakian girls left from those who had arrived on the train with her.

Besides, today was a good day. Today she could tell that he wasn't going to hurt her. All she had to do was stay quiet until it was over with, although it was impossible to forget the first time.

———— ❧ ————

She stood, her toes curling against the cold concrete floor as she watched what was happening to the women in front of her. She'd seen only one other girl be spared so far; the rest of them, all Slovakian and many from her own village, now looked more like young boys, with not a blade of hair left on their heads.

When he came close to her, she could barely breathe, and she wrapped her arms more tightly around herself, embarrassed by her nudity. But this guard didn't try to grope her, he didn't laugh, he simply met her gaze and smiled, before barking something in German that she didn't understand.

But what she did understand was him gesturing for her to continue on. She was to keep her hair. She didn't have to wait in line to be shaved. The other girls stared at her, and as she walked past, one of two to still look like the girls they'd arrived as, she couldn't help but wonder why.

She curled a lock of hair around her finger that night, shivering in her bunk, and a friend from home tucked tightly to her and stroked Lena's head, as if comforted by the silky feel of her hair, too. But it wasn't until the next day that she realised what it meant. She'd arrived a naive girl, someone with little knowledge of the things men desired, but she soon learnt what it meant to be spared one simple thing. It meant she wasn't to be spared something else, that the rest of the women would be.

When Untersturmführer Becker had walked along the line of women at roll call the next morning, he had singled her out for work in Canada. And that was when it had started. The first day, no one knew the work they would be doing, no one understood the horrendous working conditions at Auschwitz-Birkenau or the impossibly small rations of food they'd be given. By the end of the week, Lena had been alone. No one wanted to speak to the girl who was being given extra food, even though she smuggled little pieces of bread and sausage back to their block whenever she could – it was never enough to go around. They certainly didn't want to be friends with the girl who worked inside all day.

But there was something else that changed by the end of that first week, too. For Becker took something from Lena that she could never, ever take back: her innocence. And no matter how much she tried to forget it, how much she tried not to think about what he'd done to her, what she had to do in order to stay alive, she couldn't erase the smell of him from her skin.

Those were the days she wished she were working in the ponds or the fields, just like all the other girls. And that was before she'd seen his temper.

———— ❦ ————

Becker wasn't in a hurry today. Once his uniform was back in place, the knot of his tie impossibly perfect and his hands smoothing away invisible creases from his lapel, he took out a small package from his jacket and passed it to her.

'Thank you,' Lena said, careful to keep her movements steady, to not show him how desperately hungry she was. The sausage wrapped inside the package made her mouth water, and there was a piece of potato and a slice of bread, too. It was an entire meal – she would have preferred to wrap it up and save some for later, or to share it with Emilia as they curled up for bed – but Becker expected her to eat it in front of him. He'd think her a pig if he saw her tuck the food in her undergarments, and she knew he wanted her to show her gratitude. He wanted her to look at him when he gave her something, to understand why she was being given things other girls weren't.

'You know I can do things for you, Lena,' he said, as he leaned against the wall and watched her.

She chewed, slowly, as she watched him. Lena's stomach clenched, the amount of food more than she'd had in days, but she was determined to eat every bite.

'I appreciate the food you bring me,' she said, quietly, flashing him a small smile. He seemed to like it when she showed gratitude. 'This is all I need.' She didn't want to be in his debt for anything else.

'But do you have family, Lena?'

She found it hard to swallow this time. 'I have a sister,' she said. 'My parents, and a sister.'

He stroked his thumb and forefinger over his chin. 'Only you were sent here? They are not with you?'

Lena nodded. 'My sister was spared.' She stayed still, trying to stop her body from shaking as he studied her, as she prayed that her sister would never have to experience what she had. The thought of him or any other guard touching her innocent little sister made her want to be sick, to even imagine Becker doing to Dana what he'd done to her.

'She is still at your home?'

She cleared her throat, not certain she wanted to answer his question, but not believing she had another choice. 'I believe so.'

'Hmm,' he said, stroking his chin. 'I shall send her to you and allow her to work in Canada too, if she arrives here. I will do that for you, Lena. See, I am kind, am I not?'

'Thank you,' she whispered, hoping that Dana never arrived at Auschwitz. She would do anything he asked of her, anything he wanted, if it meant keeping her sister safe. It was for that reason she forced herself to smile up at him and tell a lie. 'I will never forget your kindness.'

Becker smiled, but he didn't seem to want to talk any more. Instead he pushed off from the wall where he'd been standing and inclined his head towards the door. 'It's time to go.'

She quickly ate the last two bites of food and hurried ahead of him. Next time, he might not be so nice, but she was grateful that he'd been happy today. It would keep her stomach full for days, and this time, she had no bruises to nurse. She only hoped that he didn't start to ask her more questions about her sister.

———— ⚬⁓⚬ ————

It was Sunday, and that meant the one day they didn't have to stand in the cold for hours for roll call, or spend the day working. It also meant that she was able to find her way to Zofia, although sometimes her friend wasn't there. The tattooists had to work whenever there was an arrival of new prisoners, and sometimes that meant every single day of the week.

Thankfully, today wasn't one of those days. She saw Zofia and lifted her hand in a wave. Zofia was afforded some privileges the other girls weren't, including extra rations and better living quarters.

'Lena,' Zofia said, opening her arms and embracing her. Zofia's body felt much slighter than it had months ago, but she wasn't a walking skeleton like so many of the other girls. The small amount of additional rations they both received made all the difference; it gave Lena hope that maybe they both had a chance at living and making it out of the camp one day.

'How are you feeling?'

Zofia frowned. 'As if I'm a clock counting down to something terrible.'

Lena wrapped an arm around her and leaned close. 'We have a midwife in our midst.'

'Oh,' Zofia said with a sigh, sounding uninterested.

'I asked her whether she might be able to help you,' Lena said. 'With your condition.'

Zofia eyes met hers, understanding passing between them. 'She can do such a thing?'

Lena nodded. 'I think so. She said she would help you and any other woman, in any way she could.'

Zofia seemed to be digesting her words. It took a moment for her to respond. 'She might be able to, to—'

'Yes.'

Zofia hugged Lena, tightly, and she hugged her back, imagining that it was her sister in her arms. That she was back home, that Dana had run out to embrace her.

'Thank you, Lena. If she can help me, if this works . . .'

'She will,' Lena said. 'I trust her, and you can, too.'

Lena wiped the tears from Zofia's face, her fingertips red from the cold.

'You're certain she won't tell the guards?'

'I promise. Emilia is the closest thing I've had to a friend in all the months since you left our block. If she can help you, she will.'

Zofia's head touched her shoulder as they stood together. A small ray of sunshine broke through the clouds.

'Come on, I'd like you to meet her today. She said the sooner she sees you, the better.'

Zofia squeezed her hand and they slowly walked towards the hospital block, side by side, huddled together as the wind curled around them in search of Emilia.

———— ❦ ————

'Lena said you might be able to help me.'

Lena looked hopefully at Emilia as they huddled together outside the hospital block. She hoped she hadn't promised too much, seeing the hope on Zofia's face.

'It's true, these things can be done,' Emilia said, pressing her hand firmly against Zofia's stomach. Lena watched as her friend's mouth turned downwards, but she couldn't tell if she was simply concentrating or whether she was concerned about something.

'You've done this before?' Zofia asked.

Emilia shook her head. 'No, not like this. But that doesn't mean it can't be done.'

Zofia looked terrified, and Lena stood closer to her, her hand against her friend's back.

'There is a doctor here, an obstetrician in fact, and he will know what to do,' Emilia said, taking a step back as she addressed them. 'I need you to trust that I will do everything I can for you, to help you through this.'

'You don't think I'm terrible?' Zofia asked, and Lena gripped her hand tightly. 'For not wanting this child?'

Emilia touched their hands, too. 'No, I don't think you're terrible. I think you want to stay alive, and I also think that bringing any baby into this place is the terrible thing. Look around you. How many mothers with children do you see here?'

Emilia's smile was kind, but Lena could see how tired she was, the daily toll of her work and lack of food starting to show, her face seeming more lined than it had been even a few days before.

'Let me speak to Aleksy. I know he'll be able to assist me, and perhaps we can start helping other women, too?'

Lena was about to answer when Zofia gasped. 'This doctor you speak of, he's a man?'

'Not all men are brutes,' Emilia replied. 'Aleksy is a good man, one of the best I imagine, and he might be the only person here who can help me with your request.'

They stood for another few minutes, before Emilia said goodbye and disappeared into the hospital block, leaving Lena and Zofia alone.

'If I were your sister, would you trust this woman to help me?'

Lena nodded. 'If you were my sister, Emilia is the only person other than myself and you that I'd trust in all of Auschwitz.'

It was no exaggeration. Emilia was like no one else she'd met before; her determination to help other women seemed unwavering. If Emilia said that she and this Aleksy could help, then Zofia could trust her, without a second thought.

CHAPTER TWENTY-ONE

EMILIA

It had been days since Emilia had seen Aleksy, and as she stood outside for a breath of fresh air and saw him coming along, she found herself smiling. There was a sadness about him, as there was about most of the people she encountered each day, but it was his story that she was most curious to know.

'I was hoping to find you here,' he said.

'It's been a quiet day today,' she said. 'No births, so I've swept out the block for the hundredth time, although somehow it still seems filthy.'

He indicated for them to go inside, and she followed him in, smiling as he held the door. Such little gestures were so noticeable in such crude surroundings, and she realised that she'd never felt nervous around Aleksy. She'd spent most of her life surrounded by women, had rarely been alone with a man other than her father and brother, and yet he somehow seemed able to put her at ease. Perhaps it was a skill he'd learnt as an obstetrician.

'Will you get in trouble, for being here?' she asked.

'Not if I can give a reason.' He smiled. 'Perhaps I will have to say I was worried about your competence, so please don't take offence if I do.'

She laughed. 'None taken. And to be perfectly honest, I do feel incompetent here, every day. It's hard not to, given the circumstances.'

It was only then that she realised she'd laughed. That she was smiling. Her cheeks hurt from the action – along with forgetting what it felt like to have a full stomach, she'd almost forgotten how good it felt to be happy.

'Emilia, I was given something, when I first started working here,' Aleksy said, before reaching into his pocket.

Her eyes widened when she saw it was a knife, a piece of fabric tied around the blade.

'I know it's not much, and there are so many more things I wish I could give you, but it's a start.'

Emilia stared at the knife. It *was* helpful, but to make an incision without also having other tools at her disposal . . . Aleksy held it out and she reached for it, her fingers curling around the handle. It may well have been the most thoughtful gift anyone had ever given her.

'Thank you,' she said.

Aleksy nodded, standing there in the middle of the room, his eyes on hers, as if there was something on his mind, something he wanted to say. But she knew it was time to ask him about her predicament, or more correctly the predicament of the woman who needed her assistance.

'Aleksy, what I'm about to say may come as a shock, and I want you to know that it's not something I would ever suggest under normal circumstances.'

'We're far from normal circumstances, Emilia, so please, speak freely. Nothing you can say will shock me, not here, not after what I've seen and heard.'

He shifted slightly, and she followed his gaze as he glanced over at the door.

'I would like to know your opinion on offering terminations to the women here.'

His eyebrows shot up. 'You're suggesting you terminate pregnancies? Here?'

She took a step closer to him. 'That's precisely what I'm suggesting, only I would need your help to understand exactly *how* I could perform them. It's not something I have experience in.'

She thought of Zofia, the tattooist who'd looked at her with such pure desperation when she'd come to visit with Lena, asking if she could help her, and then she looked up at Aleksy, into his eyes. And all she saw was compassion, a man who was dedicated to easing the suffering of others, and she knew she hadn't been wrong in trusting him. She held the knife in her hand, the one tool she would need.

'I will show you, Emilia. I will show you how to do it.' He reached for her, his hand over her shoulder as he gazed into her eyes. 'I will never judge you for doing this. You would be saving a life by helping this woman, and any others you choose to help. What's happening to mothers and their babies, what those women endure before they're taken . . .'

'You truly believe I would be doing the right thing?' It went against everything she would usually believe in, but how was this different from assisting a woman back home with tea to end her pregnancy? Those women usually sought help because they couldn't afford another mouth to feed, and she'd never once refused to help them in the earliest stages of pregnancy.

Aleksy's eyes met hers. 'I believe it would be a great gift to the women here at Birkenau, what you are proposing. A way to save them from certain death.'

He patted her on the shoulder before heading for the door, and she decided to follow him, stepping out once more into the cold, her arms wrapped around herself as they said goodbye. But the sight of two guards and another man walking towards them made them both freeze.

'It's Mengele. Look at him when he speaks to you, and tell him what he wants to hear,' Aleksy murmured. 'Try not to be too afraid. He's like a wolf, he can smell fear.'

Emilia quickly hid the knife, tucking it in the waistband of her skirt and praying it didn't slip down past her hip while she was standing in front of him.

'*Herr Doktor*,' Aleksy said when the man approached them.

'Gorski, what are you doing here?'

'I came to check on the midwife,' he said. 'I wanted to make sure that she was notifying me of any pregnancies, so that I could inform you.'

Mengele's eyes narrowed, and Emilia fisted her palms to stop them from shaking. She watched as the doctor touched his gun, slowly taking it half from his holster. It only made her tremble all the more, and she knew that he was trying to show them the power he wielded, that they were only alive because he let them be.

'This is true?' Mengele finally asked, addressing her.

'Yes,' she mumbled, before forcing herself to speak louder. 'It is true, *Herr Doktor*.'

'What did he tell you?'

She could hear the shortness of Aleksy's breath, knew he was as nervous as she. 'That the pregnant women would receive additional food and milk if they were reported to you.'

He took his hand from his pistol as she stared at him. 'Good. We have noticed there have been babies born, but no notification of their pregnancies. Who is to blame for this?'

'Many of the women choose not to disclose their pregnancies until they are in labour,' Aleksy said. 'It makes it difficult for us to get word to you.'

'You're suggesting this is my fault?' Mengele asked, his hand moving to his waist again, where his pistol was holstered.

'No sir, it's merely the reason I came here, to remind the midwife of her obligations. I thought perhaps she could help to spread the word, among the women, not just the pregnant women but all the women in her barracks.'

He seemed to lose interest in them then, dismissing them both as he continued on, towards the next block. *Block 25.* It was the infamous sick block, the one everyone feared being sent to, and Emilia gulped when she thought of the order he'd likely make after he looked in there. If he even bothered to look at all.

He stood at the door of Block 25 and yelled something to the guards with him, before circling back to the small hut alongside, the one she'd been forced into that first day she'd arrived.

Emilia watched him go inside, remembering the cruelty from the midwives. They would follow the doctor's orders, whatever they might be.

'You are right, we will be saving women from certain death if we can do this,' she whispered, her fingers on Aleksy's arm when she turned back to him, realising that he'd been watching, too. 'It is the right thing to do.'

'*You*,' he said. '*You* will be saving women, Emilia. All I'm going to do is teach you how to do it.'

Aleksy seemed to stare at her fingers, as if he was unsure of her touch, or perhaps unused to the contact. But when he lifted his gaze, she could sense his relief at what she'd agreed to.

'I have asked myself ever since I came here, whether I would do what I once chose to do again, if I had the choice.'

'And what would you choose?' she asked.

Tears filled his eyes. 'I would choose to save lives again, Emilia. I would choose to help everyone I could, because it's the right thing to do.'

She nodded and took a deep breath, wishing she could comfort him as he wrestled with his memories, but not knowing how.

'I'll come looking for you, next Sunday,' he said. 'We will perform the first one together, with the knife I've just given you, but it will be risky enough to do one with you. After that, you must do them alone.'

Emilia wished they could walk together, that they had longer than stolen moments here and there. But of course they couldn't, and she needed to make it back for roll call, and more importantly, dinner.

'Oh, and Emilia?'

She was surprised to hear his voice again and looked up.

'You will need to ask your friend Lena to help you, with things to trade,' he said. 'The only way this will work is if you can do the terminations in your own block, where no one will suspect anything, and to do that, you'll need to bribe your *kapo* and any block elders.'

She nodded, understanding what he was saying. The block elders held a position of power, appointed to maintain order and discipline. If she couldn't bribe them, then her plan was destined to fail. Emilia shuddered at the thought of what she'd decided, but Aleksy was right. It was the kindest thing she could do for the women in the camp, and to spare those unborn babies a cruel death upon birth.

And when she thought about Mengele and his apparent fascination with pregnant women, she knew she didn't have a choice. She only hoped she would be as capable as Aleksy seemed to think she was, and that Lena could indeed provide things for them to use as currency, and not just for her friend Zofia. Without Lena, her plan would prove impossible.

Emilia walked slowly towards the hospital block, where she now spent so much of her life. It already felt like home in a way, or at least she tried to think of it like that. She welcomed the women there, brightly telling them that it was the safest place in Auschwitz-Birkenau they could be, and she wasn't lying. She went to great lengths to protect the women, to treat them with the dignity they deserved, and so far she'd managed to see each labour through without being interrupted, even though it broke her heart to know those babies would become prisoners. Although if she were honest, she did live in fear that one of the midwives from the next hut would seek her out and try to force her to follow their orders. The thought they might find out what she was planning terrified her.

She thought back to the first time she'd seen them, and the way they'd often come out to watch her as she passed in the morning, as if they thought they could frighten her. Emilia was secretly terrified of them, but she never even gave them the satisfaction of looking in their direction, continuing on and letting herself into the hospital each day. She kept the women's hospital as clean as could be, although still the vermin came in, desperate as they scuttled inside looking for food, gnawing on the walls to make their way through. She shuddered at the thought of what they'd find next door, for she'd heard rumours that in Block 27 they plagued not only the deceased bodies but those of the sick, too.

Up ahead she saw Aleksy, noticing that his hair was starting to grow a little. She knew he'd have it shaved by the following week, often it was on Sundays that they shaved their heads, but today it looked almost normal. Emilia touched her scarf, wishing she could feel the bump of her once-thick head of hair, instead feeling only bone.

'Hello Emilia,' he said, when he was closer.

'Good morning,' she replied.

'We are meeting your patient today?'

She smiled when he did the same. 'We are.'

'You look worried.'

'I'm terribly worried,' she confessed, taking a deep breath. 'I'm terrified that I might do it wrong, that I might hurt her or cause irreparable damage—'

'Please don't worry,' he said, his smile reassuring. 'I will teach you, you have nothing to worry about.'

'With simply a knife at my disposal?' she asked.

'With simply a knife,' he said. 'People have used far worse, and with untrained hands at that.'

She shivered, despite the fact the sun was shining. Even when it was warm, she still felt cold, a result of losing so much weight so rapidly since she'd arrived.

'You don't need to be afraid, Emilia. What you're doing, what you've chosen to do, it will help so many women. It will give them a choice, and choice is something of a rarity behind this wire.'

Their walk was slowing, feet shuffling across the dirt. 'The pregnant women here, do you believe that most of them have been raped?'

'I believe that many of the women are raped by the guards and *kapos*,' Aleksy said. 'But even more arrive pregnant and don't disclose their condition, especially if they don't have other children. Some may not have even known they were expecting before they arrived.'

She hadn't thought about how many women would have been in the early stages of pregnancy upon arrival.

'You know, part of me wonders if the guards would turn a blind eye if they found out. I mean, it's almost like we'd be doing our part to keep the women working.'

'Or perhaps they have enough prisoners arriving each day and they're happy for any excuse to take a life? Or perhaps Mengele's fascination with pregnancy is such that he'd have us executed himself?'

Emilia thought of the women in her block and wondered whom she could trust. News of the service they were offering would spread by word of mouth, and quickly, and she didn't doubt that there would be demand for it. It was hard enough surviving without the added strain of carrying a child. And this might be a way she could help large numbers of Jewish women, too, in secret. If she could do it in the women's hospital or even her own block, if the other women were prepared to support her . . .

'I've heard about you, Emilia,' Aleksy said. 'About how you were caught, about the lengths you went to, to help those around you. Is it true you were smuggling babies out of Poland?'

She was surprised by his words. How did he know about her? Who would have told him what she'd done? Although she supposed word spread quickly through the camp.

'I was a small part of a movement that was much bigger than just me,' she said. 'But I did what I could. I promised my mother, before she passed, that I would continue her work. That I would serve the women who needed me.' She looked up at the sky, blinking away an unexpected rush of tears. 'She would have been brave. My father wanted me to stop, he didn't want me to put myself in danger, but I knew what my mother would have done; she wouldn't have even considered letting women labour without her assistance, no matter the risk.'

They started to walk again, not heading anywhere in particular, heads bowed as they spoke quietly to one another. Ravens flapped overhead, sounding out their horrible croak.

Walking was particularly tiring without proper nutrition, every step taking something from her depleted body. But she didn't want to stop, didn't want to give Aleksy a reason to leave her side. There was something reassuring about him that gave her comfort. Perhaps it was because they were dedicated to the same work, or his quiet manner, the way he spoke to her.

'The Jewish families in your neighbourhood, they were in hiding?' Aleksy asked.

'They were. But the night I was caught, when they found me—' She choked and had to clear her throat. 'I will never forget that night. Because of me, they were found. They were taken. The things the Gestapo did, their brutality—'

Aleksy's hand slipped against hers then, his palm flat to hers.

She fought against the tears, the torrent of emotion that made her want to scream, that was bubbling up inside her with such ferocity she could barely keep it down. Something about his gentle touch made it even harder to stifle.

'We often blame ourselves for things that are out of our control,' Aleksy said, softly, his hand still holding hers. 'But tell me, how can you be to blame for the brutality of the SS? For the cruelty of the Gestapo? How is it that we find a way to blame ourselves when it is them we should hate? Whom we should blame?'

'What you're saying is true, part of me knows that, but the other part? It questions whether I did enough, what I could have done differently so that things didn't end that way.'

They looked at one another for a long moment, and when he lifted his hand she thought he was going to touch her, to cup her face in his palm. Instead, he stopped himself.

'Have you left someone behind, Aleksy?' she asked.

His eyes met hers, telling her all she needed to know.

'Yes. I left everyone I ever loved behind. Because of what I did, the people I chose to help, they were taken from me. It's why I'm not scared of what could happen to me in here, because there is nothing left for me on the other side of that fence.'

Emilia wished she could tell him he was wrong, but who was she to tell a man who'd lost everything that he still had something to live for?

'Come on,' she said. 'You can talk me through the procedure in the hospital block. Zofia will be waiting.'

———— ❧ ————

Emilia had been feeling perfectly fine earlier, despite her nerves over what they were about to do, but she was no longer feeling so well. Her skin was suddenly on fire, and her throat was aching for water, for anything to relieve the painful dryness in her body.

'Emilia, what's wrong?' Aleksy appeared before her, his eyes searching her face.

'I'm not feeling well,' she admitted, leaning heavily into the wall as she started to feel faint.

'Come here, lie down a moment.' Emilia let Aleksy lead her to a bed, and she saw Lena and the tattooist arrive just as she lifted her legs.

'Just for a minute, I'll be right soon.'

She was like everyone else who knew the realities of the camp; the last thing she wanted to admit was that she could be sick. It was better to keep going, because you never knew when the SS doctors would order a selection. It usually happened when numbers in the camp fluctuated too high, leading them to cull the weakest and send them to the chimney, which always began in the hospitals. Block 25 was usually the first to be emptied out, but sometimes there was no warning in the other hospital blocks either. Sometimes they took away hundreds of patients.

It took her a moment to realise how many women were in the room, and when she looked around, she sat up.

'There's more than double the number of women in here today,' she said.

'The flu is starting to spread,' Aleksy said, his face sombre. What the women were suffering was most likely typhus, an immediate death sentence, so they always did their best to disguise it as the flu. 'But it appears they're not all here because of that.'

Emilia sat up, keeping her palm flat on the side of the bunk to steady herself.

Lena cleared her throat. 'Emilia, they're here for the other procedure. Zofia isn't the only woman who needs your help today.'

She swallowed, her mouth even drier. 'They are all here to see me?'

A handful of women were staring back at her, not unwell but clearly needing help with another condition. Emilia took a deep breath, wishing she didn't feel so unsteady, especially given what she was about to do. She'd been prepared to help one woman today, and instead it seemed they were to help many.

'I just need a moment, and I'll be ready to begin.'

Aleksy came closer, crouching beside her, his knees pressed into the dirt floor as he covered Emilia's forehead with his palm.

'You have a temperature,' he said. 'We could get them to come back another day, we don't have to—'

'No, today is the day, we don't want them here with the sick patients any longer than they have to be,' Emilia said. 'If I could just get some water, I'd be fine.'

'You could take this.' The aspirin tablet was sitting in the palm of his hand, and Emilia knew how quickly it would ease her headache and help reduce her fever. But she couldn't take it.

She closed Aleksy's fingers around the pill. 'Please, put it back in your pocket. We need to save those for the sickest of our patients, of which I am not one.' She took a deep breath before forcing her legs to move, swinging them out so she was sitting on the bed, facing the women gathered, who were all in their first or second trimester of pregnancy.

'I need you to understand what I'm going to be doing to you today,' she said, addressing them all in a voice that was barely a whisper.

They all blinked back at her, their eyes wide as they listened, no doubt terrified of what she was going to do, *how* she was going to do it. In all honesty, she was terrified, too.

'You can see how primitive our conditions are here,' Emilia said. 'We have no anaesthesia and no way to sterilise our tools. This procedure should be safe, but there are always risks involved, especially here.'

She'd trained herself not to see her surroundings, to not think about the conditions she was working in each day, because there was nothing she could do about it. All she could do was her best.

'I will get each of you in turn to climb onto the stove here, and I'll perform it as quickly as I can. I'm very fortunate to have the guidance of an obstetrician here at Auschwitz-Birkenau, Dr Aleksy Gorski. He is going to be teaching me today, and then I will be able to help other women, even in their own blocks instead of having to risk coming here.'

She wished the stove were working, that they had wood to light it, as the heat would have been welcome and it also would have meant she could sterilise her knife properly, instead of using only a small cup of cold water to scrub it with. But at least it provided a good place for birthing and termination procedures.

──── ◦◦◦◦ ────

It had been a long day. Emilia was having to force herself to stay on her feet, and she felt as if she was going to collapse. She held out a hand to steady herself, knowing that she needed to rest before she simply slipped to the floor.

Aleksy appeared then, and she wondered if she'd imagined him. Was he really here with her? She blinked and reached out her other arm, staggering a little, but suddenly there were arms around her, guiding her to one of the lower bunks.

'I'm fine,' she whispered. 'Please, I'm—'

'You're not fine,' came a mutter. 'Now lie down and have this.'

She did as she was told, but quickly held up her hand. 'No,' she said. 'I won't take it.'

'I've been trying to get her to take an aspirin since this morning, but she keeps refusing.'

Emilia blinked, taking a few moments for her focus to right itself. 'Aleksy?' she asked.

'Why didn't you let the nurse help you today? You're sick, Emilia, and you need to rest.'

'I just need more water, and a lie down for a few moments,' she mumbled, before closing her eyes, her headache easing a little once they were shut. 'Why are you here? Won't your absence be noticed?'

When he didn't answer straight away, she forced her eyes open and sat up a little.

'Aleksy?'

'I only wanted to tell you how proud I am of you,' he said, gently stroking her forehead. 'What you did today was incredibly selfless. You risked everything to help your fellow prisoners.'

'So many women here would have done the same if they could have,' she croaked. '*You* would have done the same.'

His smile was small. 'I have nothing left to live for,' he said. 'Whether I live or die, it means nothing any more.'

She let his words settle, not certain what to say. He wasn't asking for her pity, he was telling her his truth.

'Rest,' he said. 'As word spreads, there will be many others who need you.'

Emilia collapsed back into the uncomfortable straw as her head started to thud again, closing her eyes and praying for sleep to find her.

When Emilia woke, she immediately felt something soft beneath her head. She might not have noticed it before, when she was used to soft pillows and the comforts of home, but here it was the ultimate luxury. She lifted her head, propping herself up on her elbows as she looked around.

'It's good to have you awake.'

Emilia swung her legs down from the bunk.

'Take it slowly, you've been here for a few days.'

She looked around as a nurse came towards her. How long had she been sleeping?

'I have this for you. Your friend Lena smuggled it here herself, and she insisted I give it to you when you woke.'

It was a bottle of water, and Emilia almost leapt out of bed to grab it, her throat was so dry. Instead she sat and waited, her hand shaking as she took the lid off and took a few slow sips. It was heavenly, liquid gold as she gently took another mouthful. But she was careful with how much she had, offering the bottle back to the nurse.

'Please, have some,' she murmured. 'And share it with the others, too.'

The nurse pressed it back into her hand, lifting it slightly, and Emilia took one more sip, even though it would have been easy to gulp down the entire contents of the bottle.

'Where did this come from?' she asked, taking the soft piece of fabric that had been under her head. She could see that it was a man's shirt, folded neatly into a square.

'Your friend Lena, and the other girls that work in Canada. It seems you have a lot of people who care about you here.'

'I do?' She carefully set her feet on the ground and stood, shaky to begin with as she looked around.

'You do. Word has spread about what you're prepared to do, for your fellow prisoners. It takes time to establish trust here, especially among the women who've been here the longest.'

Emilia understood, of course she did. She'd seen how close many of the women were, but they'd had no reason to trust her in the beginning.

'I should get back to my block. What time is it?'

'Have this first. Lena made me promise that I'd give this to you the moment you woke, once you'd been given the water.'

The nurse presented her with a piece of stale bread, and some sausage.

'Please, have some with me,' Emilia said, as her stomach rumbled.

'You haven't eaten in days, you need it, to get your strength back.'

Emilia nodded and ate the food, finding it hard to gulp down despite how hungry she was. But she left half for the nurse, despite her protestations.

'My friend Aleksy, the doctor?' She said his name shyly, not wanting to make it obvious how much she thought about him, how much he'd come to mean to her. 'Have you seen him?'

'He's been very worried,' the nurse said with a wry smile. 'But don't worry, we told him you were too well loved for anyone to let anything happen to you.'

Emilia hugged her before slowly shuffling towards the door, knowing that her survival depended on her ability to show the *kapo* that she was well, that whatever illness she'd had wasn't going to take her. But most of all, she needed to see Lena, to hold her in her arms and make certain she was all right, and to thank her for the food she'd left behind.

When she finally made her way back to her block, Emilia stood at the door for a long moment, only going in when she saw an SS guard walking down the road from the corner of her eye. She did not want to face him, not when she was still feeling poorly.

What she didn't expect upon entering was the gentle clapping of hands that built around the room, the women's voices fading as they all seemed to stare at her. But it was Lena who leapt from her bunk like an acrobat, throwing her arms around Emilia as if she had all the energy in the world.

'Why is everyone clapping?' Emilia whispered in her ear.

'Because everyone knows what you'll do for us,' Lena said, turning Emilia around and pressing a kiss to her cheek as the women looked on. 'Because we all prayed that you'd survive.'

Women were getting down from the bunks now, surrounding her, and Emilia found herself most uncomfortably the centre of attention. Women tried to pass her pieces of food they'd saved, some of them offering half their evening ration or even all of it, but she refused every piece. Except for one of the Canada girls who wore a red head scarf. She was one of the girls who'd come to have a termination; she would never forget any of their faces.

'Please, take it,' the woman said. 'Otherwise I'll feel that I owe you, for how you helped me.'

Emilia looked at the piece of sausage and her stomach lurched, and she eventually took it, closing her palm around it to eat later. She would share a bite with Lena when the lights were out and they were tucked close to one another in the bunk.

After talking with the women and promising to help any of them, or anyone else in the camp, she tucked herself back into her usual spot alongside Lena.

'Lena, is Zofia recovering well?'

'Everyone from that day is well,' she said. 'You're something of a hero throughout the camp now, Emilia. Word spread quickly.'

She held Lena's hand, hoping that word hadn't spread too far. The last thing they needed was for the guards to discover what she'd been doing.

'I can see you're worrying,' Lena said. 'But you don't need to.'

Emilia watched Lena as she smiled, appearing pleased with herself.

'I've found out exactly what the *kapos* want. So long as I can smuggle things from time to time out of Canada, they will keep our secret.'

'Thank you, Lena. You're a true friend.'

Lena tucked close behind her, and Emilia kept hold of her hand, hoping that come morning she felt well enough to go back to work.

'Before I forget, Aleksy gave me something,' Lena said, leaning over her. 'He made me promise that I would give it to you.'

She opened the piece of paper, dirty around the edges, no doubt from the days Lena had had to keep it hidden. But what was on the page brought tears to her eyes.

It was a drawing of a lake surrounded by trees, a picture that must have taken him hours to complete. But what touched her the most was *what* he'd chosen to draw, because it looked like the place she and her brother and father had buried her mother. It looked like home.

She folded the page and held it to her chest. She must have told him about it when she'd been feverish. Emilia only hoped she hadn't said more.

'Aleksy is a good man,' Lena whispered.

Emilia pushed herself more tightly into her friend, trying to get warm. 'He is. He's a very good man.'

'I have to remind myself sometimes, tell myself what my father was like. What my uncle was like, because otherwise . . .'

Lena's voice drifted away. 'Because otherwise you will start to think that all men are like *him*,' she said for her. 'Is that what you were going to say?'

Lena was silent, which told Emilia she'd been right.

'There are many beautiful, kind men in the world, Lena. We have to remember that. This place . . .' She paused and blinked away tears. 'It makes us forget what life was like before, but we can never forget.' They lay in silence, as darkness blanketed the room, and Emilia wished she'd looked at the drawing for longer, while she still could. 'We can *never* forget.'

Forgetting about the life they'd led before the war meant giving up hope of ever going back. And she was never going to stop believing that they could survive until the end.

Forgive me, Mama. I made a promise to you, that I would safely deliver every pregnancy brought to me. But I think this is why I was brought here, to ease the suffering of women. I cannot let them face death because of the child they carry. I cannot let these children be born into a world where they will be killed at birth, or allowed to die of starvation. There is no way for them to survive here, and because of that, I've been left with no choice. I will help every woman, whatever she decides. For how can I not?

CHAPTER TWENTY-TWO

LENA, 1944

Lena knew simply from looking at him that today was going to be bad. Becker's eyes were narrowed and when he came for her, he prodded her roughly in the back with his stick. She stifled her cry and hurried forwards, scrambling on the floor as she fought not to fall. The other girls they passed all kept their eyes down, no doubt grateful that they hadn't caught the eye of any of the guards or SS men.

When they were alone, the door shut and locked behind them, Becker smacked her clean across the face. Lena went flying backwards, hitting her back on the wall. But she didn't have long to right herself before his fingers were around her throat, pinning her against the wall she'd just been thrown against.

'Someone has been stealing,' he hissed, his spittle landing on her face. 'Someone has been stealing from Canada and trading.'

She swallowed, or at least tried to. His hold on her was so tight, she was struggling to breathe.

'Are you trying to make a fool of me, Lena?' He tightened his hold. 'Do you think I'll be promoted if anyone finds out my little wench has been stealing from under my nose?'

Lena felt as if her eyes were going to pop from their sockets, and she must have gone very red in the face because he suddenly let her go, his fingers leaving her neck as he stepped back. He ran them through his usually perfect hair, sweeping it back off his forehead where it had fallen.

She slithered to the floor, gasping for air.

'Get up!' he screamed.

Lena scrambled against the wall, doing as she was told.

'Have you been stealing?' he asked.

She shook her head. 'No,' she whispered. 'I would never steal. Whatever I take, I give to you. I promise.'

His lips curled upwards in what she could only think of as a snarl. 'And what do you have for me today?'

Lena slipped her hand inside her brasserie and produced two small diamond earrings. They were still stained with blood from whoever's ears they had been ripped from.

He snatched them from her and slipped them into his pocket. 'If not you, then who, Lena? Someone must pay for this.'

She shook her head. 'I would never lie to you.' Lena touched her throat, her fingertips whispering against her skin. 'I don't know who would do such a thing, but I work on my own, you've seen that. I stay away from the other girls.'

His eyes narrowed and his nostrils flared as he breathed heavily. 'You are certain? If you do not tell me, I shall decide myself.'

Lena clenched her nails into her palms and tried not to cry. 'I promise you, I do not know.' *It was me, you bastard!* If only she were brave enough to spit at him and tell him what she was thinking.

He nodded and left the room then, and Lena shut her eyes, praying he wasn't going to do what she thought he might. There was a scuffle and a scream from the other side, a loud thump that made her cringe, and then the sound of a door slamming. She waited, hoping nothing was going to happen, before two gunshots suddenly pierced the air.

He'd just killed two women with whom she had been working moments earlier. Her body started to tremble, and she bent over and vomited in the corner, unable to help herself.

Becker returned then, smiling as he came towards her. Lena wanted to run, she wanted to get as far away from him as she could, but she was like a cornered animal with nowhere to escape.

When he reached out to her, she turned her face away, scared, but this time his touch was tender.

'Lena, let me see,' he said, tracing his fingers across her skin. 'I didn't mean to hurt you.'

Yes, you did. Just like you enjoyed shooting those poor girls out there.

'Forgive me,' he said, as his fingers travelled down her top, lifting it at the edges and exposing her stomach.

When he paused, she turned her face and opened her eyes, wondering why he'd stopped.

'I fear I have been giving you too much extra food,' he said, and she couldn't tell if he was serious or trying to be funny, given how hungry she was. Even the mention of food made her want to scream. 'Or you're pregnant.'

Pregnant? Her hand fell to her stomach and she lifted her eyes, meeting his gaze. It had been so long since she'd seen her body, since she'd touched it, that she hadn't even noticed. Becker pressed into her, not seeming to care.

'What did you expect from a young virile German?' he asked, laughing as he unbuckled his belt. 'I'm surprised it's taken this long.'

A tear slid down her cheek. She closed her eyes, tried not to think about the life growing inside her. And as she always did when Becker came for her, she thought of Dana, of how grateful she was that her sister had been spared the horrors of Auschwitz. And of men like Becker.

—— ༒︎⁓༒︎ ——

They'd known about the order for days now. The town crier's message had circulated fast throughout the village, that unmarried girls were to come forward to work for the Third Reich. Her parents had insisted that they wouldn't comply, and Lena and her sister watched from a little window upstairs as most of the other families did as they were ordered and sent forth their girls.

The knock at the door wasn't so unexpected, but it was the person who knocked that took the family by surprise. Lena tucked tightly against Dana, hidden beneath their childhood bed, the springs catching in their hair as they tried to hear what was being said downstairs.

'They are not here,' she heard her mother say.

'We both know you are lying. Please, do not make this harder than it has to be.'

'I've known you since you were a little boy, I've known your mother my entire life!' her mother cried. 'How can you do this to us? How can you come here and ask for my daughters?'

There was silence for a long moment, and Lena shuffled nearer to try to hear better. Dana tugged her back, holding tightly to her hand.

'Then give me one,' the man finally said. 'I cannot leave without one, you know I can't.'

'You are asking me to choose between my daughters?' It was her father now, his voice shaking with anger.

'If you will not choose, then I will do it for you.'

Lena turned to her sister, seeing how frightened she was. They were not so different in age, but Lena was the eldest and had always known that it was her duty to look out for Dana, to protect her and care for her.

Now, she reached out and touched her sister's soft, silky hair, only a shade darker than her own. She smiled as they stared back at one another, before leaning closer and pressing a kiss to her cheek.

Dana's eyes were like saucers, impossibly wide. She blinked back at her.

'I love you, Dana,' she said, as tears began to leak from her eyes. 'I would do anything to keep you from harm.'

'Lena, no!'

'Don't forget me. I'll be home soon enough.'

She wriggled out from beneath the bed as Dana tried in vain to catch her legs and hold her back.

'Lena, wait, I'll come with you! You can't go alone.'

Dana was beside her by the time she'd reached the door. 'No,' Lena said, gently stroking her sister's cheek. 'It would break Mama's heart for both of us to go. I'll do this, for both of us.'

Dana flung her arms around Lena and they stood for a long moment, as Lena breathed in the scent of her sister's shampoo and committed the feel of her hug to memory.

'I love you,' she whispered, as she walked bravely down the stairs, at the exact moment the policeman was trying to force his way past her father.

'Lena! Go back upstairs!' her mother cried.

'No, Mama, I will go,' she said, holding her chin high. 'We all know he's not going to leave without one of us.'

Her mother's arms were around her now and her father had begun to sob, and when she looked at the young man who'd come for her, she knew that he wasn't the monster her parents thought he was. If he were, he would have insisted on taking both of them.

'You will need to pack a suitcase,' he said. 'I shall wait outside.'

When she turned around, she saw Dana standing at the top of the staircase. 'I will do it. You take your time saying goodbye.'

Less than twenty minutes later, Lena walked out of the door of her house, looking over her shoulder only one last time and raising her hand in goodbye to her family. They walked mostly in silence, until they stopped at another house and two girls she'd known from school joined them, falling into step beside her.

'It won't be so bad. I've heard you're all to work in a shoe factory.'

Lena took out a sandwich from her suitcase at their next stop, savouring every mouthful of the food her mother had made her and wishing that she had her sister by her side. But when she looked back in her bag, she saw something else. She carefully opened the papers there, surprised by what she'd found. They were identity papers, giving her a new surname. Forged papers.

She swallowed, her mouth suddenly dry. They were papers that would protect her, prevent anyone from knowing she was a Jew. She carefully tucked them back into her bag.

Those papers could very well save her life.

———— ❧ ————

When it was over, as Lena drifted back from her memories, and Becker finally passed her the food he'd brought for her, he gave her the strangest smile.

'I have news that might be of interest,' he said.

'News?' *Please, don't let Dana be here. Please don't let the news be about my sister.*

'There is a special new initiative for babies.'

The food in her mouth was suddenly almost impossible to swallow. Her sister might be safe at home still, or perhaps hidden away elsewhere, but she had a feeling her baby wouldn't be safe. Not here.

———— ❧ ————

'Lena, what's wrong?' Emilia said quietly, holding her in her arms as she might a child. Lena instinctively curved her body against Emilia's, her eyes shut to block everything else out. The bleakness of their quarters, the other women crammed in around her, *everything*.

She sobbed, unable to stop herself, and Emilia only held her tighter. Lena knew she needed to control herself, to stop crying before the *kapo* or block elders saw her. She'd been trading with them, but that didn't mean she trusted them not to beat her in front of the others for breaching the silence curfew.

'Shhh,' someone hissed from another bunk.

'Lena, tell me what's wrong?' Emilia whispered again. 'I can't help you if you don't tell me.'

Lena snuffled for a moment, catching her breath from her tears, before taking Emilia's hand and placing it on her stomach. Emilia's palm was flat there for a heartbeat before she realised, before her friend went still.

'Lena?'

'I'm pregnant,' she murmured.

'You're pregnant.' Emilia echoed her words as Lena nestled even tighter against her.

'What am I going to do?'

'Do you have any idea how far along you are? When this might have happened?'

Lena was silent as she burrowed closer into Emilia. She didn't know when the baby had been conceived, it could have been any time in the past months, but the way her stomach had suddenly begun to protrude . . . Emilia pressed her palm to Lena's stomach again as they lay there in one another's arms. *I want to go home.* It was all she could think, that she just wanted to be with her mother, to return to the home and family she'd never stopped yearning for.

'Am I too far along? For you to . . .' Her whisper was barely a murmur now. '*You know?*'

220

Emilia was silent, but she started to gently smooth her hand over Lena's hair again then, and Lena knew, without her even replying. She knew it wasn't going to be possible.

Her skin itched from the bugs that plagued them all still, that lived in their bedding and tormented them all night. Bitter air berated them from the window up high that was forever open to expose them to the elements. If she'd ever tried to imagine what hell might be like, this was it. Only she couldn't imagine that she now had to add *pregnant* to her list of ailments.

'Emilia?'

Emilia's hand stopped moving over her hair, telling Lena she was listening.

'The SS man, he told me something tonight.' She paused, knowing she had to tell Emilia. 'He told me that all the babies born here will now be tattooed after birth, prisoners at Auschwitz along with their mothers.'

'They won't be killed any more?' Emilia whispered back. 'The mothers won't be taken to their death?'

'I don't think so. I think they will simply both become prisoners now. I think that's what he was trying to say.'

Emilia said nothing. Lena wrestled over the next part, wishing she didn't have to tell her.

'What is it? What else did he tell you?'

Lena stifled a cry, surprised that Emilia had been able to tell that she was withholding something. 'That all suitable babies will be taken by the SS, for placement in Aryan families.'

They could have heard a pin drop in the block it was so silent. Lena hadn't realised until then that anyone else had been listening to them, but she heard more than one gasp.

They spoke into one another's ears.

'Do you think they'll take my baby? Do you think they'll want her to be a Nazi?' She paused. 'I just know she's a girl, Emilia. I can feel it.'

221

'Lena, my love, I don't know. Who could know what those monsters will decide to do?'

'But how will I ever find her, if we survive this place? How will I ever know who she is? How will she ever know who I am, if they take her?'

Emilia continued to hold her as she cried, her hand circling Lena's back, and as she finally began to drift off to sleep, Lena wondered if perhaps Becker might look after their baby. He might have been angry tonight, but the child would be his own flesh and blood. Surely he wouldn't let it be taken? Hadn't he always said he'd look after her?

———— ⟨ひ⟩ ————

Lena didn't get the chance to talk to Emilia until the following evening. It wasn't as cold as it had been, and they stayed outside to talk for a moment, walking slowly side by side, before they had to go into their block.

'How are you feeling?' Emilia asked.

Lena shrugged. She swung between a deep sadness that threatened to swallow her whole, and a little glimmer of hope.

'I would like to talk to Aleksy, to see what he thinks about how many months pregnant you are,' Emilia said, her voice low. 'It's so much harder to tell here, due to how little weight any of the women are carrying, but I should think from my brief examination last night that you could be perhaps five or even six months.'

Lena shivered as she listened to Emilia's words. *Six months?* She couldn't believe she could be that far along already.

'Lena, I've been thinking about something you said last night, about the babies being tattooed.'

She nodded.

'I expected that a tattooist would come to mark the babies who will be staying in the camp?'

Lena nodded again. 'That was my understanding.'

'So this tattooist could very possibly be Zofia? It would be unlikely for them to send anyone else.'

'I'm not certain I understand. What would it matter who made the tattoo?'

Emilia stopped walking.

'What if we could convince her to mark the other babies, the ones chosen for German families, before they're taken? To secretly tattoo each mother and baby, with an identical mark?'

Lena grinned. 'Emilia, that's a wonderful idea!'

'The way I see it, is that Zofia owes me,' Emilia said. 'I wouldn't usually ask for a favour, but in this case, I'm more than prepared to tell her that she needs to do something for me.' Emilia cleared her throat and placed her hand on Lena's shoulder. '*For you.*'

Lena stared back at her. 'For me?'

'Lena, I believe your baby will be taken,' Emilia said. 'The father is German, and look at you with your fair features and light-brown hair. I imagine your child is precisely what they're looking for.'

'He would never be so cruel, not to me,' Lena cried. 'He told me that he'll look after me. That there are things he can do for me, and I've been thinking about it all day. I know he won't let his baby be taken.'

Emilia kept watching her, but she didn't say anything. She didn't have to; her expression told Lena exactly what Emilia thought.

'You don't believe me? You don't think he'll want to save his own child?' She heard the quiver in her own voice, and she pulled away from Emilia, taking a few steps back.

'Lena, it's not that I don't believe you, but I think it would be naive to assume that a man who is capable of being a part of all of this, who has treated you so callously for so long, would be capable of helping you. I don't think you need me to tell you this.'

Emilia's words cut through and Lena turned away, running towards the block even as Emilia called out after her.

'Lena! Lena!'

But she didn't turn around. The way Emilia had looked at her, the pity she'd seen in her eyes – she didn't want to see it again.

She didn't want to hear what Emilia had to say. Once she had the baby, it would be different. She would be the mother of his child and he would see that, he would want to protect her.

The gong went then, and Lena was surrounded by other women as they made their way to their beds. She was tempted to find another spot, especially when Emilia appeared behind her, but she knew that wouldn't be so easy.

'Lena?'

She climbed up and curled into a ball.

'Lena, please, don't be angry with me. Just think about what I said, about what we could do, just in case.'

She stayed silent for a long moment before turning around, her eyes searching Emilia's face.

'I just want to go home,' she whispered. 'I can't take it any more, Em. I just want to go home.'

'Shh, Lena,' Emilia murmured, as she stroked her face, and Lena tucked even closer as if Emilia were her own mother comforting her. 'Tell me about home, tell me about your family, Lena.'

'My family?' She hadn't spoken aloud about her family since she'd arrived, but she'd held those memories so tightly, could still hear her sister's laugh and her mother calling her for dinner.

'Yes, your family,' Emilia said. 'Tell me what you are most looking forward to. Tell me everything. We need to keep those we love alive, so we never forget what we're living for.'

Lena elbowed her sister and they both began to laugh. The boys who'd been waving to them were still staring, and Lena caught Dana's hand as they walked away. This summer had been different; all the boys seemed to notice them now, and if their father saw the attention they were getting, he'd be furious.

'Come on, if we come home without anything for dinner, Mama will never forgive us.'

They'd been sent out to do the shopping, expected to return with cheese, pork and potatoes, and so far they hadn't even made it to the butcher.

Dana's head fell to Lena's shoulder as they strolled, the boys long forgotten.

'What do you think, about the whispers of war?' Dana asked.

'I think that men like to talk about such things,' Lena replied. 'But we're safe here, Dana. Papa will never let anything happen to us, you know that.'

'But what—'

'It is nothing more than the talk of worried old men,' she said, letting go of her sister's hand and linking their arms instead. 'Now, what do you say we go past the bookstore.'

'The bookstore?'

'I heard Henrich is working there over summer,' she said with a grin.

'Did you think Henrich might have some book recommendations for you?' Dana teased.

'Why Dana, that's precisely what I was thinking!' They both laughed, and that laughter only increased when Dana bent to pick a flower and tucked it behind Lena's ear.

'You know, I also heard that Henrich has a younger brother.'

'Well, perhaps I might like a visit to the bookstore, too.'

They strolled under the warm rays of morning sunshine, heads bent close together as they gossiped and giggled about whether they'd see

Henrich and his brother. She and Dana were separated by only eighteen months, and most people who met them presumed they were twins, with the same light-brown hair that fell in waves over their shoulders, their eyes a vivid blue and so unlike their mother's dark brown.

'Promise me that even when we're married, we will always be best friends,' Dana said. 'I want our children to grow up as if they're siblings, to be like us.'

Lena pressed a warm kiss to her sister's cheek. 'They will be, Dana. And we will always be me and you, I will never let anything come between us.'

Her sister was everything to her. They slept in the same bedroom despite their mother reminding them that there was space for them each to have a room, sharing everything with one another.

'How do I look?' Lena asked, smoothing her hands down the front of her dress as she faced her sister.

'Beautiful,' Dana replied, her voice a whisper, reaching up to brush a strand of hair from her sister's face.

They didn't know then that within days their country would join the war, and that life as they knew it would change. Forever. Or the fact that their mother was Jewish would have such terrifying ramifications for their entire family.

CHAPTER TWENTY-THREE

Emilia

'Aleksy, I'm going to ask her, when she comes to tattoo the first prisoner baby,' Emilia paused, considering the enormity of what she was about to say. She, who'd never expected anything in return for helping others, was about to attempt blackmail. 'Zofia owes us. I'm going to tell her that I helped her when she needed me, and that now she has to help us.' It didn't sit comfortably with her to ask anything of anyone, but she was determined to do this. Zofia was her only chance, so she would do anything to convince her. Although it might not come to that; so many within the camp were prepared to do the most selfless acts to help others, and for all she knew, Zofia was one of those women.

Aleksy frowned at her as he passed over a small handful of aspirin and helped her to set up a bowl of water. She longed to drink from it, but they would save it for the patients suffering a fever, or to dip a precious piece of cloth into, to make a cold compress.

'I came here to see for my own eyes that you'd recovered,' he said. 'When I thought you might . . .' His voice trailed off and he cleared his throat.

'I'm fine. It would take more than a little temperature to have me sent to the sick block.'

He didn't appear amused by her joke. 'Emilia, I've lost someone I cared very deeply about before, because of a risk I chose to take. I can't—'

'This would be my risk, not yours,' she said, interrupting him as she refolded some tattered pieces of blanket that she planned to use as bandages.

'The terminations are one thing, they can be done in a way to minimise risk, especially if Lena can keep bribing the *kapos* for you, but this is different.'

They looked at one another.

'Emilia, the punishment for this would be death.'

She saw the worry in his gaze. They both knew he was right.

'If we're not taking risks to help others, we're not doing enough. Isn't that what we both said?' She paused. 'Aleksy, you and I know we could die here tomorrow. There is every chance we won't make it out of here alive, so don't we have an obligation to do whatever we can, while we're still here?'

He was silent as she walked through the block, looking at the women in her care, as if he wasn't ready to answer her yet. His walk had become a shuffle, the way most of them got around; too tired to lift their feet properly, almost too exhausted to move at all. Only they were lucky, because sometimes they received extra rations, and Emilia the best cup of soup available, stirred before serving to ensure there were little pieces of vegetable floating in it. The women all looked at her differently now, even spoke to her differently, and after the way they'd treated her while she was unwell, the care they'd shown, she'd realised just how essential her services were. Before, she'd wondered if she'd imagined the change in attitude towards her, but now she knew for certain.

'When Zofia arrives, I am going to ask her, I've made up my mind,' she said, when she came back past him. 'Aleksy, I have to try. At least for Lena. I can't let them take her baby without trying to do something.'

'And what if this tattooist tells the SS of your plans? What then?'

Emilia could see from Aleksy's eyes how nervous she'd made him. And he was right, it was risking a lot to ask. But what else could she do?

'Would you prefer me to let them take those babies, with no way for their mothers to prove their identity one day? What if they have the chance to look for them after the war? If one day this camp is liberated and we can go free?'

Aleksy shook his head and reached for her hands, folding them in his. She imagined that before the camp, his hands would have been soft and warm, but now his skin was dry, his fingers bony.

'My wife was killed before my eyes, by the same monsters who hold us here.' Tears slipped from Aleksy's eyes and slid down his cheeks. She pulled one hand away from his and gently touched his tears away.

'They killed my son, too. He was only a toddler, still too young to know what was happening, but old enough to be calling for his papa and wondering why he didn't come. They were all I had, and yet I couldn't protect them. I don't want to make that mistake again.'

Emilia held his hand, her heart breaking as he spoke. They'd all lost so much, had so much taken from them.

She watched as he closed his eyes, as if he were trying to purge the memory. Or perhaps he was trying to hold his family there, to remember that they'd once lived.

'In the beginning, I cried every day and wished we could have stayed together,' he said. 'But then I realised what would have become of them, if we'd all been sent here. The way my son would have suffered for endless minutes as the gas choked the life from him, my wife either by his side, or perhaps separated from him because she looked strong enough to be put to work. She would have screamed for him, never forgetting the look in his eyes as he was taken away, as she heard the stories of what truly happened to all those children, why they didn't bother to mark them with a tattoo upon arrival. Because they were nameless, faceless, *worthless*.' He shook his head. 'Now that I know, I am grateful they never came here. Because this is hell. The depraved things they can do to a human being here, they know no bounds.'

She digested his words, understanding his pain.

'Still, I know that it was I who failed them.'

'If I'm caught, it is my own fault, not yours,' she said. 'You're scared that I will suffer the very worst pain, and that you will feel responsible for it, but I am not your responsibility.'

He let go of her hands and placed his palms on her shoulders. 'That doesn't mean I won't do everything I can to protect you, Emilia. You have to be careful, we both do.'

She looked up into his eyes. 'I will be careful, you have my word. But I can't not try, Aleksy. I have to do this. I have to do something, at least for Lena.'

'I know you do,' he said, as his hands dropped away. 'That's what scares me.'

They both knew that she would never stop with Lena's baby. If it were a success, this was only the beginning.

———— ❦ ————

Emilia knew she would never forget the first time she saw a baby tattooed. The act itself was different from when she'd had her numbers etched onto her skin, and she instinctively rubbed her thumb over the smudged blue-green ink on her arm as she remembered.

Her skin had been unmarked until she'd arrived at the camp, and she still hated the sight of it.

'You can try to feed him as soon as it's over,' Emilia said, trying in vain to soothe the mother. She was only young and it was her first baby. All of the mothers were exhausted after labour here, their bodies spent from something that was difficult at the best of times. But these women were so depleted; it seemed almost an impossibility that they should be able to carry a baby, let alone birth one. Some of the women she'd seen recently had barely acknowledged their baby after the trauma of birth, unable to lift their heads, let alone their arms to hold an infant.

But today, today gave Emilia hope. These babies might all starve to death in the camp, it was certainly a possibility, but they were also being given a chance that most other infants had not. If the Allies came for them soon, if the war turned in their favour or somehow they survived until the end, at least these children weren't going straight to the chimney.

'I don't like doing this any more than you like watching,' Zofia said. Emilia could see the tattooist's eyes were full of tears, and she'd watched how much her hand had been shaking as she'd tried to hold the needle. They no longer wiped the ink across the scratchings now, the numbers had been known to blur too often from that original procedure; now the needle scratched and inked at the same time.

'I know you don't take pleasure in it,' Emilia said. 'We all do what we have to do here, to stay alive. What would happen to you if you refused?'

The woman placed her tools in her bag. 'They would kill me, you know they would. I'd be lined up against the wall.'

'Then you have nothing to apologise for. You're only following orders.'

Zofia gripped her bag and turned for the door, but Emilia moved in front of her, knowing that this might be her only opportunity to ask. *Do it for Lena. You have to do this, you have to try.*

'Zofia, you came to me for my help once, and now I would like to ask you. For *your* help.'

The other woman looked surprised. 'What is it that I can do for you?'

'They are taking some of the babies, the ones you don't mark. They are to be given to Nazi families, to raise as their own.'

'You're certain of this?'

'I am certain,' Emilia said. 'The orders came straight from the SS doctors.'

They stared at each other for a long moment.

'What is it you want me to do? What exactly are you asking of me, Emilia?'

'I'm asking you to secretly mark those babies, somewhere that won't easily be noticed, and to tattoo their mothers with the identical mark. In case they ever have the chance of being reunited.'

She hoped she hadn't made a mistake, and Emilia held her tongue, not wanting to remind Zofia that she owed her. Instead, she said: 'Some of the women here are too far along for me to terminate, or they're too scared to go through with it. I'm trying to give these women a choice about their baby, the same way I gave you one.'

Zofia shifted her weight from one foot to the other, but she didn't walk away. 'How would we do this? How would you get word to me, if I were to say yes?'

Relief spread through Emilia. 'Dr Aleksy Gorski, in the main camp hospital. He would help me to contact you when we need your help.' She paused. 'He is the doctor who was there that day, who helped to show me what to do for you.'

'I remember,' Zofia said.

They stood in silence.

'You won't tell anyone what I'm doing? This will stay between us?'

'It will be our secret,' Emilia said. 'I would suffer as greatly as you if we were caught.'

'Emilia, the risk, what they would do to us—'

'It is Lena's baby,' Emilia said. 'I believe that Lena's baby will be the first one taken. You would be doing this for her.'

Zofia's skin paled. 'This is for Lena?'

'It is for Lena,' Emilia repeated.

'Then I will do it,' Zofia whispered. 'For Lena.'

'If it goes well, you will consider doing more?'

Zofia simply nodded before leaving, her bag clutched in one hand as she pushed open the door, and Emilia felt a flutter of excitement in her stomach for the first time since she'd arrived at the camp. They could take everything from them, strip a human down to almost nothing, but there was something about hope that gave a person strength. And now, she was prepared to fight for these women and their babies, until her very last breath.

Starting with Lena.

CHAPTER TWENTY-FOUR

EMILIA

LONDON, 1995

THURSDAY

'It sounds like you were very close to Lena, that she became a special friend of yours,' Hannah said, as she took off her jacket. 'Did you remain friends until the liberation of Auschwitz?'

At that moment, as Emilia went to open her mouth, as she remembered Lena and all the years she'd thought of her, she froze. Hannah lifted her arm to touch her hair, the skin of her armpit visible, leaving her in only a silk tank top. Emilia's voice caught in her throat. It was faded, but the placement of the mark, the colour of it, the shape. She blinked, and then again. Her mind must have been playing tricks on her. Because it looked like . . . *no.* Her mind wasn't what it used to be, she wasn't thinking clearly. She was imagining it. She was seeing things that weren't there. Was that a tattoo?

Hannah dropped her arm, and when her eyes met Hannah's, she saw they were filled with tears.

'Your mark, your . . .' Emilia's voice faltered as she looked over at Lucy, who looked blankly back at her, not understanding what was happening. 'I'm sorry, I think talking about the past has made me confused. I thought, I mean when you lifted your arm . . .'

'Emilia, you're not confused,' Hannah said, her eyes fixed on her as she reached for the tape recorder and turned it off. 'I haven't been entirely truthful with you.'

Emilia placed a hand to her chest. Her breath had caught in her throat, and her pulse began to race.

'Mum?' Lucy's chair fell back as she leaped towards her. 'Are you okay? What's wrong? Is it your heart? Do I need to call an ambulance?'

'No, I, I—'

'I think that's enough for today,' Lucy said sharply. 'My mother—'

'No,' Emilia said, surprised by the strength of her own voice. 'Please, tell me. I need to hear you say it. I need to know, the mark under your arm, that it is what I think it is. That I'm not imagining it.' She was starting to see things more clearly now, understood that Hannah had wanted her to see it, that she'd removed her jacket and lifted her arm for a reason. She might be a confused old woman at times, but the placement of that mark, that part of her past, was something she doubted she'd ever forget.

'Emilia, I have a personal connection to Auschwitz-Birkenau,' Hannah said in a low voice. 'I believe I was born there, and the mark you just saw, I think that perhaps it was you who was responsible for placing it there. I wanted to see how you'd react, to know if you truly were the midwife I've been searching for all these years.'

Emilia swallowed, tears welling in her eyes as she thought of all the babies they'd marked, all the babies they'd tried to save. And now all these years later, one of them was seated before her. 'You were raised by a German family?'

Hannah nodded. 'I was. My mother passed away almost ten years ago now, and it wasn't until she was in hospital, on her death bed in fact, that she confessed that I'd been adopted. Until then, I believed her to be my birth mother.'

Emilia shook her head, her heart still pounding. 'She told you how she adopted you? Where you'd come from?'

'She only told me that my parents were listed as unknown, but that I was chosen as being suitable for Aryan adoption, despite not being German. It didn't take long for me to begin to piece together what had happened after that, especially when I read about the tattoos that some of the babies were given at Auschwitz.'

Emilia leaned forwards and gently lifted Hannah's arm again, squinting as she stared at the faded blue mark that was entirely indistinguishable. 'We imagined that the tattoos might help mothers and children be reunited. That we would be able to achieve miracles, I suppose. Everything we did, it was to save mothers and babies.'

'You saved many lives, Emilia, and I believe that's what most people would like to know about you. It's why I want to share your story with the world, in your own words.'

Emilia looked away, lost in her thoughts again, her memory clouded by what had happened so long ago.

'Who could have imagined that almost all of those women would die? That there wouldn't be any mothers left to reunite?' She wiped away tears that had begun to slip down her cheeks. 'I don't believe anyone now could imagine the horrors, could truly understand what it was like to see so much death. To fight so hard, knowing that so few would survive.'

'Emilia, I know this is terribly upsetting, talking of what happened, but may I ask you one final question before I go?'

She slowly turned, meeting Hannah's gaze, wanting to finish the story now that she'd already told so much of it. 'You may.'

'Would you tell me what happened to Lena? I would very much like to hear the rest of her story.'

Tears flooded Emilia's eyes and she reached for a tissue as Lucy came over and wrapped her arms around her.

'My poor, darling Lena,' Emilia said with a sigh. 'I've tried so hard to put what happened out of my mind, but not a day has gone by that I haven't remembered what he did to her. In the end, she had nothing left to lose.'

CHAPTER TWENTY-FIVE

LENA

AUSCHWITZ-BIRKENAU, 1944

Lena held tightly to Emilia's hand as she lay on the stove, gritting her teeth against another contraction that made her stomach clench more tightly than she could ever have imagined possible.

'Tell me about your sister,' Emilia said, as she stroked her forehead. 'What are you looking forward to doing with her, when we go home?'

Lena cried out and gripped Emilia's hand more tightly. 'I can't stand the pain. I can't do this, Emilia. I can't—'

'All I want to do,' Emilia said, talking over her, 'the one thing I keep imagining, is stepping through the door into my house again. I can see my father waiting, the look on his face when he realises that I've come back. If I close my eyes, I can see myself standing at the stove, I can smell the garlic sizzling in oil, ready to place fish into the pan. My brother is there too, and we're joking that we both need fattening up, while my father sits at the table, watching us, smiling at his children being together in his house once more.'

Lena forced herself to do the same, to imagine herself at home, what it would be like, what she would do, as Emilia let go of her hand and went to stand between her legs.

'I want to lie beside my sister, beside my Dana, in our bed, shoulder to shoulder, like we used to when we were girls,' Lena said, gritting her teeth before continuing. 'I want to hear her voice, I want to talk about the boys we want to marry, I want to pretend like none of this ever happened.' She started to cry then and Emilia moved to stand by her again, leaning over and cradling her in her arms. 'I want my mother to stroke my hair as I fall asleep, I want to eat her *pierogi* and listen to her singing in the garden.'

Emilia stroked Lena's hair, brushing it from her face, gently touching the back of her fingers to her flushed skin, just as Lena imagined her mother would have.

'You will be back with your family one day, Lena. We have to believe that, we have to believe that this is only a moment in time for us.'

Lena opened her mouth to speak then, but a gasp came out instead.

'Push, Lena,' Emilia instructed, moving back down. 'Lena, I need you to push as hard as you can on the next contraction.'

'I can't,' she sobbed. 'I can't do it any more.'

'You can do it,' Emilia said. 'You need to do this for your baby, Lena. You need to do this so your family can have you home again.'

The next minutes felt like the longest of her life as she cried out, bearing down as hard as she could until finally she could collapse back onto the stove. It was over.

'It's a little girl, Lena, just like you said it would be,' Emilia murmured, as the baby let out a cry that told her what a fighter she was. 'She's beautiful, just like her mother.'

Lena pushed up onto her elbows, her hair clinging to the sides of her face, skin red from the exertion. 'It's a girl?'

'It's a girl.' Emilia carefully passed Lena her baby, pressing a kiss to her head as she stared at her daughter in wonder, before cutting the umbilical cord with her knife. 'It's not over yet though, we have the afterbirth still to come. You'll feel another contraction and it should pass easily.'

'You can't let them take her,' Lena whispered. 'I know I said he wouldn't, but now that I've seen her, now that she's here . . .' She swallowed away her tears. 'What if he does?'

Emilia leaned forwards and hugged both of them. 'I can't promise you anything, but I do need to find Aleksy, to see if he can send word. I have planned for this, Lena.'

'Zofia will come?'

Emilia nodded. 'Yes, Lena. If they come for your daughter, if she is taken, then we only have so long for Zofia to help us, but she's said she would and I have no reason to doubt her.'

'Thank you.' Lena stared in wonder at the little girl in her arms. Becker had always said he'd look out for her, he'd never once said that her baby might be taken, and she was certain that when he saw her, when he gazed into her beautiful eyes that he'd let her keep her daughter. But she also knew that he was prone to anger, and if he wasn't in a good mood . . . She pressed her lips to her child's forehead, not wanting to think what might happen then.

'I'll be back soon,' Emilia said, gently touching the baby's downy head with her fingertips before she left. 'I promise.'

'Emilia?'

'You asked me what I was looking forward to doing, once this was all over. When I go home.'

Emilia smiled down at her.

'I'm looking forward to introducing you to my family,' she said. 'I want them to know that you helped to keep me alive here, that I couldn't have survived without you.'

'Lena, don't say that, you—'

'I don't want my family to know what happened to me here,' Lena interrupted. 'I don't want them to look at me as if I'm broken, for my parents to know that they were right to hide us, to not trust what would happen.'

'Then we won't tell them,' Emilia said. 'It's as simple as that.'

Emilia stared down at her for a long moment before turning away, and Lena watched until she couldn't see her any more before returning her attention to her daughter, and falling in love all over again as her little hand caught around her mother's finger.

I will never let anyone take you, my love. I promise.

CHAPTER TWENTY-SIX

Emilia

Emilia kept her head down, wanting to be as invisible as possible, her eyes darting to look at the tower as she passed it, knowing that the guards didn't need an excuse to shoot her. Sometimes they fired shots because they were bored, other times they played cruel games and taunted the prisoners to do something that would result in their death no matter what choice they made.

When she reached the infectious diseases block, a guard approached her, taking his gun out, his fingers dancing across the barrel.

'Where do you think you're going?'

'I'm a midwife, and one of my patients is experiencing complications,' she said quickly. 'I need Dr Gorski.'

The guard didn't lower his gun.

'Dr Mengele has told me to report directly to Gorski, he has a special interest in babies born here and I am to immediately inform him when a new baby is born, especially one that might be suitable for the Third Reich.' She paused, keeping her gaze slightly lowered.

She breathed a silent sigh of relief when the gun finally went back to his side, but to her disappointment he was the one to thrust open the door.

'Gorski!' the guard yelled.

Emilia glimpsed Aleksy as she peered in through the door, saw the drawn look on his face when he looked up from the patient he'd been bent over. She'd noticed the change in him recently, the way he seemed to be slightly hunched, his body more frail. She suspected that he gave the little extra bits of food she found for him to his patients, even though they needed him to stay strong. There were only so many doctors in the camp, after all.

He came towards the door, slowly, as if he were in pain. She smiled at him as she stood behind the guard, hoping he was all right.

'Dr Gorski, we have had another baby born,' she said. 'I was told to advise you of any that might be suitable.'

He nodded. 'Thank you, I shall inform the SS doctors immediately.'

'Unfortunately I think the baby needs to be checked by a doctor. Could you assist me?'

They'd practised what they'd do when Lena had her baby. Aleksy would use the excuse of needing to inform the SS doctors to leave the Birkenau hospital and head for the main building, which would allow him to give Zofia the signal that she was needed. It would also give Emilia time to rush back and give the mother her options, to explain to her what might happen and ask for her blessing to mark her child. It seemed simple, but she knew only too well how easily things could go wrong.

How easily they could all lose their lives for trying to save another.

Emilia turned and started to walk away, but the guard's call made her freeze, her legs trembling.

'Halt!'

Emilia slowly turned, swallowing hard as she did so.

'Lift your top.'

He raised his gun and she did as he'd asked. She knew better than to resist or take too long to follow orders. The humiliation was something she'd suffered enough times to be able to stomach, but seeing Aleksy standing, watching what was happening from behind the guard, almost broke her. But, bless him, he smiled, staring into her eyes, never dropping his gaze, as if trying to give her strength.

The guard gestured with his gun for her to remove the rest of her clothes. Emilia stood, trying to stop her teeth from chattering, her body from quivering in the cold wind, as she stripped outside, for the world to see. The guard watched in his warm fur coat, one eyebrow raised as he seemed to enjoy her discomfort.

But instead of cowering, Emilia kept staring back at Aleksy, drawing on the strength he seemed to give her. They could strip her naked, humiliate her, make her feel worthless, but unless they killed her, they couldn't stop the work she was doing in the camp.

'Get dressed,' the guard eventually said, spitting on the ground before turning.

Emilia finally looked away from Aleksy, seeing him hurry from the corner of her eye, and grateful that she'd been let go, especially with Lena waiting for her. She presumed he'd been searching her skin for marks – they were still on high alert for typhus – and if he'd asked her to turn, he would have seen a tell-tale mark on her back from when she'd been sick that could have resulted in her death.

Now all she had to hope was that their plan worked, because it wouldn't be long before the guards came to claim Lena's baby, and it would break all their hearts if she was taken before the tattooist had time to make her mark. She hurried back, thinking of her mother and wishing desperately that she could speak to her, just one last time.

⸺ ❧ ~❧ ⸺

'I'm not going to come today. I think it's time for you to go on your own.'

Emilia stopped at the door, seeing that her mother was still sitting at the kitchen table. Steam rose from her cup, telling Emilia that she'd only just poured it. Her mother's black leather bag was sitting on the other chair.

'I'm not ready to go on my own,' Emilia said, as panic began to rise, a tide in her throat that she could barely gulp down.

'My darling, if you weren't ready, I wouldn't send you.'

She watched her mother sip her coffee, casually, as if she'd asked Emilia to run to the store for her, not birth a baby on her own.

'Mama, please, I—'

'Emilia, you need to do this now, while I'm still here. You need to learn to trust your instincts.'

'But what if something goes wrong? What will I do? What if the baby—'

'My darling, you've trailed after me for years, you've been the best assistant midwife I could have asked for, but there's nothing more you can learn from me.' She rose and reached for her daughter, cupping her cheeks and placing a gentle kiss to her forehead. 'There's nothing that you can't do. You've learnt everything I know, and it's time for you to trust your instincts.'

Emilia sighed. She was right. Her mother was always right.

'It's important that you do this, that you take this step now.'

What she wanted was to curl up in her mother's lap, to have her stroke her hair and whisper to her as they sat in the sun. But she wasn't a child any more, she was a woman, a midwife, *and there was a baby being born.*

'We were made for this job,' her mother said, sitting back down at the table and gesturing to her bag. 'That is yours now. Just as my mother gave it to me when I was ready, I am giving it to you.'

Emilia fought against the emotion in her chest as she curled her fingers around the sturdy leather handle, familiar from all the times she'd carried it for her mother, from all the years she'd watched her collect it every time she left the house for work. Because this wasn't just about taking over her mother's role as midwife, this was about acknowledging that her mother was sick and wouldn't be alive for much longer.

'I look forward to hearing all about the baby you deliver today, Emilia. Remember that you are capable of great things, so long as you believe in yourself and your ability to help others. It's a gift that the women in our family have, it's running through your veins, now all you have to do is trust.'

Her mother's smile lit something inside her, and she smiled back. She could do this. She'd learnt from the best, and it was time for her to trust herself; she was like a baby bird being pushed from the nest when its mother knew it was ready to fly.

Only this baby bird knew that her mother didn't have much longer on this earth, not now that her body was ravaged by illness. She'd had to prepare for that, grieve the years they wouldn't have together, and accept that she needed to be grateful for every day they still had.

'I'll be waiting right here, Emilia.'

She blew her mother a kiss, finding it hard to imagine a day when she wouldn't be waiting, when that chair would be empty, when all that remained was the ghost of a memory that she hoped would never be forgotten.

Emilia's eyes kept finding their way back to the door. She didn't know when it would happen, when Lena's baby would be taken.

Would they take her when she was only hours old, knowing how unlikely it was that her mother would be able to provide milk for her anyway? Would they wait a few days? She knew Lena was either delusional or simply very naive to think she might be allowed to keep her, especially given her daughter's fair, downy hair and pale skin.

It was going to be awful whenever it happened, but if it happened before they had a chance to mark her . . .

The door opened with a bang, making her jump. Lena grabbed her hand, and she felt physically sick. If they were caught, it would be the chimney for all of them: Lena, Aleksy, Zofia and her.

'We don't have long.'

The words were spoken by Zofia. Her eyes darted around the room as she entered, and Emilia was relieved to see that Aleksy had accompanied her. It was he who shut the door, standing there and staring at Emilia as if he couldn't believe they were actually doing it, but the moment Zofia ran to Lena and threw her arms around her, Emilia knew they'd done the right thing. If they were caught, then so be it; they all cared for Lena, they had no other choice.

'Where am I marking her?' Zofia asked, as she openly wiped away her tears.

'Mark the baby first, on the underside of her big toe,' Aleksy instructed.

'Or behind her ear,' Emilia said. 'Won't it be seen too easily on her toe?'

'Why not her armpit,' Lena said, surprising Emilia when she spoke. 'It might look like a little birth mark there?'

They all stared at one another.

'Quickly,' Zofia said. 'I need to know where.'

'The armpit,' Emilia said, which received a raised brow from Aleksy. She would tell him later that it was likely the only choice

Lena would ever get to make about her child. She wouldn't get to name her, or choose her clothes; she would likely have to spend the rest of her life not knowing where her daughter was or what she was doing.

'I will do four small dots on the child,' Zofia said. 'The same four dots will be given to Lena.'

Emilia gently brushed Lena's tears from her cheeks as Zofia opened her bag.

'Hold her as still as you can,' Zofia said.

The baby began to cry as the needle was raised, and she saw Lena bravely blinking away fresh tears while she softly sung under her breath to her daughter. Emilia stood over her and watched, and Aleksy helped to hold the baby still. It was over very quickly, and almost immediately Lena had lifted her top, exposing her own armpit and receiving the same four dots in the same formation.

'I must go now,' Zofia said. 'If they ask why I was here, if someone has seen me—'

As if on cue there was a loud noise outside, followed by men's voices. Lena shrugged back into her top, her baby cradled against her, no longer crying but with her little fist pressed to her mouth.

'Aleksy, you are checking over the baby for me,' Emilia whispered. 'We are seeing whether she might be suitable for—'

The door opened. An SS doctor stood there, his eyes narrowed as he appeared to survey the room, two guards behind him, one with a menacing-looking Alsatian on a leash. For as long as she lived, she hoped that once she left the camp she would never see one of those dogs again. She'd seen them rip women apart since her arrival, kill on command, and she'd been witness to multiple deaths from infected bite wounds.

'What is going on here?' the doctor asked.

'Dr Rohde,' Aleksy said, in greeting, as if it were the most normal thing in the world for him to be there. 'We've had a baby born.' Aleksy stood in front of them all, as if he might somehow be able to protect them. 'The midwife asked me to check whether she should be tattooed or not.'

'You thought you would be the one to make the decision?'

Aleksy stepped back, closer to Emilia.

'No sir. I wanted to check the baby's health, to ensure the child was well.'

The doctor moved past them and Emilia glanced at Zofia, who'd taken a few steps back. They had a number of women in the barracks, some with infected or partially frostbitten feet, others who simply needed the rest and were shivering together while they tried to sleep. But the woman the doctor had gone to was coughing, and Emilia knew when the SS doctor looked up what he was about to say.

'Why is that woman here? Send her to Block 25.'

'But she's not so bad, she just—' Emilia was cut off.

'Would you like to join her?' he asked, glancing between her and Aleksy. 'Gorski, check all the patients for rashes. I want the infected gone before I leave. We are trying to keep babies alive now, at least the ones we want, and I don't want to risk them becoming sick.'

A hush descended across the room, and Emilia saw tears begin to roll down Aleksy's cheeks as he looked to her, as if seeking her permission to follow the order.

Lena's baby began to cry then, and Emilia watched helplessly as the SS doctor picked her up, taking the blanket off that they'd wrapped around her and examining her.

'You are Slovakian?' he asked Lena.

Lena nodded.

'The father?'

'Is German.'

'Very good.' The doctor put the baby back in Lena's arms and then proceeded to look inside the infant's mouth, before looking at her eyes and then listening to her heart. Emilia was certain Aleksy was eyeing his stethoscope with envy; it was such a basic tool to a doctor, but still one he'd been denied here.

'She is healthy and her complexion is excellent,' the SS doctor declared. 'She will be the perfect first baby for our new initiative.'

'Will you allow the baby to feed from her mother for the next couple of weeks? Perhaps she could be moved to the SS hospital?'

The doctor looked at Aleksy as if he were mad when he spoke, and Emilia knew how much he'd risked by speaking directly in such a way.

'The baby will be taken immediately,' he replied. 'You are not needed here.'

She watched as Aleksy shook his head, as if he were about to say something else that might get him killed.

'Then you will take her. Wrap her in the blanket and follow me.'

'No!' Lena cried, clutching her daughter to her chest. 'No! I won't let you take her!'

'It was so much easier when we took them straight to the chimney after birth,' the SS doctor said with a sigh to one of the guards. 'Perhaps we should consider that again, to prevent this hysteria.'

Lena screamed so loudly that Emilia shut her eyes against the visceral sound of pain.

'*Untersturmführer* Becker will never allow this!' she screamed.

'Becker?' The doctor smiled. 'Why, it was Becker who told me there would be a suitable baby born soon.'

Lena's screams abated to sobs, as Emilia tried in vain to console her.

'What is she doing here? Who are you?' The SS doctor turned his attention unexpectedly to Zofia, who'd been standing silently against the wall, clutching her bag, as if she'd hoped not to be seen.

'I am one of the tattooists,' she said, and Emilia heard the shake in her voice. 'I came in case the child needed to be given a number.'

'You will be called when you're needed,' he said, dismissing her and pointing towards the door. 'There are new arrivals coming in today, I expect you're wanted. Go!'

Emilia hoped that Zofia hadn't been scared off, that she would still return when they needed her. They needed a better system, a better way to make sure they could tattoo each baby before anyone even knew of its birth.

'Did you not hear me? Doctor, take the child!'

Aleksy reached for Lena's baby, but as her screams filled the room once more, Emilia watched in horror as the SS doctor took one of the guard's sticks and set upon Lena, smacking her across the shoulder. She continued to resist, her spindly arms holding tight to her baby, eyes wide now and almost animal-like.

The doctor's hair fell onto his face as he raised the stick again, his cheeks stained red as he smacked Lena's shoulders once again, looking like a true madman, before landing a blow to Lena's head that sent her reeling back, her skull making a sickening crack against the back of the stove where she now lay still, unmoving.

'Take the baby!' he screamed. Aleksy tugged the infant from Lena's arms, holding her against his chest as his eyes met Emilia's. And just like that, he was part of Lena's pain, unable to do anything other than follow the order he was given, or face the end of a guard's gun.

'Please,' came a whisper, as Lena lifted her head. 'Please, let me keep her a little longer. Don't take her.'

The doctor passed the stick back to the guard and seemed to survey the room, looking at each of them in turn as he pushed his hair back from his face.

'That dog can teach her a lesson,' he said. 'Let him have her, or take her to the wall.'

Emilia inhaled, glancing at Aleksy who was desperately trying to soothe the crying baby.

'Please sir, I am in need of an assistant,' Emilia said, moving forwards, in much the same way Aleksy had once saved her. 'So many wretches are getting pregnant, and I could do with the help.'

'You are the midwife?'

'I am. It is just me birthing the babies, since Dr Gorski here was taken to the main hospital.'

She knew she was holding her breath but she couldn't help it.

He looked down his nose at her. 'She has experience?'

'Yes sir, I believe she does. She told me so during her labour.'

'Fine,' he said with a wave of his hand, as the guard shoved Aleksy towards the door. 'But if she doesn't follow orders or she makes a fuss again, the guards will come for her. If she doesn't do it herself on the fence first.'

His smile haunted her the moment she saw it, the image of Lena dead on the fence imprinted in her mind. He knew the pain he was causing Lena, he knew that what he'd done could push her to take her own life, and it seemed to amuse him.

When they'd finally left she hurried to Lena, cradling her in her arms before checking the back of her head. The blood was starting to dry, caked in her hair, her head no doubt throbbing in pain.

'Lena, one day you will be reunited,' she whispered to her, her lips touching Lena's hair. 'One day you will hold your child in your arms, you will tell her about this day and how hard you fought for her, and she will tell you about all the days you missed her.'

Lena was silent now, and Emilia wished there was something she could do, something she could give her, for the pain.

When Lena pulled away from her, curling into a ball on the hard stove, Emilia crouched beside her.

'You should have let them kill me.'

Her whisper shocked Emilia. She immediately placed her hand on her shoulder.

'You don't mean that, Lena. You can't possibly mean that,' Emilia said. 'What about after the war? What—'

'I'm never going to see her again. Just leave me.'

Emilia stood, dabbing her own eyes with the back of her fingers.

She tried to tell herself that Lena was only tired, that she didn't truly want to die. But in truth, Emilia was the one who was tired. It was the kind of tired she could never have imagined before, the kind of tired that had seeped into her bones, making it almost impossible to lift her head, let alone help others day in and day out. She sat down on one of the empty bunks for a moment.

'He comes for me when I'm working,' Lena said, her voice so soft that Emilia could only just hear it. 'You've never asked me. All these months, you never asked me which officer the father is, who it is that hurts me.'

Emilia sat up, her vision slightly blurred as the room spun around her. She took a moment to right herself. 'I never asked, because I wanted you to tell me when you were ready,' she replied in a low voice. 'I didn't want you to have to talk about something painful if you didn't want to.'

Lena never lifted her head, still curled up like a child, her hair falling over her shoulder and partially covering her face.

'The first time, he smiled at me. He came and talked to me, before asking me to follow him into another room. I thought he was being nice to me, that perhaps he was going to help me.'

'Is it always the same man?'

'It's always him. Sometimes he's kind, but sometimes he's not. I thought that once he saw his baby, maybe he would help me, like he always said he would, that maybe he would let her stay with me.'

'I'm so sorry.' Emilia's heart was breaking for Lena all over again. 'I wish there was something I could do.'

'He tells me I'm only alive because of him. That I only have my hair because of him.'

Emilia listened, crawling across the ground now to Lena and sitting heavily against the stove, reaching up for her friend's hand as it dangled towards her. It was too much effort to rise.

'I'm not going to let him touch me again,' Lena whispered. 'Next time he touches me, I'm going to kill him for what he's done.'

Emilia knew something was wrong a few days later when she saw the guards talking to their *kapo*. She was always careful of her – despite her willingness to trade in the past, Emilia had never trusted her. Lena hadn't been back there since she'd had her baby, giving her head scarf to another girl who was grateful to work inside instead of doing back-breaking labour, but some of the others had started helping Emilia. They all knew she only traded in order to get medical supplies, and no one knew just when they might need to be treated for an ailment.

But the way the *kapo* turned, her hand raised to shield her eyes from the sun as she surveyed all the women walking with their cups in hand, Emilia knew something was about to happen.

The *kapos* and block elders were given a level of comfort and privilege that most of the rest of them weren't; they had beds to themselves and were given extra rations of food. And most of them abused their power in the worst of ways, taking pleasure in beating the women in their care, lashing out at them as if they were SS guards. Some tried to be kind when the guards weren't looking, but most did not.

The *kapo* pointed past Emilia, and she turned and saw that it was Lena she was looking at. She froze, watching as Lena approached, her steps tentative. Emilia caught her hand before she passed her.

'Just wait. Don't go over until they call you.'

She could see the tightness of Lena's jaw, the way her bony hands dug into hers.

'I don't want to die,' Lena whispered back, as her bottom lip began to quiver. 'I've always thought I would face it, when I had to, but I want to find my daughter. I need to make it to the end.'

'And you will. You will.'

'But if I don't, if this is it . . .'

When they called Lena's number, Emilia let go of her hand and watched her move away towards the *kapo* who raised her hand as if to strike Lena, only to be kicked out of the way.

'Don't mark her,' one of the guards snarled. 'He won't like it if she has a mark on her.'

Emilia's heart sank. So that's where Lena was being taken. He wouldn't like her face marked, but she doubted he'd care about her broken heart or private parts that would still be tender from childbirth. Her body needed rest, not to be used by a man.

She stifled her own anger, forcing a smile when Lena looked back at her, a rifle behind her as she was marched away. She would be back. That was the only thing she had to hold on to.

No matter what he did to her, how he tried to break her, Lena would be back.

'It's been a day since they took her.'

She was sitting with Aleksy. It was Sunday, and she hadn't spoken to him since Lena's child had been taken. Sometimes they passed one another in the distance, and they'd follow each other with their eyes, never wanting to make their personal connection obvious in case it was used against them somehow. But today, they'd been able to find a moment together, and some of the other women from her block were keeping watch for them.

Although it was Sunday and few of the prisoners were working, the chimney was back belching smoke again, a reminder of how quickly their lives could be extinguished. It seemed as if they were killing more people every day, the sheer number of prisoners taken from the camp, or those that arrived being sent straight to the gas, increasing all the time.

'Don't look at the smoke,' he said. 'It doesn't do us any good thinking about who's in there.'

'I have this silly feeling that I'd know, if she was. That I'd feel it somehow.'

Aleksy sighed. 'Maybe you would? I think we have to trust how we feel sometimes.' She nodded.

'Like when I decided to risk my life to save a brave young woman.'

Emilia smiled. It wasn't something she did very often these days, but when she did, it was usually with Aleksy. He seemed to lighten something inside her when she spent time with him.

'I don't know how I'm still alive,' she said.

They sat in silence for a little longer, as she remembered that day, the image of the two German women inside that hut imprinted in her mind forever. Whenever she passed it she walked as quickly as her scuffed feet could carry her, knowing what was likely still happening in there. It gave her great comfort to know how many Jewish women she'd personally helped though, sometimes performing her terminations in the women's blocks instead of the hospital, with the other girls forming a half-circle so that her work couldn't be seen if someone were to walk in. At least they wouldn't have to suffer in that ghastly birthing hut.

'It's strange, seeing babies in the camp now,' Aleksy said, and she followed where he was staring at a mother slumped forwards on the ground, a baby in her arms.

'And children,' Emilia said. 'There's something haunting about seeing children here now, especially knowing that they could come for them at any time.'

Aleksy touched her hand, and she let him, moving her fingers so that they were against his.

'They came for the Roma families, you know,' he said. 'They lived just near my block, I heard it happen in the night, and by morning when I looked for them, they were all gone. Every last one of them.'

'They came in the night?' she gasped.

'They did. All the mothers, children,' he said grimly. 'They were all taken.'

In the beginning, she'd thought that he considered her a colleague of sorts, especially when she'd found out what had happened to his wife, but the way he'd reached for her hand, the way he looked at her sometimes, made her wonder if it meant something else. Which was ridiculous, she knew that. They were barely alive, barely surviving, their bodies ravaged by starvation; it was her imagination getting the better of her.

'Have you spoken to Zofia?' Aleksy asked. 'I was worried she might be too scared to come back again, after what happened.'

'Zofia was terrified, but she said it was worth it. She will help us whenever she is able.'

Aleksy sighed. 'That is good news. I was worried Lena's baby might be the first, and the last.'

'I don't know how long we'll get away with it, before someone figures out what we're doing, but we have to try.'

'So long as the tattooist keeps coming,' Aleksy said.

'If Zofia can't, if something should happen to her, I'll find a way to do it myself. Or Lena will.' *If she ever returns.*

Aleksy stood then, and she let him help her to her feet. He kept hold of her hand for a long moment, before leaning forwards and pressing his lips to her cheek. They were chapped and rough against her skin, but she still leaned into his touch.

'She will come back, Emilia,' he murmured, before pulling away. 'Lena is stronger than you realise.'

CHAPTER TWENTY-SEVEN

LENA

Lena was struggling to see through her eye. It had swollen over so much that she could barely blink. When Becker had sent the guards for her, when she'd seen his face, she'd known it was going to be bad, but she hadn't known the brutality he was truly capable of.

She stopped, her fingers catching on a button as she searched yet another coat for treasures. The memories of what he'd done to her earlier that day circled her mind.

———— ❦ ————

'You dared to say my name when the baby was born?'

Her lip quivered as she pressed herself against the wall, trying to hide from him, wishing she were invisible to the brute she'd once thought capable of kindness.

'I'm sorry,' she whispered. 'I thought you would help me. I thought—'

'You thought I would help to save a worthless girl?'

Lena lifted her head, staring into eyes filled with rage. 'She was your daughter!'

The crack of his knuckles against her eye socket took her by surprise, as did the way her body crumpled in a heap on the ground.

Her tears fell freely when he hauled her up by her hair, his fist tight to her scalp.

'You said you'd help me,' she murmured.

Becker released her hair, smoothing it instead of tugging it, the fingers he curled beneath her chin surprisingly gentle.

'Look what you made me do to you,' he muttered. 'You should know not to make me angry.'

She tried to stop the tears leaking from her eyes, tried to look at him, but it wasn't the pain from her eye making her cry, it was the pain of her loss. Her breasts were leaking for the baby they yearned to feed, her body still ached from the trauma of what had happened to her, and her mind . . . She shut her eyes as he began to fumble with her skirt. He could do whatever he wanted with her, so long as no one took away the memory of her daughter.

Lena lifted her head and stared out of the window, knowing she would be reprimanded soon for her slow work, but no longer caring. As they often did, the new arrivals streamed past behind a wire fence as they were walked to their death.

In the beginning, Lena hadn't been able to watch them. It was too painful knowing their fate, especially when so many of them were children. Many of the women in Canada couldn't eat the extra food they found in pockets, sick to their stomachs that they were eating food from the condemned, as ash clogged the air outside.

Today, she stood and watched as a young boy fell to his knees, his mother desperately trying to get him to move, an even smaller boy on her hip. The woman was sobbing, encouraging to get the child to do as she said, but he wouldn't stop screaming.

Lena looked at the bottle of water she'd found only minutes earlier. She'd had a few sips herself and had planned on taking what was left for Emilia, but she decided in that moment to give the water to the child.

She glanced around and quickly let herself out of the door, hurrying over to the fence.

'Take this water!' she called out, in Slovakian and then in Polish, hoping the mother understood.

But as she threw it, Lena froze. A young woman stepped forwards to help the mother on the other side of the fence, her hand outstretched to help the boy, a girl with chestnut hair a shade darker than her own. *Dana.*

Lena stepped closer, her fingers curling around wire in front of her as she stared at the woman. Could it truly be her?

'*Dana?*' she called.

Her sister looked up at her, her cry of disbelief when she met her gaze sending a stab of pain through Lena so deep that she almost fell to her knees.

'Lena!' she screamed. 'Mama, Papa, it's Lena!'

A sob erupted from inside her as her mother and father turned to face her. She hadn't even realised it was them; when she'd seen Dana, she'd had eyes only for her.

'Lena! What are they doing to us? Where are they taking us?' her mother cried.

'Lena, why are you so thin? Why are you behind wire? What happened to your eye?'

Her tears flowed freely as she reached her arms through the wire, as her sister clutched one hand and her mother the other. But it was her father who truly broke her heart; his face was drained of all colour, his eyes showing his defeat. He knew. He knew he could no longer protect his family, that there was nothing he could do. It was a look she'd seen countless times since arriving; the devastating moment when a person realised their life was no longer theirs.

The guards were coming to see what was happening now, why the line had stopped moving, and Lena knew she didn't have long with her family.

'Lena, we were hiding in the countryside, at our uncle's house, but they found us and brought us here in a cattle cart,' Dana said, her fingers tight around Lena's. 'Why are they doing this? Where are they taking us?'

Lena smiled, even though her body was screaming in pain, choosing in that moment not to scare them. 'It's not so bad here,' she lied. 'We'll be together soon, I promise.'

The guard's scream pierced the air again, his stick striking her father hard across the back.

'*Ocko!*' she cried, as her sister continued to cling to her through the fence.

'Lena, I'm scared.'

'I'm sorry,' Lena whispered back, her eyes filling with tears as her mother pulled her sister and father from the fence. They stumbled away, all of them looking back at her over their shoulders.

When Lena turned, she saw two SS men coming towards her. *Becker.* His face was expressionless, but she saw the way the other guard lifted his stick, prepared for her to resist.

'*Untersturmführer* Becker,' she said, bravely looking him in the eye as her voice wobbled. 'That is my sister. My family have just arrived.'

'Get back to work!' he barked.

The two men stopped near her as she fell to her knees, her hands clasped together. 'Please, please save my sister. I beg of you! You said—'

His big black boot landed squarely on her chest, kicking her to the ground. Dust caught in her throat as she lost her breath, and fought to right herself. Lena looked over her shoulder when she heard a scream, knowing it was her sister, knowing she'd just seen what had happened to Lena.

'Martin, please!' she cried. 'She's only seventeen, *please!*'

He used his stick to strike her face then, her jaw reeling with the impact, but it was when he caught hold of her hair and began to drag her across the dirt that she understood the extent of what he was capable of. She fought against his hold, screamed and kicked and flailed as he continued to haul her behind him, knowing her family could see what was happening to her, as powerless to help her as she was to help them.

'I will teach you to utter my name,' he snarled.

'Please,' she cried. 'Please, do anything to me, but don't let them take my sister.'

Not my Dana. I can't live without Dana, I can't.

CHAPTER TWENTY-EIGHT

EMILIA

'Lena!'

Emilia gasped when she saw the silhouette of a woman standing in the doorway. It took her a second to realise who it was, that it was her Lena. She moved as quickly as her stiff legs would allow, swinging them down from the bunk and catching Lena just before she collapsed to the ground.

The low murmur in their block hushed to silence, as Emilia cradled her, keeping her arms around her as she surveyed her injuries. Lena's lower lip was severely swollen, making it almost impossible for her to shut her mouth, and one of her eyes matched it, leaving barely a slit for her to see through. As she lifted her hand to stroke Lena's hair, she stopped herself, seeing the clumps that were missing, ripped straight from her scalp.

Whoever had kept Lena these past two days had certainly done their best to break her. Emilia could see bruises on her neck, and she hated to think what the rest of her body would look like if she was able to examine her properly.

'Lena, who did this to you?' Emilia spoke in her ear. 'Where have you been?'

Lena just shuddered and leaned in closer to Emilia.

Emilia looked up at the women staring at them from the bunks. They were still silent, still watching. She was certain they weren't envious of Lena now, and she angrily wondered if they finally realised what Lena had been through since she'd arrived, the treatment she'd regularly been subjected to.

'Come on, let's get you into bed.' She helped Lena up, her arms aching with the effort of trying to lift her. Some days it felt as if her spindly arms might snap, the skin stretched over bone now, almost unrecognisable as the strong, supple body she'd arrived with.

Lena didn't speak, but she let Emilia guide her, and some of the other women moved from the bottom bunk to help lift her up. Once she was there, Emilia crawled up behind her, taking the half piece of bread she'd saved from dinner and pressing it into Lena's hand.

'Eat this,' she said quietly.

Lena shut her eyes and turned her head away.

'Please, Lena, you need to have something,' Emilia said, as her own stomach growled at the sight of the food. 'Please. For me.'

Lena didn't move, so Emilia touched a small piece of bread to her lips.

'No,' she croaked, turning her head again.

Emilia tucked the bread back into her top, hoping that she could convince Lena later, and if she couldn't, then she'd eat it herself in the morning.

'Lena, is there anything I can do for you?' she whispered. 'Please, let me know how I can help you.'

A single tear slid from Lena's eye down her cheek.

'Lena,' Emilia murmured, tucking tightly to her, wrapping her arms around her as she tried to give her both comfort and body heat.

'Just let me die,' Lena finally mumbled.

Her words washed over Emilia, the pain in her voice, the shudder that ran through her friend's body into hers.

'Don't say that,' Emilia murmured. 'Remember what we talked about? Remember what we're going to do when we leave here? Your family—'

Lena pulled away from Emilia, her shoulders shrugging forwards, her back hunched.

The next morning, Lena was still silent. Her face looked even worse in the daylight, her skin turning purple as the bruise deepened, and Emilia could see that there was dried blood behind her right ear and covering one of her hands as well.

Emilia walked beside her as they left the block and watched as she grimaced when she went to the toilet. There was little she could have done to ease her pain, but at least if she'd talked to her, she would have known what was wrong, or what was hurting the most.

At breakfast, Lena held her cup of coffee and looked off into the distance, taking a few painful-looking sips before giving her cup to one of the new girls. But despite her silence, she did follow Emilia to the women's hospital block and let a new doctor who'd recently joined them look over her.

Emilia checked the pregnant women in their care, taking pulses, listening to breathing, including one who had come in the night before with severe stomach pains. She would likely be having her baby before the end of the day, and Emilia talked to her for a few minutes, before making her way back to Lena.

'Do you know what happened to her?' the doctor asked in a low voice.

Emilia shook her head. 'She won't speak to me. I wish I knew.'

'I've cleaned her up as best I can, and put salve on her open wounds, but—'

'The same bastard SS man who got me pregnant decided to teach me a lesson, that's what happened to me.'

Emilia exchanged glances with the doctor, before dropping to her knees and taking Lena's hands into hers.

'He raped you, so soon after childbirth?'

Lena turned her face away.

'Lena, may I examine you? Or perhaps if there's damage down there, given how soon—'

Lena looked away, her eyes shut. 'Just leave me.'

'Lena, please,' Emilia said, still holding her hands. 'Let us help you, let us look after you.'

'Why? I have nothing to live for. I'd rather die than let him come back for me.'

Emilia hugged her, as the doctor stood and watched, hovering as if she wanted to be there to help when Lena was ready.

'Lena, you have your family to live for, you—'

As she spoke, Lena turned, her face drained of colour. 'They're all dead, Emilia. I have nothing, *nothing*, to live for any more. Don't you understand? I have *nothing*!'

'Who's dead?' Emilia asked, holding tightly to her hand, trying to understand. 'Who are you talking about, Lena?'

'My family,' Lena said, her voice thick with emotion. 'I've always been able to see the people arriving from the window in the room I work in, I watch them make the long trek, the ones who don't get numbers.'

The ones who are condemned to die. Emilia listened to Lena, scared of what she was about to say.

Lena cried, her body shaking as she whispered.

'I didn't recognise them straight away. I was watching this little boy as he cried, his mother tried to drag him along, but he kept wailing and refusing to move. And then I saw someone step out of line to help.'

Lena looked away again, and Emilia found herself holding her breath.

'They're gone. My family is gone.'

Anger rose in Emilia's throat, as she imagined the scene Lena was describing, listening to the pain her friend had experienced. Now she truly understood why so many women threw their bodies against the electric fence, why they felt there was no reason left to live. There was only so much pain and suffering a person could be subjected to.

'I fought him so hard he ripped out chunks of my hair. Then he used his stick on me. All over me, every part of my body, until I couldn't cry any more. Until I lay there and gave up.'

Emilia shivered at the thought, understanding what he'd done to her body. Lena had only just had a baby, and instead of being allowed to recover, she'd been raped and tortured.

'He told me he'd put another baby in me, that it would be taken just like the last one. And the only thing I could think, the only thing I knew for certain as he had his way with me, was that I'd die before bringing another baby into this world.'

'Lena, you're like a sister to me,' Emilia said. 'If there's anything I can do, anyway I can help you to heal . . .' She swallowed. 'I will do anything you ask of me. *Anything.*'

Lena cleared her throat and stood, as if now that she'd shed her story she no longer wanted to think about it.

'I want to help all the pregnant women,' Lena said, looking Emilia in the eye. 'Let me take the risks, let them kill me if we're discovered.'

'Lena, please,' Emilia said, reaching for her.

But Lena pulled away.

'This is all I have left,' Lena said. 'Please, let me help. Let me do anything that needs to be done to save the babies born here. Let me die here, Emilia, but let it not be for nothing. Let me die saving a child. *Please.*'

Emilia studied her friend, looked over her face and tried to imagine the pain she was suffering.

'All right,' she said. 'All right, we will let you take the risks. But if you want to stop, if it becomes too much—'

Lena's eyes met hers. 'Every termination, every baby born, every tattoo, I want to be part of it all.'

But as Lena stepped away from her, Emilia wondered if she was ever truly going to have her friend back. Lena was broken inside, her body and her mind, and sometimes, Emilia knew, there was no coming back from that kind of pain. That there was nothing wrong with accepting death when there was nothing left to live for.

'There is something else you can do for me.'

'Anything,' Emilia said, before realising that Lena was staring at her knife.

'I want you to cut off my hair,' Lena said.

Emilia nodded.

'Of course.'

It had been days since Emilia had seen Aleksy, and she was pleased when he arrived. Being with Lena, holding her through her nightmares and seeing the pain etched into her face had been almost too much to bear. But Aleksy always managed to make her feel better somehow, reminding her that there were kind men in the world.

'How is she?' Aleksy asked, looking past her to Lena. Emilia watched, too. She was almost unrecognisable with her short tufts of hair sticking up in every direction. Her eye and lip had healed now, a mottled green bruise the only remaining evidence of the trauma she'd been through.

'She's working here every day, assisting me with terminations, although there aren't as many of those now as there were. Same with the labours, she's tireless. She wants to help everyone, and she's always the one who goes to alert Zofia now.'

He nodded, turning his attention to her. 'And you? How are you?'

She smiled back at him. 'I'm alive,' she offered.

'One day,' he said. 'One day, when this place is only a memory—'

There was a shout outside just before the door was flung open, flooding the barracks with light. Emilia squinted, seeing two guards standing there, and she instinctively reached for Aleksy's hand, catching his fingers in hers. Her breath came in little pants, her body shaking. The guards looked around the room.

'There she is.'

Emilia watched in horror as they turned their attention to Lena, who stood, wide-eyed, looking back at them.

'He's not going to be happy with her hair,' one of them said. 'Who did this to you?'

The guard turned to look at her and Aleksy, but Lena spoke up.

'I did it to myself,' she said. '*I* did this.'

'Come on,' the guard said, taking out his stick. 'You're coming with us.'

'No,' Lena said, calmly, as if she'd been ready for them to ask and had already decided she wasn't going.

The other guard laughed and took out his gun, lifting it.

'What did you say?'

'I said *no*.' Lena's nostrils flared, the only indicator that she was scared.

Aleksy tightened his fingers around Emilia's, his silent warning to her to stay still. She was too afraid to move anyway, but as she stared at Lena, as she saw the guard lift his gun and aim it at Lena, it took all her strength not to run to her. To throw her body across hers and protect her friend. Emilia gulped, bile rising in her throat.

She knew what she had to do. She knew she had to stand there, that she was powerless against the guards with their guns, when she didn't have the strength to so much as run at them, but it didn't stop her feeling like a coward.

'She thinks she can refuse!' one of the guards said.

'You would like us to take you here, on the floor?' the other one said. 'In front of your friends?'

Lena looked at her then. She looked past the guards, and her eyes met Emilia's, her smile bittersweet. They stared at one another as if they were the only two people in the room. That beautiful smile that had given Emilia hope when she'd first met her, when they'd first walked together and Lena had shared some of the food she'd found.

Emilia wanted to scream, she could see what was going to happen; she knew in her heart that it was the final time she would see Lena smile.

CHAPTER TWENTY-NINE

LENA

'Take it off.' The guard stepped towards Lena, using his gun to prod at her and inch up her flimsy shirt. '*Now.*'

Lena spat at him, her saliva landing on his face, dripping slowly down his cheek.

'I'm not doing anything for you fucking bastards.' She barely recognised herself as she heard the boom of a deep voice, a voice that made her want to scream for what he'd done to her.

Lena looked over at Emilia, at the truest friend she'd ever had, before lifting her chin and looking instead into the eyes of the man who'd taken everything from her. He walked towards her with such purpose, his black leather boots quickly covering the ground. *This is not a good day.* That's what she would have thought if it were just the two of them, if they were alone and he had that look on his face, his eyes narrowed to half their usual size.

It almost happened in slow motion. Lena looked from Becker to the guard closest to her, at the pistol on his hip, at the way he'd turned slightly away from her when he heard the call of his superior.

This is for my sister. This is for my baby. This is for stealing everything I ever loved from me.

Lena launched forwards, her hand connecting with the gun, lifting it as she stumbled, her bare foot catching on the guard's boot. But she didn't feel the pain of her toes crumpling against the hard leather, or the crack of the other guard's stick against her back. All Lena could see was the man she hated, and as she lifted the gun, their eyes met.

His eyes were no longer narrowed. Now, they were wide, his fear palpable, and she smiled as she squeezed the trigger, as he waited too long to reach for his own, as if not truly believing that she could be capable of such an act.

Lena watched his body fall to the ground and she squeezed the trigger again to make certain she'd killed him, that he wasn't going to rise again. To make sure he would never, ever be able to hurt her again.

But as she stared at his fallen body, she stumbled, bending forwards when a sharp pain pierced her. Lena touched her abdomen, crying out when her palm came away bright red, sticky and wet with her own blood.

'Lena!' The scream sounded too far away, but she knew it was Emilia. She tried to call back to her at the same moment as another bullet entered her stomach and sent her falling.

Lena tried to move, tried in vain to lift herself, as she heard someone calling her. *Dana.* She smiled when her sister's words wrapped around her, as everything went black.

CHAPTER THIRTY

EMILIA

SIX MONTHS LATER

The months after Lena's death were the longest and most pain-ful of Emilia's life. She'd seen death more times than she cared to remember in the past six months, witnessed suffering for the past few years beyond what she could ever have imagined, and mourned the death of her mother just as the war began. But she'd never, ever experienced the pain that she suffered after her friend's brutal, senseless death.

It was a Sunday today, and she'd forced herself to rise, to put one foot in front of the other and go outside. The sun was shining, and she wanted to feel the warmth of it on her body, to try to feel alive again, to remind herself why she needed to live. Almost every day she wondered if it wouldn't be preferable to simply wither away in bed.

'Emilia.'

Aleksy's voice was the most familiar to her in the camp, and she turned to see him ambling towards her. When his hand touched hers, she found herself wishing that he would hold her forever. His friendship had come to mean so much to her, and she couldn't stand the thought of losing him, too.

'Don't look,' he said, as they walked.

The moment he told her not to, of course she did. And he'd been right, she shouldn't have, because it only made her wonder all over again whether it was even worth fighting, whether it was worth the effort for any of them to try to stay alive each day. The bodies on the fence hadn't been removed yet, they wouldn't be until later in the day, a reminder to them all of how bleak their existence was, of how many people had woken before daybreak and decided it was no longer worth the fight.

'I don't think I can go on,' she said, as they turned their backs and let the sunshine touch their faces. 'I can't stand another day here.'

'Your life is too valuable,' he said, his voice barely a whisper, a rasp just like hers was now. They were all severely dehydrated, and it made every word painful to expel.

She blinked back at him. 'But is it?'

'Emilia, without you, who would all those women turn to in their time of need? Who would care for them?'

His words washed over her, and in truth it was the only reason she hadn't chosen to join those women on the fence after Lena's death. Not to mention she knew it would break Aleksy's heart.

'Emilia,' he said, as they stood facing the forest that was the camp's namesake. She looked at the towering birches waving at them in the wind, and wondered if she'd ever be free again. 'I've already lost my wife. I can't lose you, too. I can't.'

She would have cried, but her eyes were bone dry. Every movement, every emotion, hurt her now, but what she could do was lean into him, to show him that she'd heard his words.

'We have to be stronger than we've ever been, we have to survive this,' he whispered. 'For Lena. For her family. For my wife.' His breath shuddered from his lips. 'For my son.'

'I keep seeing her. I keep seeing her standing in front of me. Is that how you feel about your child?' She swallowed. 'About your wife?'

'There was nothing you could have done. There was nothing any of us could have done to save Lena.' His face crumpled. 'My family were killed because of my actions, but could I have truly made any other choice? Could I have lived with myself if I hadn't tried to save everyone I could? We have done our best in the face of evil, Emilia. We must hold on to that.'

'Then why do I still feel like a coward for not doing more?'

Aleksy pulled her against the side of the barracks, against his chest, holding her as she tried to catch her breath against him. It had been so long since she'd been held by anyone; since Lena had died, she'd missed the feel of her body tucked close to hers at night, missed the way they'd held hands after dark to comfort one another, when the memories of what they'd left behind had become too much. But now, with Aleksy's arms around her, she realised that she wasn't alone. Not yet. Not with him still alive and prepared to fight for her.

'Keep telling the women your stories, Emilia. Keep reminding them of what they have to live for,' he said. 'We have to keep the past alive, and believe that we will have a future. That those of us who survive this place can hold someone to account, one day, somehow. That their lives count for something.'

'What if it's too painful to think about the past? When we don't know if the past will still be waiting for us when we return?'

He held her hand, carefully, as if he were holding a bird in his palm. 'The lives we saved here, the things we did to make the lives of others better in some small way, we can't ever forget that, Emilia. If we survive this place, at least we will be able to tell others what happened here. At least we might be able to find those babies that were taken, to finish what we started.'

'I miss her so much,' she said, as a single tear leaked from her eye. 'It's almost impossible some days without her.'

'We will never forget her. We will never forget how brave she was.'

'Or what she did with me, what she risked to help me.'

They both smiled at the memory of their friend, and Emilia leaned into Aleksy, her left arm wrapped around herself to protect her thin frame from the biting wind.

Aleksy lifted her hand, the one he'd been holding, and pressed his chapped, dry lips to her skin. He was a good man, and she only hoped that if they did survive, she'd get to see him again.

'I'm going to make you a promise, Emilia,' he said. 'That if we both survive here, I will come looking for you.'

She smiled at him, her eyes meeting his. 'I'd like that, Aleksy.'

Before they parted, she studied his face and asked him a question she'd held back for some time.

'Why did you risk your life to save me, that very first day?' she asked.

His smile lit his eyes. 'Because you reminded me that all wasn't lost. Or perhaps you reminded me of the person I once was, before all of this.'

Aleksy held her gaze for a long moment, before shuffling away, and she didn't turn until he'd disappeared from her line of sight entirely.

It had been a year almost to the day since Lena had died. Keeping track of the days had seemed impossible in her first months at the camp, but since Lena had passed, Emilia had scratched a mark on the wall of the hospital barracks. But when she'd arrived today, counting the marks as she always did, she was startled by the sound of gunshots. One after the other. The last time she'd heard that, the

SS guards had been celebrating the new year by shooting a hundred prisoners for fun.

'Quickly, we need to hide,' she said to the patients who filled the beds. 'Something terrible is happening out there.'

The guards very rarely fired that many shots – they almost never executed large groups of prisoners in the open. They preferred to do it against the wall, closer to the crematoria, if they were going to murder en masse with their guns, so it wasn't so far to move the bodies.

'What's happening?' someone cried.

Another patient with a baby was whimpering, but Emilia hushed them all.

'We must be silent. Curl against the far walls, use the blankets to hide yourselves,' she said. 'I'll try to find out what's happening out there.'

She'd barely made it to the door when Aleksy appeared, his body low to the ground.

'Get inside!' he ordered.

'Why? What are they doing? What—'

He pushed her through the door. 'You have your knife?'

She nodded.

'Keep it close to you, and hide. We both need to hide.'

They curled together onto an unused bunk, pulling the blanket up over them, a blanket that she recalled Lena smuggling out of Canada for one of the pregnant mothers in her care a month or so before her death.

'They're executing hundreds, right out there in the open,' Aleksy whispered. 'And thousands more are being rounded up; they're marching them straight down the road and out of the gates.'

'Away from here?' *Away from Auschwitz?* 'But why?'

Aleksy's breath was warm against the back of her neck, his arms wrapped protectively around her.

'I don't know,' he said. 'I honestly don't know.'

It seemed like hours as they lay there, listening to gunshots and the shouts of guards. Voices came close to their door and then disappeared. But it was when she smelt smoke that Emilia wriggled from Aleksy's grip, needing to see what was going on. There was a small window, but it was covered in grime.

'Emilia,' Aleksy cautioned, as the baby in the block with them began to cry.

'I need to see,' she said. 'What if they set us on fire?'

When she peered out of the door, it wasn't the blocks near them that were on fire, nor the crematoria, but Canada. The place where Lena had worked for most of her time at Auschwitz-Birkenau was going up in flames, the black smoke curling into the sky.

But most alarming of all was the bodies littered everywhere. It appeared they'd been shot as they ran, as they'd tried to take cover from the gun-toting guards.

'Emilia?'

She stood back so he could look past her at the devastation, at a sight she could never have imagined.

'Where is everyone?' he asked.

She took his hand and stepped tentatively outside, slowly looking around.

'I think they've gone.'

A single gunshot echoed out, and Emilia looked up and saw that there was still a guard in one of the towers. She pulled Aleksy back into the cabin with her and shut the door, her back pressed against it.

'We need to stay hidden,' she said. 'If they forget about us, if they don't know we're here . . .'

Aleksy nodded, but then he started to cough, and she led him back to the bed, wishing she had something she could give him. But when they were tucked against the far wall again, she lifted his top to check his skin, seeing the tell-tale rash of typhus on his abdomen.

'No,' she whispered. *The illness that he'd used to save so many. It wouldn't be fair for typhus to take his life.*

He took her hand, his eyes swimming.

'You made me a promise, Aleksy Gorski, a promise that I'm going to make you keep.'

He leaned heavily against her as he began to cough again, and she held him as tightly as her weakened arms could muster. Another round of shots rang out, each one making her shut her eyes tighter, praying that the next bullet didn't come through their door.

CHAPTER THIRTY-ONE

EMILIA

LONDON, 1995

FRIDAY

As they sat, their dinner plates still on the table, the recorder long since turned off, Lucy poured them all another glass of red wine. It had been a day full of emotion, but after so long keeping her memories buried, Emilia felt lighter somehow, as if now that she'd finally spoken of the past, she'd in turn let it go. Although, there was a pain inside her, a catch in her chest that she knew she'd hold until her very last breath.

Lucy smiled at her and Emilia settled back into her chair, grateful she'd chosen to stay. Earlier, she'd almost wished she'd been alone with Hannah, but now she was pleased her daughter had been there to hear what she had to say.

'Mum, what of your Aleksy? Did you ever see one another again? Did he survive to see the liberation of Auschwitz?'

'We were so fortunate not to join the death march, that we were able to hide and stay behind, and we didn't even know then what would happen to all those prisoners,' she said. 'But we were only just alive, like so many others, we were like walking skeletons by then. There was a saying back then, that most of those still living had one foot in the grave, barely clinging on to life. Not many were left behind, the rest were marched out of the camp gates into the snow, but we would have refused to leave those who needed us, and I think they simply didn't bother with the sick or dying.'

Emilia pushed back her chair then and slowly rose, walking to the fire on unsteady legs and taking a photo frame from the mantel. She stared into the eyes of the man she'd married, imagining him beside her now. She could almost feel his hand resting on her shoulder, his warm breath against her cheek while he whispered in her ear.

'And when the soldiers came to liberate the camp? Was Aleksy still alive then?'

Emilia looked at her daughter for a long moment, closing her eyes. She saw him in her mind, as she looked into a dark-brown gaze that she'd never forget for as long as she lived.

It's time. After all these years, it's time our story is told, Aleksy. I only wish you were still here beside me. I wish Hannah could have met the man who risked everything to save so many women and their babies. I wish our daughter could have looked into your eyes and known what you were capable of, what you did for so many.

'He did survive,' she finally said. She turned, placing the photograph on the table, her hand shaking as she let it go. 'Lucy, Aleksy was your father.'

She watched Lucy staring at the photograph before looking up at her, her eyes shining with disbelief.

'My father? But Mum, all these years, and his name, I . . .'

Emilia sat beside her daughter, reaching for her hand. *I wish you were here to tell her with me. I wish it wasn't me telling our story alone.* 'Your father wanted to start a new life,' she told her. 'After the war, we'd both lost everything. Everyone we'd ever loved had perished, we only had one another, and we decided to start again.'

'So he changed his name?' Hannah asked.

'He did,' she said. 'He felt it was the only way to live life again, to start afresh as new people. So he took his middle name, which was Jakub, but he changed the spelling to Jacob. I wasn't ready to give up my name, but I simply became Emmy to almost everyone.'

'It was his choice to never speak of your past?' Lucy asked.

She sighed. 'It was, although I was happy to forget, too. Sometimes, though, late at night when everyone else was asleep, I'd hear him cry, and we'd hold each other and say the names of all those we remembered, all those women who disappeared and never came back. And we'd remember Lena and wish she were still with us.' Emilia paused. 'We lived our lives for those women, knowing how fortunate we were to have survived, but also trying to repent for the part we played, in the babies who never had a chance to live. For the guilt we felt, even though we both knew with all our hearts that we did what we could.'

'To the mothers and babies of Auschwitz,' Hannah said, quietly.

'To the mothers and babies of Auschwitz,' Emilia and Lucy repeated, as they all gently touched their glasses together and took a sip of their wine.

They were the women she'd never forget. Even a thousand years of living could never erase the memory of what she'd experienced, or the lives she'd seen extinguished as if they'd never deserved the right to live in the first place.

She only wished Aleksy could have lived long enough to see the woman standing before her, one of the babies they'd once risked their lives for, who'd survived despite it all.

I'm so proud of what we did, Aleksy. I only wish we could have one more moment together, one more cup of tea, one more evening of standing side by side in the kitchen.

Aleksy was another part of her memory that never evaded her, and as much as it pained her, she knew just how fortunate they'd been to not only survive, but to live the beautiful life they'd had the privilege of enjoying together, when so many others they'd known and loved had not.

EPILOGUE

EMILIA

POLAND, DECEMBER 1945

The knock at the door was unexpected. Many of the houses around hers were derelict, the gardens that were once plentiful now forlorn, and many of the neighbours she'd known for her entire life had either perished or hadn't yet returned home. Emilia hadn't encountered a visitor more than once or twice since reclaiming her home.

She walked slowly to the door, her body still moving as if she were a much older woman, despite the weight that she'd slowly added to her bones over the past months. Emilia clasped a hand to the shawl around her shoulders as she opened the door. But her hand quickly fell away and instead covered her mouth when she saw who was standing there.

'Emilia.'

His voice. She gripped the door as her legs wobbled, fearing she might slip to the ground as his familiar voice washed over her.

'Aleksy?' she whispered. 'It's really you?'

He stepped forwards, holding out a hand, tears brimming in his eyes. 'It is.'

Emilia reached for him, her fingers clasping his, palms pressing together. She remembered the last time they'd held hands, the moment the camp had been liberated; it already felt like a lifetime ago.

'*Emilia?*'

This time he said her name as a question, and he seemed to search her face as she blinked back at him. She slowly lifted her other hand and placed it against his cheek, her fingers trembling when she touched his skin. His arms slowly came around her as hesitantly as she'd reached to touch him, and they stood like that for a long moment, slightly apart and looking at one another, until she eventually stepped into his embrace, her cheek to his chest.

There was so much she wanted to say, to ask him, but the emotion of seeing him again seemed to have stripped her of the ability to speak. She felt Aleksy's body tremble and she clutched his shirt; they stood together and cried at her front door.

When their eyes were no longer damp and she found the courage to step away from him, Emilia stared bravely into Aleksy's eyes.

'I have never been so happy to see anyone,' she said. 'Truly, I never thought I'd set eyes upon you again.'

Aleksy nodded, and she took his hand and led him through her home.

'How?' she asked, when they stepped into her kitchen. 'How are you here?' She gestured for him to sit and put water on to boil, before sitting beside him and folding her hands in her lap, not sure whether to reach for him again or not.

'You told me about your village.' He smiled. 'I still had the image of your favourite place by the lake, the one I drew, in my mind.'

The picture. Of course. 'You've been in hospital all this time?'

He smiled again. 'No. I *was* in hospital, I was suffering from typhus when we were liberated, and my recovery took months. But after that, I stayed on to help there.'

'Of course you did.' She sighed. 'You would give the clothes off your back to a person in need.'

'I couldn't bear the thought of going home, the very idea of going back to my house, of remembering what had happened there, of seeing it . . .'

Emilia watched as he looked away, clearing his throat, his pain palpable.

'And your family?' he asked, turning his attention back to her.

She shook her head. 'All gone. My brother was killed in an ambush from what I've been able to piece together, and my father passed away shortly before the liberation.'

'I'm sorry,' Aleksy said.

'So am I.' She glanced out of the window, almost able to picture her mother standing by the washing line and her father bent over in the garden. 'Sometimes I wonder how I survived Auschwitz, only to come home to find my entire family gone.'

'Emilia,' Aleksy said, leaning forwards in his chair and taking her hands in his. 'I came here because I couldn't imagine a life without you in it, because I miss you terribly.'

Tears filled her eyes again, although she quickly blinked them away. 'I feel the same,' she said. They'd known each other through too much hardship for her not to be honest with him, not to make it clear how she felt in return.

'Emilia, what I'm going to ask you, I wish it could be more romantic, but there is a pain inside me that hasn't yet healed.' She listened as he took a deep breath, his eyes never leaving hers.

She wasn't certain what he was about to say, but she wanted to hear the rest. And when he reached for her, she took his hand.

'I want to start a new life, somewhere far from here, somewhere I can move on from the past and try to live my life again. We survived the unthinkable, you and I, and it doesn't seem right not to at least try to make the most of it, to live for all those who perished.'

Aleksy touched her face, his fingertips tracing from her cheekbone down to her jaw, before falling away.

'Emilia, will you marry me?'

She stared into eyes that were so familiar to her, eyes that had found hers at some of the most brutal, traumatic moments of her life. The eyes of the man who'd become her closest friend during her last months of incarceration.

'I promise I will do everything I can to give you the life you deserve, to be the husband you deserve,' he said. 'To love you and care for you, for as long as we have together. To build a new life and leave the past behind.'

'Yes,' she replied, not sure whether to smile or cry. 'Yes, Aleksy, I will be your wife.'

His smile made his eyes crinkle in the corners; his face was fuller than it had been, although still haunted by their time incarcerated. But it was the tentative way he leaned towards her that filled her heart, the way he waited for her, showing her the same kindness that he'd shown countless times at the camp. And she knew then that marrying Aleksy would give her a chance to move on from a past that might otherwise consume her.

Emilia closed the distance between them and gently pressed her lips to his, their touch feather light, before pulling away slightly and touching their foreheads together.

'Will you leave here with me?' he asked.

She closed her eyes, seeing her family, knowing they'd want her to live her life instead of clinging to their ghosts in the house they'd once shared.

'I want to live,' she told him. 'I want to live for Lena, for my parents, for my brother. I want to live my life for all of them.'

'So do I, Emilia. And the only way I know how, is with you.'

Despite their closeness, the bond they'd shared at Auschwitz, Emilia hadn't ever allowed herself to dream of what Aleksy could one day be to her, hadn't been able to think past their daily survival.

'I would like to cook for you,' Emilia said, smiling at Aleksy as she stood and brushed her hand across his shoulder. 'All those years imagining food, now we can actually eat it.'

As Aleksy laughed, coming to stand beside her and tying an apron around her waist, she turned in his arms and stared up into his eyes.

'We can be happy, you and I,' she said. 'Despite it all, despite the pain, despite our loss, we will make a life together.'

He smiled down at her. 'For all those we've lost.'

She leaned into him and pressed her lips to his again, before whispering against his skin. 'For all those we've lost.'

AUTHOR'S NOTE

I want to start by saying that although much of this story is inspired by, and based on, fact, it is very much a work of fiction. The topic of Auschwitz deserves to be treated with the utmost sensitivity, and as an author it was a daunting prospect to write about it. When I first came up with the concept for this book, it was my editor Victoria who gave me the confidence to write it. I was worried not only about the subject matter, but in my ability to write a story that balanced the horrors of Auschwitz with a sense of hope – that even in the midst of such atrocities, some people did live to tell their stories of what happened at the infamous camp. Their tales of survival are exceptional, and creating a fictional story inspired by history felt like a terrifying prospect. In all honesty though, the moment I started writing, I knew it was a story that I needed to tell – these characters felt so special and real to me! I never forget my characters, even years later I still think of them sometimes, but I know that Emilia, Lena and Aleksy in particular will stay with me in a way that others have not. Their story was steeped in such tragedy, but something about the way they revealed themselves to me, the way they spoke to me, feels truly unique.

Aleksy and Emilia's story was inspired by many incredible people that I discovered during my research. I spent months researching Polish doctors, midwives and social workers who spent time at

Auschwitz, and who risked their lives to save others, both inside and outside the camp, and others who worked tirelessly from their villages throughout the war. I'd like to mention some of those real-life historical figures here, in case you'd like to research them further: Polish doctor Eugene Lazowski was determined to save as many people as possible, and managed to fool the Nazis into believing that his town was in the midst of a typhus outbreak. It kept the Germans away for some time, and he did this by creating false positive results, injecting *Proteus* OX19 directly into patients. Part of Aleksy's earlier story was very much inspired by Lazowski.

Before her incarceration, Polish midwife Stanislawa Leszczyńska smuggled false documents and food to Jews inside the Warsaw Ghetto. She delivered thousands of babies in the worst conditions at Auschwitz, and refused to drown Jewish babies. It is estimated that of the 3,000 babies she delivered, all of the mothers survived childbirth, but half of the infants were drowned, 1,000 died of starvation and about 30 survived. The remaining babies were sent to Nakło for Germanisation.

I was also hugely inspired by Hungarian Jewish gynaecologist Gisella Perl, who performed terminations for pregnant women at Auschwitz, to save their lives and avoid them from being experimented on. She had no tools or anaesthesia, but she was prepared to do anything she could.

And last but not least, I have to mention Irena Sendler, a Polish social worker who saved the lives of more than 2,500 Jewish children. She smuggled them from the ghettos and risked her own life over and over again, before finally being caught. I'm pleased to say that she survived. Having been sentenced to death at the infamous Pawiak prison, her fellow Żegota (Polish resistance) activists managed to bribe officials to release her.

ACKNOWLEDGEMENTS

For those of you who've read my books before, you'll know that I frequently thank the same group of people, and this time is no different! First, I need to say a huge thank you to my editor, Victoria Oundjian. Victoria, you gave me the confidence to write this book, and to really push myself with my writing, and I'm so grateful that you did! It was a very dark, emotional book to write, but I'm so proud of the end result. To editor Sophie Wilson, thank you for helping me to shape this book, for knowing just how far to push me while at the same time offering such genuine encouragement. The three of us have worked on so many books together now and I'm so grateful to have you both in my corner! I'd also like to extend my thanks to copy-editor Sadie Mayne for her extraordinary attention to detail, as well as proofreader Swati Gamble.

To my team at Amazon Publishing UK, thank you! This is my tenth historical novel I've written under the Lake Union imprint, and I couldn't imagine a better home for my books. Thanks to Sammia Hamer for having the confidence in me so many years ago when we first worked together, and to my author relations team for always being there. Thank you also to my long-time agent, Laura Bradford, for your ongoing support and advice.

I would also like to say a special thank you to author Yvonne Lindsay, the absolute best daily writing partner! How would I ever have written this book without you making me set the timer each day? And to authors Natalie Anderson and Nicola Marsh, thanks for all the emails and daily support!

To my family, thank you for helping me to live my dream. To my husband Hamish, thanks for listening to my endless discussions about my books; to my boys, Mack and Hunter, for always understanding when I have to 'write just one more sentence'; and to my parents, Maureen and Craig, for their ongoing support.

And finally, thank YOU, my amazing readers! It is because of you that I get to write every day, to create characters and write the stories of my heart.

Soraya x

Read on for an exclusive extract from Soraya M. Lane's novel *The London Girls.*

PROLOGUE

London, 29 December 1940

Smoke curled through the air, threatening to choke Ava as she slowly opened her eyes. She reached out a hand, fumbling in the dark, clawing at the ground as she tried to drag her body from the hard road beneath her.

Where am I?

She blinked, the black skyline in the far distance punctuated by large, rising clouds of white smoke that she knew could only mean one thing. *Bombs are falling on London.*

The ringing in her ears was so loud she could barely think; a high-pitched scream that made it almost impossible for her to piece together what had happened.

Ava finally hauled herself up, frantic now as she realised she'd come off her motorcycle on the road and could be hit by a vehicle at any moment. The blackout meant that the roads were the most dangerous place to be as night fell, with most vehicles forced to drive without lights. She couldn't remember what had happened, how she'd ended up on the ground, her body flung so far from her bike. Had she hit something? Had a bomb been dropped near her?

I was riding straight and then . . . Her mind felt like a sieve, unable to piece together the moments that had left her on the ground.

She searched for her torch, barely able to see as she shuffled across the road. Eventually her foot connected with something hard and she bent to collect it, grateful to discover it was what she'd been looking for. She turned it on, banging it against her leg when it didn't immediately work, and then suddenly there was a pool of light around her, illuminating the crash. *There was a tree.* It all came rushing back to her then: the explosion that had sent her careering sideways; the fallen tree trunk she'd seen too late; swerving across the road, her front wheel clipping the trunk and sending both her and the motorcycle flying up into the air.

Ava's breath caught in her throat, rasping as she hurried to inspect her bike. She wiped at her face, eyes stinging as she hauled her motorcycle up, her light positioned between her teeth now, and desperately tried to start it. But it was a waste of time; the front wheel was pushed back into the frame, and even if she could have started the engine, she never could have ridden it. It was a mangled mess.

She hauled the motorcycle off the road, arms screaming in pain as she used all her strength to move it, hoping it would look salvageable come morning, and she checked the satchel across her body, sliding her hand inside to make sure the document was still there. Her head was spinning and she lifted her hand to it, wondering if perhaps she'd hit it. When her hand came away sticky with blood, she realised there was a good reason for how woozy she felt. Her head had started to pound and she was finding it difficult to balance, let alone walk, her ears still ringing and making it almost impossible to think. She stood in the dark, her light turned off now for fear of being seen from the sky as more booms echoed out, more than she'd ever heard before, and she tried to ground herself, tried to keep her feet steady as she focused on breathing in and out.

You deliver those documents, even if it kills you.

Ava had never forgotten the words relayed to them during their training, and as she set off down the road on foot, her canvas satchel firmly across her body, bombs falling behind her and wreaking havoc on the city she loved, she wondered if it was to be her last dispatch. Every time she was sent out with a memo, she knew she was carrying an order or piece of information considered crucial to the war that was highly time-sensitive; they all knew they were risking their lives every single time they set out. She'd just been lucky up until now.

She forced her legs into a run, like a newborn foal trying to gain its balance as she stumbled along, determined to do her job even if it took her all night. How much time had passed? She wracked her brain, trying to remember where she'd been, how long she'd been riding for before the crash.

Devonport. You were trying to get to the shipyards at Devonport, in Plymouth. You know the route like the back of your own hand. You can do this.

She stopped for a moment, turning her light on to get her bearings again. She was still miles away, but so long as she could walk, if she could just keep moving, she could still make it before morning. *I'm not going to let anyone down. I can do this.*

Another boom sounded out so loudly that she felt it reverberate through her feet, the ground shuddering with the force of it as she propelled herself forward again, as she refused to accept defeat. But in that moment there was something scaring her more than the bombs; she could smell smoke, and it was becoming thick in the air, filling her nostrils, sending a shiver down her spine as she realised what was happening.

London wasn't just being bombed. It was on fire.

If ever there was a night she was in danger of losing her life, it was tonight.

PART ONE

CHAPTER ONE

THREE MONTHS EARLIER

AVA

Ava stood in front of Norfolk House, running one palm down her tailored navy uniform to smooth any creases. She'd caught the Tube and then walked from the station as she did every morning, and she wished she could have lingered a little longer in the morning sun. Two weeks ago she'd been moved from the Navy section to a temporary posting, on loan to a dashing general who had a penchant for working late into the night. The hours were long, which meant she was frequently exhausted, but she'd loved every minute – working so closely with a man like him wasn't exactly a hardship. Her heart skipped a beat as she walked, the way it always did when she knew she was about to see him.

She squared her shoulders and entered the building, which was already a hive of activity. There were men and women from all three services stationed there and it didn't seem to matter what time of the day she was there, it was always busy – war never slept.

'Morning,' someone called out as she headed for the stairs.

Ava smiled at a fellow Wren, their fashionable Women's Royal Naval Service uniforms setting them apart from the other working women in the building. She knew it was the not-so-secret reason why so many young women wanted to join the Navy – because the uniforms were so smart – and she'd heard the waiting list was a mile long now. If only she could tell them all just how much work the job actually was, it might reduce the list by half. But she knew many of the girls would still apply, simply because they weren't likely to encounter any objection from their parents. It had certainly been that way for her; her mother loved bragging to her friends that her daughter was a Wren, and her father had been more than happy for her to join. As far as they were concerned, it was the most prestigious posting a woman in London could have.

Ava smiled to herself as she pushed open the door to the section she'd been assigned, walking through to General Armstrong's office. She hesitated, lifting her hand to knock on the open door before entering. As he did every morning, her boss waved her in before she even had the chance to tap her knuckles against the wood, somehow sensing her presence – it wouldn't have mattered if she'd arrived two hours early, she would bet he'd already be there.

'Good morning, sir,' Ava said, making her way to her desk and setting her things down, lingering just a moment longer than necessary when she felt him watching her.

'Morning, sailor.'

She giggled, feeling a familiar heat in her cheeks as his eyes appraised her. He'd said it so many times now that she shouldn't still find it amusing, but for some reason she loved the way he called her *sailor*. In the beginning, Ava had wondered if he simply couldn't remember her name, and it wasn't lost on her that, despite being part of the Navy, she was never going to see the water, but she loved their little morning joke all the same.

'Sir, the Chief of Staff's conference begins in thirty minutes,' she said, forcing herself to keep a straight face. 'I have all your notes from yesterday evening ready for you.' She slowly walked around and then leaned over him, straightening the papers on his desk. 'Would you like a cup of tea beforehand?'

General Armstrong sat back in his chair, and she could tell his eyes never left her. 'You always seem to know just what I need,' he said. 'But a half-teaspoon of sugar today, sailor. Just don't tell my wife, she'd be furious if she knew.'

'Your secret's safe with me,' Ava said with a smile. *Sugar in your tea isn't the only secret I'm helping you keep from your wife; I doubt she'd appreciate the way you're looking at me right now, either.*

Ava left her bag by her chair and quickly headed to their staffroom to make his tea with the requested half-spoon of sugar instead of his usual carefully measured quarter. He had a secret jar that she'd taken on her way past his desk; she'd never asked where it came from although she guessed the black market, as he always managed to keep it more than half-full. She'd missed being in the Navy section with the other Wrens to start with, but the general had certainly made her time with him interesting. Whenever she was around him, her pulse raced and her stomach fluttered; for her it had been love at first sight. The moment she'd walked into his office – his dark brown eyes never leaving hers as they were introduced, his hand holding hers for a second longer than was polite – she'd fallen for him. She knew in her heart that he felt the same, especially when he came up with excuses to keep her late each night, always offering her his driver to ensure she got home safely. As far as she was concerned, it was only a matter of time before he told her how he truly felt – surely he didn't lend his chauffeur-driven car to just anyone? She only hoped he made his feelings clear before her time working for him came to an end.

Ava was back at her desk within minutes, shuffling papers and making sure she had everything for the meeting, in between quick gulps of her own hot drink. From the moment their meeting began, she'd be taking notes and typing, the day always a blur of preparing for the next meeting of section heads, and as much as she knew the general liked her, she was also well aware of his expectations when it came to her work. The more she did for him, the more secret smiles she received when they were alone.

Soon they were making their way downstairs, Ava following a few steps behind the general as he greeted countless people by name until they were ushered into the large meeting room. There were as many women as men seated, all with pens poised to begin taking notes in shorthand. Despite the glamorous uniforms, the Wrens stationed at Norfolk House were doing little more than secretarial work.

The meeting began like it always did, and Ava did her job quickly and efficiently, barely digesting what was being said as she recorded everything for the general, until one particular memo caught her attention. She looked up with interest.

'The Navy has settled on the absurd notion of recruiting *women* as motorcycle dispatch riders, to deliver memos throughout England,' one of the men in attendance said. 'It's causing quite the stir amongst some of the ranks, but we do need to free up more men to be posted offshore. They're proposing to recruit from our existing Wrens, although I don't expect they'll have much luck. What kind of woman would volunteer to be out in the dark of night riding a *motorcycle*?'

Some of the other men chuckled and spoke amongst themselves, as if it were the most ridiculous idea they'd ever heard, but Ava sat ramrod-straight, her attention suddenly razor-sharp. She could barely restrain herself from interrupting to ask for more. She knew that women were flying planes and doing all sorts of unexpected work to free up men for service, but Wrens riding motorcycles? Now that was something she most definitely wanted to know more about! Her parents would be furious with her for even thinking it, which was one of the reasons she liked the idea of it so much, and she also liked the 'out at night' part. Independence wasn't something often extended to her by her father, but these women would have the cover of *work* to keep them out at all times. She chewed on her bottom lip as she thought it through, imagining the freedom such a job would afford her.

'We'll be circulating the memo presently to see what interest there is, but we're expecting only a handful of capable riders to apply. I doubt it'll be a position that's easy to fill, although from what I'm told there are a few speedway riders they've already begun with.'

'Women capable of riding motorcycles? I'd say it will be an impossible position to fill!' someone called out. 'What next? Shall we send them to the front lines too?'

Ava glanced at her general, desperately hoping he'd say something in support of women, but when he looked up, he seemed to find the idea as absurd as all the other men in the room did. Her heart sank. She'd somehow hoped he'd think differently.

'Good luck to them,' he muttered. 'They're certainly going to need it.'

'Meeting adjourned,' the bushy-moustached admiral in charge announced. 'See you all this evening.'

The meeting over, Ava filed her papers and followed her boss, upset with him for making it sound as if no woman would be capable of such a job. She glanced around at the other women to see if anyone else looked as excited as she felt, exhilarated by what had been announced, but no one so much as returned her gaze, all busy with their own workload and trotting after the men they were taking notes for. Typical; something exciting was announced for women, and everyone just carried on as normal, without a second thought.

I could do it, though. Excitement built inside her as she hurried down the halls, her low heels clicking as she failed to keep up with the general's long stride. *I could apply to be one of those women. There's no reason why it can't be me. What an adventure it would be! And then I'd be free to sneak off before or after my shifts to see him without anyone knowing my whereabouts.* All this time she'd been worried she wouldn't be able to see him any more when her time working for him came to an end, but this would certainly give her the opportunity.

'Sailor, I can hear you thinking all the way back there. What is it?'

She looked up, surprised to see that the general wasn't even looking at her as he spoke. Did he have eyes in the back of his head?

'Something on your mind?' he asked.

'Nothing, sir. Just thinking about the, ah – the notes I have to prepare for you.' She grimaced, knowing how easily he'd see through her lie. *Will he think it's a good idea, once I explain it to him?*

When they reached his office, the general blocked her way, frowning as he looked down at her.

'I wouldn't like to see you get hurt, sailor. Motorcycles are death traps,' he said. 'Besides, it'd be a disappointment to lose a girl like you to such an unladylike job. I'd miss seeing you around the office, and it would be such a shame for you to give up that uniform when you fill it out so nicely.'

Ava blushed at the comment. 'Sir, you're a married man! I don't think your wife would appreciate you being so forward.'

She'd had to say it, even though her stomach was dancing. *Is he teasing me, or does he truly want to be with me?* She had to know.

'Ava, my marriage is all but over. It's merely a formality.'

She gulped. 'You're truly free to do as you please?'

The general laughed. 'Do I look like a man who needs permission to do as he pleases?'

Ava gazed up and into his dark brown eyes, his hair perfectly combed from his face, the smell of his oaky aftershave filling her nostrils. She lifted her chin defiantly, despite her nerves at being so close to him, despite not being entirely certain of herself around him. 'No sir, you do not.'

She was well-used to men who liked having the upper hand – she'd grown up with one after all – but the general had certainly surprised her with his directness.

'So, can I stop worrying about you running off and riding a motorcycle?'

'You'll barely see me once I'm back downstairs, so it won't matter what job I have,' she said, trying to sound bright, not liking that he was telling her what to do all of a sudden. She hoped her attempt at lightening the situation would work. 'I think riding motorcycles sounds like quite the adventure actually, and you haven't even seen me in trousers before. You might find you like it.' She didn't have the nerve yet to tell him why the job might work to their advantage, hoping she hadn't read the situation wrong.

'I doubt very much that I'd prefer a pretty girl like you in trousers,' he muttered.

He didn't say anything else, but she could sense his disapproval resting like a heavy cloak over her shoulders. Ava settled into her chair, ignoring it as best she could, and began typing up the notes from the meeting, at the same time trying not to get carried away with her thoughts. But a motorcycle dispatch rider? A shiver of anticipation ran through her as she imagined herself on a bike, racing around London delivering messages, being free. Before the war, her aspirations hadn't amounted to more than finding a dashing man to marry and escaping the tense atmosphere of her parents' house, but now she found herself loving the freedom of having a job and doing things she'd never dreamed of doing before.

She smiled to herself as she typed, forcing herself to slow down lest she make an error and have to redo the memorandum all over again.

Somehow, she needed to find out more. Perhaps she could create an excuse to go back to the Navy section and beg the other Wrens to find out information for her? Surely she wasn't the only one excited about the opportunity?

'Sailor?'

She cleared her throat and glanced back. 'Yes, sir?'

'Have you ever actually ridden a motorcycle before?'

Ava kept her composure, not even turning to face him. She was surprised he was still thinking about it. 'No sir, I haven't.'

'Well, good, that's one less thing for me to worry about. I doubt you'd even stand a chance.'

Ava let out a long, slow breath, not wanting him to know how badly she wanted it, or how much she hated being spoken to like that. As a child, she'd liked to defy anyone who underestimated her, and nothing had changed since then. But she refused to let his words sting, not before he knew one of the main reasons she was considering it in the first place. He'd shown her so much respect in the past, which was why his rebuke about her abilities hurt all the more. It was only days ago he'd told her she was so pretty and clever, and now he suddenly didn't think she was even capable of learning something new! *Just say it. Tell him why you really want to do it.*

'Do you remember when you asked me to meet you late one night, and I had to decline?' she asked, turning in her chair and keeping her voice low.

His smile told her that he definitely remembered; it had been her first Friday on the job, the first time she'd wondered if he was possibly as smitten with her as she was with him.

'Well, imagine if I had *this* job? I'd have an excuse to be out every night if I needed one. My parents wouldn't know a thing about my whereabouts, and I'd be free to do as I pleased after dark.' She lowered her voice to a whisper. 'I have to admit, it's one of the reasons I was so immediately drawn to the job.'

She noticed the way his eyebrows raised, as if he was suddenly far more interested in her idea, and a little thrill went through her as she imagined saying yes to him next time he asked and arriving at his townhouse. She bet he wouldn't doubt her ability to ride a motorcycle if it meant she was more available to see him.

'Back to work,' he said, going back to his own papers. 'We still have a full morning ahead of us. But it's certainly sounding far more promising now that you put it that way.'

'Will you give me leave to apply then?' she asked, holding her breath, hoping she hadn't pushed him too far.

His eyes met hers and he nodded, but she knew what his long gaze meant. His permission was clearly in exchange for her saying yes next time he asked her to visit after hours, and it sent a shiver of anticipation through her body.

Ava fought against a smile as she went back to her typing, wondering how difficult it would be to apply, and then how difficult it would be to convince her parents to let her take part. Her father would likely explode; his temper was a beast at the best of times.

Riding motorcycles sounded like more fun than she'd ever had in her life before, and if it gave her something exhilarating to do each day, then as far as she was concerned, she'd be a fool not to apply. She closed her eyes for a moment and imagined the general opening his door to her, the look in his eyes as she stepped into his home after dark. Perhaps then he'd finally make his move and show her exactly how he felt, or even invite her to stay.

———— ◦◦◦◦◦◦ ————

Ava hurried downstairs, her heels beating a fast clack on the hard floor as she rushed into the Navy section, head down as she made for the tea room. On her way she saw some of the other Wrens look up and she inclined her head, beckoning them to follow her. From the corner of her eye she saw two of the women rise, whispering excuses as they followed her, and she only hoped that none of their superiors noticed her and questioned her presence. She had no good reason to be downstairs, and no excuse prepared, either.

She paced in the small room, her mind racing as she waited for someone, *anyone*, to join her. All she needed was information, and she'd thought of little else as she'd bided her time, waiting for an excuse to leave her office.

First through the door was Lucy, whom Ava had completed her training with earlier in the year.

'Tell me what you know about the new recruitment,' Ava said hurriedly. 'The female dispatch riders?'

As Lucy went to open her mouth, Catherine – another woman Ava had known for months – stepped through the door, closing it behind her and turning with a big grin on her face.

'Is this what you're looking for?' Catherine asked, producing a piece of paper she had concealed inside her jacket. 'I had a feeling you'd be crazy enough to want to apply.'

Ava reached for it, her heart skipping a beat as Catherine placed the memo in her hand.

'You're welcome,' Catherine said. 'Although you owe me a favour, all right? This isn't supposed to be distributed until tomorrow.'

Ava nodded, tucking the paper behind her back when the door opened, but it was only another Wren who'd come to see what all the fuss was about.

'What are you lot whispering about?' she asked.

'Ava here wants to ride motorcycles,' Lucy said. 'I don't think we're exciting enough for her any more.'

They all laughed, but Ava ignored them. She stared at the memorandum in her hand and slowly read the words, excitement building within her. They were looking for motorcyclists, and it appeared that they were first wanting to recruit women who already had experience; however, they were prepared to provide training if required, and that was the part she couldn't stop rereading. She had not the faintest clue how to ride a motorcycle, but she was certainly willing to learn. How much harder could it be than sitting astride a horse, anyway?

She took a big breath and looked up at the other women in the small room, who were all watching her, as if waiting for some big announcement. They likely all thought she was mad.

'Well?' Catherine asked.

Ava glanced at Catherine, then Lucy, and then the other woman, whose name she couldn't remember.

'I'm going to apply,' she said, surprising herself with how convincing she sounded.

'You're not!' Lucy gasped.

'I am,' Ava said firmly. 'Can I keep this?'

'No.' Catherine groaned when she tucked it into her pocket anyway. 'Ava, no!' she cried. 'I'll have to type it all over again.'

'I'll bring you in lunch tomorrow to say thank you,' Ava promised. 'Please?'

'Fine. But it had better be something good.'

Ava gave her a quick hug then spun around to make the cup of tea she'd come for. She had the general's secret stash of sugar in her pocket and she pulled it out, not realising immediately that the other girls had all gone silent.

'Where did you get all that sugar from!'

She slowly turned, seeing Catherine's arched brow. 'Ah, it's the general's. He keeps a personal supply.'

She watched as Catherine moved closer and took down a cup, holding it out. 'Half a teaspoonful. For the memo.'

Ava looked down at the jar, knowing it wasn't hers to give but also knowing that he'd never find out. She sighed. 'Fine. But if I disappear, you'll know why. He's very protective of his sugar.'

'How *is* it going with the handsome general?' Catherine asked, waggling her eyebrows. 'You're the envy of everyone being put on his service, you know.'

Ava shrugged, as if she hadn't fallen head over heels in love with the man. She'd certainly done her fair share of fantasising about smoothing her palm down his jacket lapel as he kissed her, and with the idea of this job rattling around in her head, her anticipation had increased tenfold.

'I can't complain,' she said nonchalantly. 'But I'll be finished with him soon, and this sounds far more exciting than sitting here at a typewriter all bloody day. Give me an adventure any day of the week.'

Catherine laughed at her, and Ava finished making the tea, walking back to her office as quickly as she could without spilling it, the memo burning a hole in her breast pocket. Despite her outward confidence, she was nervous. Being a Wren had changed her life; it meant she could leave home for long stretches every day instead of being so tightly controlled by her parents, not to mention she had her own income, which she'd never had before. She would hate to lose what she had, but surely it wouldn't affect her existing position if she wasn't accepted?

Tomorrow. I'll apply tomorrow. Although she had a feeling that applying wasn't going to be the most challenging part of her plan; now she had to tell her father.

She'd waited all night to tell them, but it wasn't until Ava's mother rose to collect the dinner plates that she finally cleared her throat to speak. Her father reached for his whisky glass, sitting back in his chair, his eyes fixed on his daughter. They weren't unused to her speaking her mind at the dinner table, but usually it turned into an argument that had her father threatening to send her packing. She took a deep breath.

'I wanted to talk to you both about a new, er, *promotion* that I've decided to put myself forward for.'

Her mother sat, still holding the plates she'd collected. 'Oh? What kind of promotion?'

'As you know, my work for the general comes to an end next week,' she said.

'You'll be back in the Navy section after that?' her father asked, reaching for the newspaper he'd left folded beside him while he ate. He glanced at her over his glasses, before seeming to switch his attention to the newspaper, clearly disinterested.

'The Navy are actually looking to recruit women for quite an extraordinary new role,' Ava said carefully. 'They need Wrens to become motorcycle dispatch riders, delivering important memorandums all over England by the sounds of it.'

'Absolutely not!' her mother cried, dropping the plates to the table with a clatter as she looked at Ava in horror. 'Of all the harebrained things you've said in your life, this, this—'

Ava looked to her father, thinking for one naïve second that he might support her, before he began to laugh. 'Ava, that's the most hilarious thing I've heard all day. A motorcycle rider? Your mother's right, it might be your most hare-brained idea yet.'

She reached for the edge of the tablecloth and clenched her fingers around the starched fabric. 'Regardless, Father, I'd still like to apply.'

He set the paper down then, and she clenched the tablecloth even tighter. 'My dear, what exactly makes you think you'd be capable of doing this job? Please enlighten me.' He sat back and smiled. 'Perhaps your ability to balance on a horse?'

Ava didn't tell him that was exactly what she thought. 'I'm also very capable at driving your motorcar,' she said, hating the quake in her voice.

'The answer is no,' he said, picking up his paper again. 'No daughter of mine will be gallivanting around on a motorcycle. It's unseemly.'

Ava looked at her mother, who just shook her head, lips pursed as she rose with the plates. They'd been delighted when she'd come to them and asked if she could become a Wren – it was something to boast about to their friends over dinner parties, after all. *Dispatch rider* clearly didn't sound anywhere near as prestigious.

'Father, if you'd just—'

His fist hit the table with such force that the remaining plates and cutlery jumped. 'I said no!' he roared. 'Do not question me. Go to your room!'

Ava straightened her shoulders and levelled her gaze on him, even as her stomach clenched with fear. She'd pushed him to anger many times, but she'd always known when to back down. Tonight, she'd already decided not to take no for an answer, regardless of the consequences.

'I am a woman of twenty years, with a prestigious job working for the Navy,' she said quietly. 'I think I'm well past being told to go to my room, don't you?'

The glass tumbler that he threw came within an inch of her forehead. If she hadn't been so used to his temper, and so adept at ducking, she would have no doubt sported an ugly scar for the rest of her life.

Her father's face was red as her mother ignored the shattered glass and rushed to the drinks cabinet to fetch him another Scotch, his eyes dark as he leaned forward.

'Unless you want to find somewhere else to live, Ava, you *will* do as I say,' he said. 'If I tell you to go to your room, you go!'

Ava rose, leaving her mother to clean up the mess as she walked to the door.

'Defy me on this matter and you'll never set foot in this house again, do you hear me?'

She turned, resisting the urge to tell him that she didn't need his damn permission, instead addressing him in her calmest voice.

'Father, this is something I feel very strongly about,' she said. 'Women are desperately needed to fill these roles, to free more men up for service, and I'm prepared to step up and do my bit. They're expecting Wrens to come forward if they're either experienced or capable of learning, and I'm certainly capable. It also doesn't change the fact that I'm a Wren because I would still hold that title, if that's your primary concern.'

'Then let them take someone else's daughter,' he muttered, downing the new drink her mother had brought him. 'As far as *I'm* concerned, this conversation is over.'

Ava turned on her heel and went to her room, closing the door and flopping down on to her bed. With or without their permission, she was going to apply. This was the last time she was going to let him tell her what to do.

ABOUT THE AUTHOR

Photo © 2022 Jemima Helmore

Soraya M. Lane graduated with a law degree before realising that law wasn't the career for her and that her future was in writing. She is the author of historical and contemporary women's fiction, and her novel *Wives of War* was an Amazon Charts bestseller. Soraya lives on a small farm in her native New Zealand with her husband, their two young sons, and a collection of four-legged friends. When she's not writing, she loves to be outside playing make-believe with her children or snuggled up inside reading. For more information about Soraya and her books, visit www.sorayalane.com or www.facebook.com/SorayaLaneAuthor, or follow her on Twitter: @Soraya_Lane.

Follow the Author on Amazon

If you enjoyed this book, follow Soraya M. Lane on Amazon to be notified when she releases a new book!
To do this, please follow these instructions:

Desktop:

1) Search for the author's name on Amazon or in the Amazon App.
2) Click on the author's name to arrive on their Amazon page.
3) Click the 'Follow' button.

Mobile and Tablet:

1) Search for the author's name on Amazon or in the Amazon App.
2) Click on one of the author's books.
3) Click on the author's name to arrive on their Amazon page.
4) Click the 'Follow' button.

Kindle eReader and Kindle App:

If you enjoyed this book on a Kindle eReader or in the Kindle App, you will find the author 'Follow' button after the last page.